D1823950

Vacuum-Packed
© 2003 Robin Newbold. All rights reserved.
ISBN: Pending

Published by nightwares LLC
Milwaukee, Wisconsin
books.nightwares.com

This text may not be duplicated or distributed in whole or in part without
prior written permission of the publisher or author, except in the case of
text excerpts for the purposes of commentary or review.

This is a work of fiction. The characters, incidents and dialogues are
products of the author's imagination and are not to be construed as real.
Any resemblance to actual events or persons, living or dead, is entirely
coincidental.

Acknowledgements

A special thanks to Daniel Wells, since the book wouldn't have been written without you. And honourable mentions — in no particular order — to Art Neslen, Kathy Hardy, Daniel Gawthrop, Warren Ockrassa and Patrick Baughan. I may need your help and encouragement for the second work in progress.

For Kitcharoen

VACUUM-PACKED

ROBIN NEWBOLD

And like all the boys in all the cities
I take the poison, take the pity
But he and I, we soon discovered
We'd take the pills to find each other

Suede, *New Generation*

CHAPTER ONE

Jamie got back to his Tower Bridge council flat on another chill, lonely day and shut the door on a smell lingering somewhere between cheap cooking and urine. The remnants of last night's sex were still sadly there, hurriedly discarded clothes in a bundle on his bedroom floor, sticky stain on the sheets that was fading fast like the memory. He felt so empty he even thought briefly about calling the one-night stand (whom he'd already forgotten the name of) but then realised he'd deleted the phone number from his mobile and doubted the guy had given him genuine coordinates anyway.

He went to the kitchen, grabbed the third-full bottle of whisky and poured himself a more than liberal dose, desperate to shut out the winter cold. Jamie took a big swig and grimaced as it hit the pit of his stomach. He saw his answering machine winking as he moved into the hallway. One message; he hesitated as he hit "play".

"Aright babe, this is Pete, bell me when you get the chance. Good news!"

The message was shouted and Jamie thought he could discern a pub in the background. He imagined "Sweet" Pete — sweet as in everything was always "sweet as a nut" — with a beer in one hand and a cigarette in the other while his mobile was perched precariously between shoulder and ear, looking every inch the Cockney chancer.

Pete owned a record label and licensed his artists' recordings to the majors. He'd been auditioning new talent in the search for a "young male singer" and Jamie had got the job. Though the boy sensed it was more about his good looks and the fact that at nineteen he looked more like a fourteen-year-old than about his singing ability. The view was reinforced on their first meeting outside the auditioning hall, which took place in a City of London pub one weekday afternoon. The record company executive had made a pathetic drunken lunge at his new signing and then admitted to being an alcoholic by way of an apology.

He was beginning to seriously question how such a desperate

man could help him but he dialled Pete's number anyway because he didn't have any better options.

"Hello, it's Jamie."

"All right," wheezed Pete, clearly shouting above the background noise of another raucous bar, one that Jamie suspected he retired to in the afternoons all too frequently. "Yeah, good news as I said. We've been invited to my mate's party tonight. He's a big record producer and he's holding a do down at his Sussex pad."

"Okay," he replied, a little too eagerly, being sold on the words "record" and "producer".

"Can you meet me at the office 'bout seven?"

"Yeah."

"Sweet as. Make sure you look pretty," Pete said, hanging up and leaving the comment ringing in Jamie's ear.

He sensed the record executive was desperate to make some kind of impression other than the wrong one since he'd already admitted in another moment of drunken candour that Ripe Records was earning the dubious distinction of the label with a single hit.

Nevertheless, keen on making an entrance, Jamie showered, scrubbed and bathed himself in perfume. He chose the tightest of white Calvin Klein T-shirts, which he'd actually washed on a high temperature to shrink even further. He complemented the look with a pair of blue Levi's that left little to the imagination and gazed at himself approvingly in the mirror with the sure knowledge he wouldn't be his only admirer that evening.

The front door was locked when Jamie reached the inexplicably numbered 89-and-a-half Worship Street in the back end of Shore-ditch, though Pete's black Jaguar XJ12 was in the driveway. He impatiently rang the buzzer, imagining him slumped over in his office recovering from another drunken stupor.

After a few moments of silence with Jamie poised to hold down the buzzer again the intercom crackled into life: "Babe, I'll be right there, I was just cleaning meself up."

Pete came out of the door looking typically dishevelled. He thrust out his frail arms to grab the youngster and gave him a peck on the cheek. Jamie groaned inwardly as he smelled the booze on the man's breath, which was barely masked by a haze of aftershave. He looked accusingly into Pete's watery, bloodshot eyes and the record company man could only look away.

"You look lovely darling," he said, still avoiding eye contact.

"Cheers," replied Jamie, wishing he could say the same about his companion. Dressed in loafers, jeans and a crumpled polo shirt with his gin-coloured, thinning hair brushed back severely over his scalp he didn't give the impression of a record company executive; to his new employee he looked like he'd given up. They walked to the Jag in silence.

Pete glanced across at the boy as he turned the engine over, already having lit a cigarette. Jamie ignored the look and sat demurely as his boss nervously blew out heavy clouds of smoke.

"Don't mind me babe," he said as they turned onto the street, but Jamie saw the tears in his companion's sad eyes. "Just sit back and enjoy the ride."

They drove in virtual silence since Pete had turned up the stereo loud enough that it would make conversation almost impossible. Jamie sank back into the black leather seat, relieved at not having to make idle chitchat as he listened to the pumping nightclub soundtrack and averted his eyes from the desperate man just inches from him, the man that had promised so much.

They pulled up outside the impressive old country house. Expensive cars littered the sweeping gravel driveway and Jamie felt slightly daunted at what lay ahead of him, while Pete sat staring through the windscreen like he didn't want to move as the engine still ticked over and the music pounded.

"Are we getting out then?"

"I s'pose we should," said Pete, finally coming to. "We don't want to hold the party up."

Jamie felt his heart beating faster as they entered the house and moved into the cavernous hallway, the walls reverberating with a heavy bass beat. Pete knowingly led the way as large, sumptuously decorated rooms flashed by, the music getting louder. They finally came to a set of ornate double doors almost bursting with sound. The record executive flung them open for the boy to take in the decadent scene under subdued lighting. It was as though every detail had been carefully considered and taken care of, he thought. The grand, smoky room was filled primarily by a white middle-aged male gathering who were sipping flutes of champagne, frantically refilled by scantily clad young waiters.

People flocked around Pete as though they'd known him forever but disappeared just as quickly, not even making time for Jamie, though he was aware he raised more than the odd eyebrow.

Introduced to many faces that were too old to be interesting he nevertheless felt relaxed as the music throbbed in his temples and gratefully accepted a glass of fizz thrust at him by some beautiful young thing.

It seemed as though Pete finally got disenchanted with standing on the sidelines and had collared a young man whom he was having a rather one-sided conversation with. He'd rudely failed to introduce Jamie to the guy, who he recognised as a member of a popular boy band. He stood on the fringes of the chatter feeling like a spare part, guzzling his champagne and glancing over at the handsome singer, trying to catch his attention.

"Hi, my name's Jim," he said eventually as he pointedly turned his back on Pete and addressed Jamie. "I'm from the boy band 999."

"I didn't know they were gay," Jamie shrieked facetiously.

"They're not," said Jim in his pronounced Liverpudlian accent. "Officially."

"Is it true they call you 'Jumbo' Jim?"

"You must have a subscription to *Smash Hits*, you daft lad," replied Jim, laughing as he unselfconsciously pulled Jamie to him, pecked him on the cheek and gave him a slap on the arse, oozing the confidence of a C-list celebrity.

Jamie was enjoying his brush with the almost famous but felt uncomfortable under the watchful gaze of Pete, who seemed to be eyeing him with a hateful and jealous leer.

"What's his problem?" he said discreetly, nodding over to indicate Pete.

"Oh, he's a bit of a joke in the industry now," replied Jim, lowering his voice conspiratorially. "The only artists he's concerned with are piss artists."

"I've just signed a bloody contract."

"Yeah he told me you're the next big thing," Jim replied, laughing cruelly. "From what I've heard he's got a mega cash flow problem and people are saying Ripe Records is about to go under."

"Why has he signed me then?"

"Look, Pete's well known as a big gambler and I think you're really his last throw of the dice," said the singer. "I've heard creditors saying he's in the red to the tune of thousands. I wouldn't expect paying if I was you."

"Thanks for the warning."

"Look, the old man is giving us the evil eye. I better be off," said

Jim. "He's probably wondering what I'm telling you."

"See you later then."

He looked across at Pete, who was swaying from side to side, busy courting yet another refill when he'd obviously had more than enough already. Jamie resented him for driving Jim away, resented him for his desperation and fixed on party smile, and hated him for being dumped at a party full of strangers and then set adrift.

"You're never going to make me famous, you're just a fucking fraud, an alcoholic!" he shouted at the record executive, who'd been busily in conversation with an older man.

Pete looked mortified, as though just one sentence was all it took to floor him, but he clumsily swung his arm and lashed out. He got lucky and his fist struck Jamie's eye. The boy was sent reeling backwards as the pain pierced through the haze of alcohol. He worriedly clutched the side of his face, feeling it swell immediately.

Pete stepped up again but was held back by the old man he'd been talking to as surrounding party guests hid behind champagne flutes as though unaware of the commotion.

Jamie looked at Pete, who was still being restrained, with utter contempt and spat in his face like he no longer existed, let alone mattered. Then he walked away and lost himself in the crowd, resolving never to see him again, though he had a horrible feeling he would.

Still stunned he felt a tug at his hand and turned around, pleased to see Jim, who sported a wide champagne smile. The singer pulled Jamie through the crowd and out of the cloying room.

"Don't worry about Pete. He likes pretty faces around but hasn't got a clue what to do with 'em," said Jim as they ascended some stairs.

"Yeah, I've just realised how full of shit he really is," Jamie replied, laughing bitterly as he felt his swollen eye.

"One way or the other he's not going to be on the scene much longer."

They reached a small landing at the top of the house and the singer opened the door onto a dully-lit room with a double bed suggestively at the centre.

"Come on, they won't miss us for a while," said Jim as he pulled Jamie onto the bed. "I saw the way you was looking at me downstairs."

The boy was slightly taken aback by the forwardness and tried to kiss Jim for reassurance but found his head being pushed roughly down to the star's crotch. It didn't take long for him to indulge in what he knew every pubescent girl in the land had been aching to do — he unzipped the singer's jeans.

Once he'd come the star was seemingly oblivious to his companion and selfishly used the *en-suite* shower first. Jamie just sat on the bed, still dazed, as he listened to the cascading water from the bathroom.

On the way out Jim offered only the weakest of smiles. As Jamie entered the shower cubicle his stomach knotted in pain and he threw up from the drink and from the shock of the whole violent night. The vomit congealed around the drain and he pulled the showerhead from the wall to wash it all away. He grimaced as he caught sight of his bloated, discoloured eye in a wall-mounted mirror.

"Come on, there's someone I want you to meet," barked Jim, all businesslike as Jamie exited the shower. It was like the previous half hour had never happened.

He followed Jim reluctantly like a little lost child back to the function room. The chat seemed to have got louder and more excitable but it just made Jamie want to cower. In this room full of people he felt impossibly lonely and wondered, not for the first time, what he was doing in a cavernous space full of strangers who weren't interested in him because he wasn't a "somebody". He signalled hopefully to one of those he could always catch eye contact with and asked the waiter for yet another drink.

"Jamie, this is George, and vice versa," said Jim, introducing Jamie to a skinny, middle-aged, balding guy.

The man's pink dome, visibly sweating under the lights, gave him an unpleasantly greasy sheen. Jamie felt himself being eyed up and down as he watched George's thin white lips chomping busily on a big cigar.

"Delighted to meet you," he said, holding out a slender hand for Jamie to shake. A chunky Rolex sat ostentatiously on his puny wrist.

"Pleased to meet you too," Jamie replied, but shyly averted his gaze as he felt George's bulging eyes creep all over his body, mentally undressing and abusing him. He let out a nervous, pathetic laugh.

"Very pretty face," said the immaculately dressed man with the skeletal-like face and accent that was impossible to place, as though he didn't want to be pinpointed. His long, thin fingers brushed Jamie's cheek and the heavy swelling around his eye.

"Just what you're looking for, George. I've tested the goods," said Jim, laughing casually.

"I'm in movies my dear. Your face definitely fits, and everything else by the looks," said George, looking intently at Jamie and puffing up his ridiculously out of place cravat. "Here's my card. Screen tests in the next two weeks. Do call me."

Jamie shifted uncomfortably, nervously stroking the business card, but he made a point of putting it carefully into his wallet and promised to call, slightly star struck by the idea of films even though he realised it wouldn't be anything warranting an Oscar nomination. George winked at the pair by way of goodbye, waving an arm in the air as he slunk back into the crowd.

Jim shrugged as Jamie looked at him forlornly, as if to say he'd done his duty of looking after the party's leper; now it was someone else's turn. The boy noticed Pete slumped in a corner passed out as people, his so-called friends, walked by without a second glance as though he wasn't even there.

The singer turned his back on the boy like he was surplus to requirements as a procession of men approached him. Jamie doubted the young, handsome star wanted to admit to himself, let alone the world, he was gay, having seen the always joshing, football-loving lad on too numerous afternoon TV quiz shows trying to plug his group's latest dirge.

Jamie felt a loathing rise up inside at his fellow partygoers but hated himself more for so desperately wanting to be a part of it. He thought Pete had been his key to the door, though now there was George. For the moment he decided to leave Jim and his attentive friends, who he felt wouldn't even notice his disappearance, let alone care.

The boy strode purposefully through the great house and out into the stinging winter air, which he breathed in great gulps. He walked on down to the main road, leaving the lights and sound far behind. He stood by the side of the black tarmac thumbing a lift back to London, back to his home, wondering what lay ahead of him. Being a young, pretty boy alone at night he knew it wouldn't take long for someone to stop; they always did.

CHAPTER TWO

When Craig had called Gay Switchboard — the free gay advice service — the counsellor had been so nice to him that he'd felt like bursting into tears. The voice at the end of the line was so soothing, caring and calm, the antithesis of his own; he believed he sounded a broken man. Even going to the shop and asking for a pack of cigarettes was an ordeal. He sensed people could tell by his tone that he was suffering a life-threatening illness, that they could see right through him.

Craig had called Switchboard when he was coming out and it'd helped. For the lack of friends he turned to them again. Okay, he had friends, but there was no one he felt like discussing AIDS with. He thought mates were people you talked superficial fluff with.

Jamie had already rejected him because HIV positive just wasn't fashionable, though Craig knew he was better off without his boyfriend of six months. He could turn his back on most people like that without it coming back to haunt him, but it was his mum and her husband Bill he was worried about.

Craig approached Switchboard in desperation and it had saved him. The counsellor, who admitted he was HIV positive too, said that revealing your positive status was like coming out all over again but "without the happiness". He'd signed off one of their intense conversations with the simple but telling line: "You've got to be tough, fucking tough. That's my advice."

As Craig sat in his small, dreary studio and contemplated telling his mum and her husband, who'd been so good to him through the trials of coming out, he appreciated how prophetic the small words of advice had been. With coming out he felt a big sense of trepidation but there was also part of him that wanted to shout it from the rooftops. Being HIV positive was something completely and appallingly different. His world had fallen apart when the doctor had broken the news in that softly, softly fashion that was neither here nor there. Really, he was handed a death sentence at nineteen years of age, or that's how he thought at the time through the endless tears.

Over the course of a few weeks and with professional medical consultation he was made aware that combination therapies could prevent him getting sick for years and he'd managed to live by the cliché "one day at a time", though some days were worse than others. At least he'd stopped destroying himself and tried to see a future.

It was the end of autumn and the onset of winter, the latter part of October. They'd had an Indian summer and Craig had basked in those glorious deep-blue sky days like he'd never see the sun again, all too aware that winter was a long, dark shadow around the corner. The past week had seen bitterly cold winds and grey skies blow in from the north — Siberian weather, they said.

Nevertheless, on this Sunday in late October with the brown leaves cascading sadly from the trees, Craig had arranged to see his mum and her husband in Regent's Park. He couldn't face a confrontational style meeting and thought it would be somehow easier to tell them in a wide-open space. He guessed it might lessen the shock but knew bitterly from experience that nothing could ease the coming blow.

He checked himself in the bathroom mirror and acknowledged that he looked tired and drawn. Craig hoped his time away in the sun — he'd decided with the help of his counsellor to do what he'd always wanted to do and travel the world — would do its job of rejuvenating him.

He had managed to get out of bed even on the hardest days but was finding it exhausting to motivate himself. The boy had declared his HIV status to the NHS since he was a nurse and had been given the all-clear, though prevented from carrying out "high-risk procedures". He saw the newfound concern of his employers as intrusive because he'd already told them more than he wanted to about his life; saving up for his trip was the spur that kept him going.

Craig smiled at his image in the mirror but even that looked unconvincing as he pulled his coat protectively around his shoulders, bracing himself for the cold day. On his way out the front door he kicked at the pile of letters and newspapers that had gathered on his mat. He hadn't opened a letter or read a newspaper since the diagnosis. He really didn't know when he was going to be able to bring himself to do anything that required more effort than switching the "on" and "off" button of the TV.

Even though his legs felt leaden Craig closed the door resignedly behind him and headed for his afternoon rendezvous. It was a bitterly cold, blustery day, as he knew it would be.

He'd planned to meet his mum and Bill in the ticket hall of Regent's Park Underground but as he sat on the Tube he hoped they'd get the wrong place and that they wouldn't be left waiting for him like he saw in his mind's eye. He imagined the couple so happy to see him, clinging to each other warmly in the cold with no idea what he was about to unleash on their contented life.

It was suffocating on the Underground, as always, yet Craig pulled his fleece around him. He'd felt a chilling cold since he'd sat in the whitewashed doctor's room and witnessed his world cave in.

He was uncharacteristically early when he arrived at the ticket hall, though only by a few minutes, and his heart skipped a beat when he saw his mum and Bill standing smiling over at him.

"Hi, how are you," she said cheerily, giving him one of her familiar embraces.

"Fine," he replied guardedly, already beginning to wonder how he could possibly bring himself to break the news. Rehearsing it over and over in his mind beforehand had clearly been no preparation.

"All right Craig, looking good as usual," said Bill, giving him a brief bear hug.

His mum's new husband was always tactile, always very welcoming (and Craig had once suspected too eager to please, but he knew better now). His strong London accent was strangely comforting but he wondered how Bill was going to cope too as they headed up the stairs and out into the street.

They crossed the busy main road where people drove purposefully by, heading for a destination, but all Craig could see ahead was uncertainty. He felt the icy wind biting at the exposed part of his face and pulled the fleece collar higher.

"Bloody freezing, isn't it?" his mum finally said as they walked three abreast, Craig in the middle.

"Yeah," he replied.

Having reached the park he noticed how the leaves were falling from the trees, how some stood skeletal-like, framed against the metal-grey sky, and felt the summer had died within himself too. Craig despaired at the way he was going to express his feelings to his mum and her husband as they stood either side, just inches away.

When they entered the comforting warmth of the park's teashop

Craig couldn't stop himself visibly shaking.

"Are you all right, love?" asked his mum with a look of concern.

"Yeah, I'm fine. Just cold."

"Okay, you two sit down and I'll get the teas in," said Bill, rubbing his hands and smiling as he walked to the counter.

He soon returned with a tray of tea and three Jumbo Kit-Kats, his chubby face flushed red with the chill.

"There you go," Bill said. "That should warm us all up."

He laid the tray with the steaming cups on the table in the cheerless little café in which they were the only punters. A sullen teenage girl manned the counter. She'd been on her mobile from the time they'd entered.

A contemplative hush fell at the table, just the girl babbling into her phone and the whistling of a radio turned down low. Craig was forming the words on his tongue to spectacularly break the silence when his mum said, "So what have you been up to?"

It was just the type of meaningless crap she was so adept at trotting out to break an uncomfortable pause in conversation. He loved his mum but Craig felt with resentment that their encounters were becoming more and more superficial.

I've been thinking about dying for the last eight weeks, nothing much, he thought, but instead said, "Oh this and that, not a lot really but I'm thinking of travelling."

"That's nice. Where?"

"Australia, India, Thailand? I'm not completely sure yet," he said with a total lack of enthusiasm, staring into his teacup.

"Oh lovely."

"I've always wanted to go to those kind of places meself," said Bill ruefully. "Never had the time or the bloody money."

Craig ignored Bill's comment and continued staring down into his mug. It was like he was in a dream watching himself from afar when he finally did open his mouth.

"I'm going because I'm HIV positive," he said as evenly as he could, his monotone masking the extreme emotion he was feeling. He held the table to prevent himself from shaking. He felt like he'd slip to the floor if he didn't hold on.

"What?"

"Mum, I've tested positive for the human immunodeficiency virus — H-I-V." He spelled out for her as though reading from a medical textbook and for the first time he turned from his teacup to look at her. He wished he hadn't. She looked shattered and her eyes seemed filled with a lifetime's worth of tears.

"You can't be," she whispered pathetically, sliding her hand across the table to hold Craig's as tears rolled down her pallid cheeks.

"Mum I was tested, I'm positive but it's okay. They say I'm lucky, they caught me early."

"Lucky?" she spluttered. "But you're going to die."

"Karen!" reproached her husband.

Craig held his mum's cold, delicate hand more tightly in his selling her an optimistic story, the one he'd been sold and was so sceptical about. Yet he had nothing else to cling to.

"Mum, I might stay free of illness for 10 years, and there are new drugs to treat AIDS. Combination therapies, wonder drugs they call them."

"We'll look after you mate, don't you worry about that," said Bill patting Craig's hand and squeezing it sensitively.

Seeing the two of them looking on so concerned he already felt prostrate in a starched hospital bed, tied to a drip and relying on a concoction of chemicals simply to keep him breathing as the walls closed in, but he was still totally overwhelmed by their support.

Under their burning, compassionate gaze his façade finally cracked and he burst uncontrollably into tears. His mum came across and held him as he shook and sobbed, wiping his tears away as though he was a helpless child. Through it all Craig could still hear the counter girl babbling inconsequentially away on her phone and he wished her dead.

"Don't worry. We'll always be there for you," said his mum. "I'll always love you."

He looked up as the tears dried and saw Bill approaching with some more tea.

"I expect you'll need something stronger than that mate," he said as he put the tray down, and Craig could see the glimmer in his big, honest eyes.

"Yeah a lot stronger."

They each sipped their tea for a few moments, none of them knowing what to say as Craig continued to cling to his mother.

"I don't want to ask you any awkward questions, love, but what happens now?" she said, staring at the table in front of her as if it was too harrowing even to look at her own son.

"Well, my CD4 and viral load counts are okay, thank God, but eventually I'll go on a course of therapy to prevent infection and protect my immune system," he said slow and methodically despite his mum's sobs. "I'll be on a battery of drugs that I'll have to take every few hours."

He looked at both of them, Karen still staring at the table and Bill gazing numbly across at his wife.

"What about AIDS? What about getting sick? You look so bloody healthy," she said, still refusing to catch her son's eye.

The line about looking healthy stung him more than ever. He had been ill — a nasty fever — which prompted him to go to his GP, who'd suggested the HIV test in the first place. He'd tested positive but his antibodies soon fought off the fever like any healthy young man's should. Craig even dared to think the diagnosis was wrong when soon after he recovered he looked in the mirror and was sickened at the image of well-being staring back. But as he stood and studied himself that day he wondered what horrifying problems he was going to be struck down with — if not immediately or even soon, then in the foreseeable future.

"People contract AIDS — auto immuno deficiency — when their T-cell count falls below a certain level. That's when the immune system is fundamentally weakened, making the sufferer susceptible to secondary infections like PCP — a lung infection; Kaposi's sarcoma — skin cancer; or, CMV — an infection that affects the eyes," he said stoically. "That's what kills in the end."

His mum and Bill looked like someone had just died along with part of themselves. A mother burying her son shouldn't happen to anyone — he knew that — but Craig also knew he had to be totally honest, so he continued as both of them openly wept.

"AIDS maybe ten or fifteen years down the line and as I said, even that is treatable with a combination of drugs. I hope I won't get sick before then."

"We'll always be here to look after you," said his mum.

"There are carers and AIDS hospices that look after the sick. Most of it is provided free by the social services," he replied hurriedly, already feeling the need to absolve his mother from what he knew would be a heavy and soul-destroying burden.

"Oh love, I'm so worried about you," she said, wailing and encasing Craig as he collapsed into sobs again too.

Bill was on hand, as always, smoothing down his wife's hair and offering soothing words. Even the waitress came over and asked whether everything was okay.

"Yes, everything is fine," said his mum. "Just a bit of a tearjerker, that's all."

"Oh," said the girl, and sloped off to the counter, phone clamped back to her ear.

They'd stopped crying at her approach and Craig's mum handed out the tissues she always carried in her handbag. They cleaned themselves up and composed themselves, though the boy noticed he was still shaking.

"Right," said Bill. "What shall we do? I feel like a drink, I don't know about anyone else?"

For want of any better suggestions they filed out of the café, all contemplating a different future. Hurrying through Regent's Park Craig kicked at the dead, browning autumnal leaves disconsolately as they headed past the imposing stucco houses. They all stayed close together as they walked but no one said a word, nothing but their breath visible on the frosty evening air.

Only a short distance was Camden's Parkway Tavern. As the trio entered the coarse interior of the pub Craig remembered enjoying the England football team's Euro '96 successes there not so long ago. He'd felt immortal then as Terry Venables' boys enjoyed the sweet taste of a 4-1 victory against a well-fancied Dutch side. He now tasted only bitterness and laughed sadly to himself at life's unpredictable twists and turns.

The pub looked uninviting, half-empty and all partied out after the weekend. At least it was warm and the three of them basked in it after the chilling afternoon.

"I'm really worried how your mum's going to cope," said Bill as they went up to the bar to get the drinks.

"I'm worried how I'm going to cope," Craig replied as Bill ordered. But it was like he hadn't heard Craig's comment or didn't want to hear as an unusually uncomfortable silence settled between them.

He looked around the bar as the bored barman pulled the pints and felt more desolate than ever. London could seem like the loneliest place in the world sometimes. People hardly spoke to each other, Craig mused, as he watched a group of men in the corner sadly, distractedly sipping their pints and watching a Premiership game on a wall-mounted TV. Each was conspicuously alone and there was no other sound apart from the overexcited chatter of the commentator trying desperately to inject some life into the dregs of the weekend before it dissolved into Monday morning. Craig had work too. He'd so wanted to resign but he needed the money to travel.

The barman handed over the drinks and change with a curt "cheers mate" and they headed back to the table, Karen watching her son return with a renewed concern in her eyes.

"I'm all right," he said sitting down opposite her and taking a welcome gulp of his pint. "Really."

"I just worry."

Bill was watching the football, obviously wanting to disengage himself from any more intense conversation, and Craig couldn't blame him.

"How often do you think about it?" she said, almost whispering, already halfway down her glass of dry white.

"Too bloody often."

"I'm so sorry," she said finally. "How the hell did you get through those first few weeks?"

"Mum, I really don't know," he replied, almost convulsing with emotion.

"How about Jamie?" she asked tentatively, as though she already feared the answer.

"He's left me."

"Wanker," commented Bill.

"Yeah," said Craig, laughing. Bill always cheered him up even at his lowest ebb.

His mum noticeably never asked for more details. While she was totally okay about him being gay she was still amusingly queasy about the ins and outs of Craig's life.

"So when will you travel?" asked Bill.

"As soon as possible," he replied. "I'm just saving as much as I can but I want to be gone before Christmas."

"We can help you out," said Bill, glancing at Karen for reassurance. "We've got a few quid spare at the moment."

"If you're sure that's all right."

"No problem," Bill said, his face breaking into a beaming, infectious smile.

For the first time in weeks Craig felt genuinely glad to be alive, though overcome by the generosity and compassion he'd received from his closest family.

"I'll get the drinks in," he said, blinking back tears as he headed to the bar, holding his hand up to signal he didn't need any help.

While he was at the counter he allowed himself to dream of the wonderful places he was going to be seeing in just a few weeks and felt just maybe things were going to be okay. He knew he needed blue skies and sunshine after the bleakness of the last couple of months.

As he walked back to their table and watched as they smiled up at him, Craig was so thankful not to be alone any more.

CHAPTER THREE

Jamie was jolted awake by the shrill ring of his alarm clock, which he leaned over and batted hard. It was a sickening reminder that he'd have to drag himself out of the warmth of his bed and meet Pete for the first time since their violent argument at the glittering house party. He looked in the bedroom mirror and grimaced in the half-light; his face still showed the ugly remnants of the black eye where the record producer had awkwardly swung his fist.

Jamie was full of hate this particular morning. He'd worked late the previous night at the trendy Saint Bar off Saint Martin's Lane in London's West End. The tips were good, particularly when he directed his sickly smile at the pissed businessmen, even if he did gob in their drinks on a regular basis. Though this was the trying season to be jolly, with hoards of falsely merry office workers on their Christmas junkets to be serviced. He had felt like putting rat poison in their turkey dinners but instead snorted some coke proffered by his friend Philippe to make himself feel superior.

Jamie walked past the multi-million pound façades of Broadgate where he supposed the City money men revelled in making the world go round. The sky was a deep, deep icy blue and he shivered as he continued on to dilapidated Shoreditch, contemplating the meeting with Pete and wondering what more there was to say.

Lost in thought, he came upon Worship Street sooner than he would have liked. In the distance the towers of Mammon glittered and sparkled, though Jamie had already experienced this street that lay very much in the shadows. He'd joined Pete one lunchtime in a couple of the seedy local pubs offering strippers for bored brokers and broken men. Everyone was on nodding terms with the record executive, sadly indicating just how much of a regular he was.

Jamie reached 89-and-a-half and went to press the buzzer when he noticed the front door oddly flapping open in the breeze. He entered the small reception, lit by a strip light that hummed cheaply; it hadn't seen a receptionist for some time so he continued on down a claustrophobic, dark hallway to Pete's office. He remembered how before their first meeting he'd been so excited and full of hope. Now he just felt numb. Even the handful of silver and gold-framed discs tacked to the walls seemed to have lost their lustre.

The heating was clearly switched on, as Jamie felt the sweat spring to his forehead, so he guessed someone was around. He knocked on Pete's door expecting to be beckoned inside but was met with silence. He knocked again, louder, nothing. He caught his breath as the stillness began to get to him but resolved that maybe his boss had passed out on booze or popped out to buy some cigarettes or simply forgotten the meeting.

Anxiously Jamie tried the door, expecting it to be locked, but it swung open freely. The first thing to hit him was the obscene, fetid smell of rotting meat that crawled up his nostrils. He instinctively put his hand to his nose and should have slammed the door shut but was instead transfixed by the horrific scene in a room that he'd never seen so still and silent, so infected by death.

Pete's body lay slumped forward over his desk, grotesquely naked, gouged wrists outstretched. Jamie's eyes followed a glorious fountain of gore thick and crimson up the white walls. The bureau was inundated with the blood that had cascaded onto the floor and the boy stepped back as though it threatened to flood over his shoes. The putrid butcher's shop stench, making him want to retch, was one he'd never forget.

"You fucking bastard," he shouted, then turned and ran as though fleeing for his life.

He was still sprinting as he turned onto Broadgate and past the elaborately decorated Christmas trees and the expensively suited City analysts.

Jamie got on the Tube at Liverpool Street and it was crowded with passengers but he didn't notice them. All he could see was Pete, or the twisted thing he'd become, wrists slashed open and blackened by blood. The image was burned into his mind like his brain had taken a photograph, one it would select at random all too often, he feared.

It was a cold day, the kind of cold that made the bones ache and the ears sting. It was as unforgiving and relentless as the wintry skies above but even though Jamie was tired and strung out he didn't want to go back to his empty flat and the half-empty bottle of whisky by his armchair. He didn't want to sit anaesthetised in front of some cheerily awful sitcom and decided to stay out because he wanted company. Well he wanted sex, at least.

He reached K-Bar, another fashionably appointed gay den in central London that to him looked suspiciously like something out of an Ikea catalogue. The doorman mumbled something which could have been "good evening", but just as likely "fuck you", supposed Jamie as he tried to ignore the intrusion and crossed the threshold.

He headed to the dark pit of downstairs where men in suits had already gathered in front of a large video screen, no doubt trying to forget another mindless day, the type of existence Jamie was trying so hard to avoid.

There were a few stray Orientals around the bar since this was the place to come if you liked "rice". Jamie didn't. Many of the boys were strangely without drinks, most very young looking and some illegally so, he thought. He'd often witnessed how the Asians loitered, waiting for the men in suits to offer them drinks and, he guessed, the contents of their wallets.

He pushed his way through the strays at the bar. He had no time for Orientals; in fact he had little time for anyone. He caught the barman's eye and ordered a gin and tonic, having to shout above the music into the boy's ear. Jamie enjoyed getting so close to someone but the barman was the typical studied professional of a Soho boy and looked straight through him as he handed over the drink. An automatic smile played on the waiter's pretty face as he delivered a silver tray of change but Jamie had already lost interest and guiltlessly pocketed the money.

He positioned himself in front of the screen as the videos poured out. Jamie enjoyed not having to think and let the alcohol seep into the dark recesses of his brain. But quickly bored he soon shifted his attention as some of the rent boys began to pair off with those old enough to be their fathers. He was vaguely concerned and imagined one of the men handing over a crumpled 20-pound note to a boy for his pain at the end of the night.

Instead of letting his imagination wander any further he took another swig of his drink, let the bitterness explode at the back of his throat and watched as a cute skinhead walked in. The boy had an angelic face, though his stance and scrappy clothes suggested he was anything but.

Buoyed by alcohol Jamie kept his eyes fixed on the lad now standing at the bar. The skinhead could hardly fail to notice the attention and looked alive to any possibilities though he scowled back, which only made Jamie more interested. He continued to glance over at the boy at far too regular intervals.

Twenty minutes passed. Jamie was about to leave but stopped expectantly as he watched the skinhead saunter over. He didn't even want to talk to him but just wanted to taste the lush lips set in a strangely innocent looking face under an impossibly rough haircut.

"Don't look at me unless you wanna pay for it," said the boy, his face contorted by hate.

Jamie felt the embarrassing sting of tears in his eyes.

"Fuck you," he shouted back impotently, since the lad had already retreated to his spot at the bar and was smiling serenely as an elderly man offered him a drink.

Jamie swigged back his gin as quickly as possible, hoping no one else had watched his humiliation, even though he saw smiles playing wickedly on the lips of those around him. He elbowed his way past people in his haste to leave. The faceless doorman ushered him out and again mumbled something that could have been "good night", but was most probably "wanker", Jamie thought.

He almost fell onto the pavement outside, flushed with uncertainty and embarrassment. It was sleeting and small ice particles spiralled from the sky and struck his face. Even the cheerful Christmas decorations seemed to mock him as he hurried to Charing Cross Underground Station.

He sat on the Tube, enveloped in silence, face to face with commuters headed back to their suburbs, their televisions and their families, he guessed. Jamie stared out of the window and found the dark emptiness more fulfilling than the boring certainty of those around him.

He got off at Clapham Common, though the train was still full as it thundered towards the grey satellite town of Modern. The boy pulled his coat tight around himself as he ascended from the station and headed for the shadowy expanse of the common, treetops illuminated a dull orange by the urban street lamps.

It was still sleeting and Jamie could hear the cars swish by on the wet tarmac and the leaves rustle as he passed the dark tree line. The traffic noise soon gave way to other sounds, more human. There was a clump of bushes and he caught a glimpse of bare white flesh writhing around behind the foliage as though the bushes offered some protection or gave some privacy to another snatched, desperate moment.

His expensively fashionable trainers had soaked through, his feet cold and wet, and mud was splattered up his trousers, but Jamie stood under the cover of a tree, waiting. He lit a cigarette and watched the glowing tip, puffing out blue clouds of smoke in a bid to win some attention.

Finally a guy loomed out of the darkness. It scared Jamie but he stood his ground. A skinhead came into focus. His heart jumped but he knew it wasn't really the lad from the bar. Their eyes locked with intent and even though he could see the man was not convincingly attractive it was too late as a primitive lust took over.

Jamie threw his cigarette to the ground, offering a weak smile, and grabbed the guy around shoulders that were disappointingly fragile. They hopelessly clung to each other and awkwardly kissed. As a last resort he ignored his own limp penis, reached to the man's fly, undid the zip and as he went down thought of the boy in K.

The skinhead pushed Jamie away as he came, cleaned himself up and ambled off into the night as though nothing had happened. An older man who'd been watching them from the shadows emerged and smiled. Jamie grimaced and the man scuttled back into the darkness like a wounded animal.

He lit another cigarette and trudged sadly to the edge of the common, his appetite for sex numbed by the previous encounter. A man passed walking his dog and he fixed Jamie with a hateful stare.

"Fuckin' queer," he snarled.

Jamie knew better than to reply and just kept on walking and, as he increased his pace, felt more unsettled and lonelier than ever. He activated his voice mail only to be told by the cold computer-generated speech that there was one message. He groaned inwardly at his mum's mock cheerful tone, reminding him to come home for Christmas dinner — like he needed reminding. He was dreading it.

He got on the night-bus and squinted at the clinically bright light. His shoes and trousers were caked in mud and the assorted shift workers looked at him with disdain as if it was obvious what he'd been up to. Jamie skulked upstairs to avoid the judgmental eyes and lit another cigarette in spite of the "No Smoking" signs. It felt like him up against the world.

He'd actually intended to spend Christmas alone but his mum's invitation put his cold, empty flat into stark contrast with the central heating and a fridge full of food in Carshalton — another characterless London suburb — though he sensed it would be a difficult day.

From past experience he knew to expect grandparents dribbling over their Christmas dinners and his parents with fixed grins and party hats as though enjoying themselves with their gay son.

His parents, Bob and Liz, had virtually disowned him when he was a baby. At the time they were both Royal Navy doctors and shipped him off to his grandmother rather than let the new arrival sink their glorious careers. Liz — because he was always instructed to call his parents formally by their Christian names — had even admitted to him that he'd been an "unplanned, unwanted pregnancy".

Nevertheless they had gloried in his modest successes, GSCEs and the like; it reflected well on them but of course, as Jamie knew, it lied. They'd even made the concession of sending him to stage school after much badgering, but only because they'd felt guilty about deserting him for all of those years, the boy guessed.

When he came out as gay that was another story, how their middle-class *"Daily Mail"* sensibilities had struggled to cope. He was shunned by his father who expressed revulsion about anal sex yet seemed fixated by it while his mother, being dominated by her husband, also pleaded horror but felt duty-bound to meet her son at least once a month and at Christmas, as she claimed it was "good therapy". To Jamie Liz could be as icy as the large diamond wedding ring on her cool, slender finger because she was so frightened of opening up and being herself.

Beneath the well-heeled façade of coffee mornings and church fetes Jamie knew his parents were very unhappy with the monotony of their lives. He also knew that Bob, who masqueraded as a mild-mannered local GP, was quite violent and hit his wife on a regular basis, as often as he played golf.

He even remembered his dad giving him a black eye on his eighteenth birthday for crashing the car, Bob's pride and joy that he waxed every Sunday morning. Jamie moved out of the house soon afterwards and always felt sick going back to the scene of his far from happy childhood.

Unsurprisingly he felt a familiarly jarring twinge as his old route to school flashed by while the cab wound its way towards his parents' house around roads boasting grass verges and double garages. It had never really felt like a home and he'd never felt comfortable in Carshalton, Jamie thought as he clutched more tightly at the last-minute presents in his hands.

The cab pulled up beside the semi framed by the finely trimmed conifers, his mum already at the door — glass in hand, smiling, nervous. Jamie quickly paid the driver and strode down the path, returning his mother's smile and giving her a peck on the cheek as he took in the whiff of alcohol. She shakily took the presents from him, smiled weakly again.

"Nice to see you," she said inanely.

"Yeah, you too," he replied as he walked into the front room where he knew his dad would be desperate to get the awkward introductions over with.

He hadn't seen Bob since last Christmas and he didn't miss him but went through the formalities and shook the outstretched hand. Jamie shrugged inwardly as he felt the cold clamminess and witnessed the impassive eyes.

"All right," Bob grunted.

"Yeah," he replied, laughing sadly to himself at the fact there was nothing to say even though they hadn't seen each other in twelve months.

Bob's face flushed with alcohol he ran his eyes over his son and Jamie could tell he didn't like what he saw because just as quickly his father's eyes reverted back to the television, already disinterested.

Liz thrust a beer in Jamie's hand, the Christmas movie sadly filling the void. He gratefully accepted the cold bottle, let the cool fizzy liquid slide down his throat in the warm and airless room. Picking at the nuts on the highly polished table he was dying for a cigarette but Bob wouldn't allow smoking in the house.

The Christmas tree lights busily buzzed on and off in the lifeless room. Bob kept his eyes glued to the TV and Jamie looked at Liz, who pointedly sat apart from her husband, a space yawning between them on the sofa. She put her hand up and nervously brushed her right eye and the boy could roughly discern the outline of a bruise. His mum caught his gaze and smiled shyly.

"What have you been up to?" she blurted out edgily.

"Oh, not a lot really. This and that."

"It's nice to see you," she said with tears in her eyes.

"You too," he said and found himself wanting to reach out and hug her, but he was worried about the reaction of his dad, who didn't like any sign of affection.

"I better get on with the dinner," she said, smiling nervously as she headed for the kitchen.

"Get us another beer love," Bob barked at his wife.

"Okay dear."

Silence fell once again, an embarrassing silence between strangers. The boy gazed at his dad but Bob steadfastly refused to return the look, seemingly frightened of being lured into conversation. Jamie knew he didn't want to know about his life, a life centred on young men with hard, athletic bodies, but he'd suffered how Bob talked so reverently about his life in the Royal Navy — a life of "male bonding and discipline", he'd enthused unhealthily often.

Jamie sometimes fantasised he'd had a shotgun when he lived in Carshalton because he'd wanted to end the misery for all of them. He often pictured his mum and dad with holes in the head — blood pumping into the deep-pile Axminster. The thought came into his mind again as he looked at Bob and realised how much he hated him.

He went upstairs to the toilet but it was an excuse to get away from the old man and peek at his bedroom. It was now an office for his dad, completely redecorated as though Jamie had never existed. He moved inside and closed the door, tracing the dimensions of the room where he grew up, where he remembered hearing the furious arguments as he cowered beneath the covers as Liz's tears flowed for what seemed like forever. He also recalled having his first sexual fantasies there and looked around, sad; all the traces of his youth had disappeared under a glossy white paint, his presence deleted.

Jamie padded back down the stairs into the hallway, attention caught by a framed picture of his grinning parents. He stood between them aged about ten, tanned and smiling with a foreign sea glistening in the background, the perfect family. Liz quietly appeared over his shoulder, looked at the image and sighed.

"What?"

"It all seems so long ago," she replied, turning her back on him and shaking her head.

He re-entered the front room and saw his grandparents had arrived. They looked almost identical, both placed in front of the television. There was a faint recognition in their eyes as Jamie said "hello" and he hugged each in turn but recoiled at the frail bodies and the unsettling smell of decay.

"Don't worry love, dinner's nearly ready," Liz said as he looked over at his nan, who sat open-mouthed, oblivious.

The slow, well-rounded, monotonous voice of the Queen came from the television and the family turned reverently to the screen, lapping up the empty, detached words while Jamie excused himself to fetch another beer.

Following the address they all sat down to dinner and the sound of clinking plates and cutlery soon filled the silence. Jamie looked at his grandparents, who picked at their dinners as though in slow motion. His mother and father sat elbow to elbow with nothing to say to one another despite being married for over thirty years. They deserved each other, he thought, and was glad he was no longer a part of it because he knew he'd end up feeling sorry for Liz again, when she was mostly to blame for the hell she was in.

"Liz, I've got an appointment this evening," he lied. "I'll have to leave soon."

"An appointment tonight?" questioned Bob rudely through a mouthful of food. "That's convenient."

"That's all right Bob, he's entitled to have a drink with his friends," his mum said meekly. "You can take some turkey home; otherwise we'll be eating it till the middle of January."

"I'm on a diet."

"A diet?" bellowed Bob. "For Christ's sake you're wasting away son."

Jamie looked away from his dad's accusing stare and noticed his grandparents still pecking at their food, wide-eyed and uncomprehending at what was going on around them.

"When will I see you again?" asked Liz.

"Just give me a call after New Year," he replied, shovelling in the last of his food and preparing for a quick exit.

"Won't you even stay for Christmas pudding?" Liz asked almost pleadingly. "We've got brandy butter."

"He's on a diet, remember," said Bob derisively, not-so lightly tapping his wife on the side of the head.

"No I really better be off, I booked the cab for four-thirty. Thanks for everything."

In some ways he loathed himself for the fact he despised his own family so much he would desert them on Christmas Day, but he was relieved when the taxi company phoned to tell them the driver was outside.

He hugged his grandparents and shook Bob's hand without a word. Liz accompanied him to the front door and he kissed his mum and promised to call.

"Thanks again," he said, but couldn't stop himself looking into her bruised eye.

By the time Jamie reached the car he heard the front door being closed on him. He sadly stared out of the window as the landscape of his youth unravelled but was thankful to be going home, away from the immaculate grass verges and the Neighbourhood Watch.

Jamie had spent the last hour making himself look beautiful for the long night ahead. New Year's Eve, a bit of post-Christmas hedonism after he'd had a bellyful of turkey and all the trimmings at his parents' house. He'd hated that day and the long evening he'd spent at home in his flat mesmerised by the false jollity of the holiday television schedule — it just made him more depressed.

He was meeting his friend, Philippe, a fellow waiter at the Saint. They could have been rivals but Jamie was so in his thrall that he couldn't bear to fight him. It wasn't often he was outshone but the French boy was just so pretty that, by his own immodest admission, it encouraged people to do "unspeakable things" to him.

Philippe had revealed his father was a wealthy architect and provided him with a healthy allowance just to keep him away. Though as far as Jamie knew it simply helped the French boy fuel a far from healthy drug habit and funded an entourage of enthusiastic hangers on.

They'd slept together once but had been too wasted to do anything, clinging to each other's finely sculptured torsos but waking up on separate sides of the bed. It never happened again because Philippe craved older, hairier guys, father figures he'd said, but he was still a friend and Jamie didn't have many of those. He was determined to hang onto the French boy even though he knew the chemistry between them was mostly of the Class-A variety.

He checked himself in the mirror and was happy with the image staring back at him as he rolled a large joint. Jamie vainly blew out large clouds of smoke at the ceiling and felt relaxed for the first time in days, glad to be going out to forget about his life for a while.

Delighted when there was a knock on his door that wasn't the postman, or worse the Jehovah's Witnesses coming to save his soul, he skipped down the hallway to let his friend in.

"You tart," said Philippe, laughing, eyeing Jamie up and down.

"Look at little Miss Thing tonight," he replied, taking in an eyeful of the pumped body and chiselled features set off by innocent big brown eyes. "Dressed to kill, aren't we?"

Philippe gave his friend a peck on the cheek only so he could relieve him of the joint in his hand.

"Oi!" Jamie shouted as they wrestled playfully with each other into the hallway, the French boy kicking the front door shut and taking a puff of the joint through giggles.

"That's not glitter on your face is it? You slag," joshed Jamie in the "mockney" accent he'd perfected so well. He'd read in one of the style bibles it was cool to sound working class and even foreigners like Philippe indulged, though it sounded utterly absurd delivered with a European accent, as opposed to simply ridiculous. "If you get your head kicked in don't expect me to save you."

"I wasn't, you poof."

They moved into Jamie's unkempt living room, which reflected the turmoil of his life. Pizza boxes and fast food cartons littered most of the surfaces.

"This looks like an episode of Men Behaving Badly," said Philippe. "Why don't you hire a maid?"

That was the French lad's answer to everything: Buy his way out of trouble. Jamie ignored him and scooped a pile of old porn off of the sofa so his friend could sit down.

"Want a drink?"

"Could I see the drinks list?" replied Philippe with a stoned giggle, still waving the joint around.

"Well there's whisky and Coke or whisky and Coke."

"Er, whisky and Coke then," said the French boy, laughing as though he'd delivered the funniest of one-liners.

Jamie rolled his eyes and walked to the kitchen to pour drinks for both of them. He heard Philippe switch on the TV as he plonked ice into the glasses.

"Stupid fag," shouted the French boy.

"Yeah, he's a wanker," agreed Jamie as he returned with the drinks and saw the object of his friend's abuse was camp comedian Julian Clarey. Even though he was gay it was just so in vogue to be homophobic since according to the glossies the "new lad" was king.

"How can you hate queens if you wear moisturizer?" said Philippe, laughing.

"Fuck off."

"Hey, I slept with a girl the other day," said the French boy. "She was delicious."

"Whatever," said Jamie, unmoved by his friend's common claims to be a "fashionable" bisexual.

Philippe ignored the derision and continued flicking channels as he stubbed out the joint.

"Come on, let's go," said Jamie, swigging back the rest of his drink and snatching the remote from his friend.

Bored with each other already, the French boy sighed like a spoilt child as Jamie shooed him off the sofa and down the hallway.

They walked along the South Bank, both braced against the cold but buzzing from the whisky and the marijuana. Jamie loved wandering along the river, watching the reflection of London's lights in the vast, muddy depths. He often wondered ruefully how he could be in a city of millions yet feel so lonely and he was glad to have Philippe by his side.

As they strolled up Embankment puffing on another joint they passed boisterous partygoers headed for an icy Trafalgar Square.

"Watch out for the bridge and tunnel crowd," said Philippe as the suburbanites swayed by, beer cans seemingly glued to their fists.

"Sad bastards," whispered Jamie, looking at the blokes who were more often than not all hair-gel and earrings, while their girlfriends invariably had big hair and were garishly dressed head to toe in what he guessed was Top Shop.

"This country's gone to the dogs."

"Shut up, you sound just like my dad," said Jamie, laughing as he inhaled the last remnants of the joint.

They slowed down around the grim, drug-addled shadows of Centre Point and stopped at a shop window, desperately trying to see their reflections so they could fix their hair and look perfect for the club crowd. There were a couple of beggars shivering in a doorway nearby looking across pleadingly for change but the two ignored them and carried on tousling their hair.

As they approached The End nightclub both winced at the snaking queue but nonchalantly approached the doorman from the left-hand side. They exchanged pleasantries with him, a very good friend of Philippe's, and were whisked inside laughing quietly at the long, shivering line as they went.

"Peasants," said Philippe as they descended into the glamorous bowels of the club like supermodels.

Jamie was still laughing when he said, "You must have slept with all the doormen in London."

"That's my secret honey," said the French boy, clicking his fingers and removing a vintage leather jacket. He virtually threw it at the girl behind the coat check.

Jamie discarded his coat in similar fashion and they both stood poised in their almost matching sleeveless tops, Philippe's only distinguished by a funky logo on the front that he told everyone he'd designed himself.

Their virtually identical buffed bodies bumped each other as they moved excitedly to the heavy double doors and the fabulous sound and light show the other side, the floor beneath their feet reverberating with the beat. Jamie and Philippe shot each other a grin as they sashayed through in tandem, determined to make an entrance.

"Do you know where to shop?" yelled Philippe above some euphoric trance anthem.

"Are you joking? I've got a loyalty card," Jamie replied, laughing. "Yeah, I know the dealers, it's good stuff."

They both lit cigarettes almost simultaneously as they headed to the immaculately lit bar and approached the attitude-laden beauty who was meant to be serving but, thought Jamie, was far more interested in looking pretty.

"Two gin and tonics," he shouted across.

The expressionless barman said something inaudible and busied himself making the drinks. He virtually slammed the tumblers on the counter as Jamie handed over a ten-pound note. He received miniscule change that looked even more worthless since it was handed over on the obligatory silver platter.

He turned around and handed the drink to Philippe, who he noted was already scanning the club for a possible mate. Jamie still couldn't help feeling a tinge of jealousy even though it had been so long since they'd slept together, but he tried to trash it from his mind as he spotted one of the dealers hovering conspicuously at the edge of the dance floor.

As Jamie approached the guy eyeballed him and waved him across to a quieter, gloomier corner of the club.

"All right mate, what you after?" he said in that busy, businesslike East End manner as though he was selling fruit and veg from a barrow.

Jamie looked at the chubby youngster in front of him and was reminded of one of comedian Harry Enfield's shiftier caricatures. He didn't know what to say to the vision in cargo pants and Stüssy T-shirt and, intimidated by the guy's easy charm, simply placed his order.

The dealer nodded and indiscreetly held up his podgy fingers to indicate a figure. Jamie thrust the notes into a grubby hand decorated with sovereign rings and received the pills in a plastic bag.

"'Appy New Year, mate," he said above the music. "But don't look at me like that again."

"What?" said Jamie, swiping the bag.

"I know you're a shirtlifter," he said. "Just watch yourself."

Wordlessly Jamie turned his back, gripping tighter to the bag, but he could still hear the dealer's cruel laughter as he tried to lose himself in the gathering crowd, vaguely unsettled.

His mood improved once he'd found Philippe and they swallowed their pills and waited for it to kick in before they could start enjoying themselves.

The pair sought out one of the huge speakers and stood in front of it, as though bees to honey. People were beginning to jam the dance floor and the excitement was rising as the music got harder, more out of control. Jamie spotted one of the "superstar" DJs gazing enthusiastically down from his decks as though tending his flock.

He was beginning to feel the rhythm lift him up when a well-built guy who was sweating heavily put his arms around him and lay on Jamie's chest like a dead weight. Peering into the stranger's eyes he asked his name but the man just stared ahead as if he wasn't there and spun back into the chaos.

He looked across at Philippe, whose hard, muscular silhouette was picked out so artistically by the strobe lights, but the French boy's blank gaze pierced straight through him. Jamie felt himself joining the ranks of the anaesthetised too as colour and sound swirled in his head and he began to dance free and uninhibited.

Finally he dragged himself away from the dance floor and ordered a bottle of water from the bar. He swallowed it down in big gulps, amazed at how good it tasted. Still clinging to the water bottle Jamie headed for the chill-out room, vaguely nodding at other clubbers as they walked by.

He sat with many others in a kind of respectful silence watching a bank of equally mute TV screens spewing out MTV. Jamie discreetly lit a small joint and watched as the smoke crawled to the ceiling amid the stillness.

His heart skipped a beat when Philippe walked in and came and put an arm around his shoulder, though neither knew what to say to one another. He handed over the joint to his friend but, coming down, felt cold and empty in the cocoon of the club as he sensed the day had already dawned and feared the glare of morning that awaited them.

Outside in Holborn they passed the homeless who were comatose in icy doorways, though the boys didn't seem to notice and Jamie certainly was too high to care. The beat still pulsed in his ears as his eyes adjusted to daylight but the morning, heralding a new year, was as grey and empty as he felt.

"So what are your resolutions?" asked Philippe as they headed down Charing Cross Road and into Soho.

"I'm going to give up drinking, drugs and smoking. And I'm going to become a monk," Jamie replied, and they both exploded into giggles, oblivious as another beggar shambled by.

Jamie noticed the muscle boys gathered around Compton Café spilling out onto the pavement, getting their coffee buzz before undoubtedly heading to another club, and he just hated them. He knew he'd become part of the scene too but as he watched the group offset nervous exhaustion with pearly grins and monotonous, neurotic chatter he couldn't suppress a large yawn. Even their permatans looked decidedly jaded, he thought.

Luckily the pair managed to grab a table inside and sat in silence as they sipped their coffee and smoked their cigarettes. Jamie wished he could get Philippe back into bed again, to have that hard, muscular body climb all over him, but he noticed the French boy was already eyeing up a man on the adjoining table.

"Oh, who caught your eye then?" he said bitchily.

"Do you mind if I talk to him?"

"Course not," spat Jamie.

"Oh, just get over yourself honey."

Looking at the spot vacated by Philippe, who already had an arm around his bulky, shaven-headed admirer, Jamie felt a tap on his shoulder. Hopeful as he turned around, he felt utterly desolate when he looked up at the tall, balding man with the bulbous eyes boring into him from above, his pink dome reflecting the café's glare.

"Hi, remember me?" the man said in a familiar but expressionless drawl.

Jamie couldn't recall the name but he knew he'd met him at the party and an image of Pete flashed horribly into his mind.

"Yeah," he said, hoping he wouldn't have to make conversation with this odd guy, a mismatch of cool and totally eccentric, the so-called filmmaker with the overpowering perfume and obscene breath.

"George," he said, getting down on his haunches and freaking out Jamie by meeting him at eye level. "Shame about Pete but I'm still on the look out for new talent. I guess you're out of a job."

"Look I'll give you a call, I've got your card," he said, flinching as the man's unforgiving stare crawled all over him.

"Tell you what, screen test next Wednesday afternoon at 3 o'clock."

"I don't know."

"I'll make it worth your while," said George, rubbing thumb and forefinger together.

"Okay," replied Jamie resignedly; he could do with the money.

"See you next Wednesday then, and stay pretty," he said, brushing a long, bony hand across the boy's cheek, but just as abruptly got up and turned on his heels, waving an arm in the air as he went.

Alone again, Jamie stared blankly into his cappuccino and realised he had no plans for the rest of the day, a day that stretched out relentlessly ahead of him.

CHAPTER FOUR

Craig arrived in the 1970's nightmare of orange and brown plastic that was Bangkok's Don Muang airport. He shivered in the icy air conditioning as he shuffled through the murky labyrinth of corridors with many signs welcoming him to the "Land of Smiles."

He didn't see too many smiles as he stood and waited nervously by the frayed plastic luggage carousel, wondering what lay outside of the hermetically sealed concrete monstrosity of the airport — wondering how a city of almost 10 million people stewing in tropical heat would look and feel.

Other passengers stood next to him that he recognised from the excruciatingly long flight where they'd been packed in like animals in transit. Craig sensed the fetid smell of the cramped pressurised cabin still clinging to his clothes and felt the cheap airline food lying uncomfortably in his stomach as he anxiously waited to experience the sights and sounds of Bangkok.

Stepping outside of the terminal building he was engulfed by the heat and the acrid smell of exhaust smoke.

"I take you Bangkok, good price," barked a man into his ear, grabbing his arm.

Immediately on the defensive he stepped back, struggling under the weight of his backpack, but the taxi driver gesticulating in front of him with the craggy old face disarmed him with a wide smile that revealed an array of crooked, yellow teeth. *Welcome to Bangkok*, he thought as he slung his awkward bag into the back of an aging Toyota painted a tacky yellow and green.

"Where you go?" the driver said from the front seat.

"Malaysia Hotel," Craig pronounced slowly and was relieved by the old man's curt nod, which presumably meant he knew where he was going, though he annoyingly repeated the name of the hotel to himself several times over.

As they left the airport for the expressway Craig was apprehensive at how alien everything felt. He caught a look at himself in the rearview mirror. It was if some white ghost was staring back at him amid the radiant landscape. The orange disc of the early morning sun was shrouded by sooty clouds of pollution, while underneath lay a swirling chaos of cars and trucks. Craig already noticed a vivid, crazed energy, as though people had been told there was no tomorrow.

They careened onto an elevated highway and the sprawling cityscape came into view on all sides. Multi-lane roads peeled off in every direction, dominated by cars, hundreds and thousands of them, shimmering in the heat. Huge advertising billboards flashed by plying all-too-familiar names like Coke and Pizza Hut, while an imposing effigy of Madonna stood like some blonde goddess — brands and images that promised to improve everybody's lives but proved a gaudy representation of capitalist garbage, he thought. Still more adverts sold the traditional culture of Thailand "sponsored by Sony" and set Craig laughing bitterly at so much Eastern promise vacuum-packed for Western consumption.

The concrete nightmare stretched as far as his eye could see, spilling over everything in its wake and dwarfing what he'd read about and so hoped to witness — the authentic and traditional Asia. What he saw instead were centuries-old temples with their attendant ancient rites set uncomfortably in a standardised, globalised urban centre.

Though as they finally left the highway — the driver belying his age by obliviously singing along to some high-energy Thai pop trash — Craig was engrossed in the minutiae of street life: The roadside stalls belching smoke, the ear splitting motorbikes weaving precariously in and out of traffic with whole families seemingly on board and the tawdry *tuk-tuks* buzz-sawing their way along. He felt exhilarated by the contrasts, the monotony of the physical landscape against the very human riot of colour and life. It was as though there was a new possibility around every corner, a city that attacked all the senses.

Arriving at the hotel, another relic of 1960's breeze-block, he fumbled around in his wallet deciphering the odd coloured notes as he calculated the right amount of Thai *baht*.

Craig walked into reception lugging his backpack. Like most of the city he'd witnessed so far, it certainly wasn't easy on the eye. At least the receptionist looked mildly pleased to see him, as did several boys skulking around the lobby who he couldn't help but notice smiling at him despite his jet lag and general disorientation.

He'd read from his *Lonely Planet* that the Malaysia was a remnant of the Vietnam War and had played host to American troops on R&R. The hotel thrived on prostitution, both sexes, and supported the local constabulary with oodles of protection money (according to his guidebook), so a blind eye was turned in all the right places.

He sensed it was an establishment where anything went, which explained the elderly clientele he glimpsed in the coffee shop, several of whom were sitting with boys who looked like they should have been at school. And it explained the boy who immediately followed him up to his room and asked him for sex. Craig declined.

The room looked like it had enjoyed — for want of a better word — a makeover in the 1970s. The brown clunky furniture, green linoleum and gargantuan air-conditioning unit were a giveaway. Nevertheless he lay down on the blue acrylic blankets and felt thrilled by the distance between him and home, at how far he had come.

As he flitted in and out of consciousness on the bed he thought of the day before when he'd left London. He'd been looking out of the grimy windows of the early morning Tube as it ground its way past the grey commuter army. Sitting there with his backpack, Heathrow-bound, he was glad not to be a part of it but he also feared being stigmatised — put in a little box with a label on: "Person With AIDS."

It may have no longer been a death sentence but a shadow that he couldn't quite shake had descended over his life when he'd been diagnosed. That day he'd stood outside the clinic shaking, mobile phone in hand, wondering who he could possibly call.

What was burned into his mind was when he'd told Jamie he was positive. He'd let his boyfriend tentatively into his Camden studio-flat even though he had actually arranged the meeting. Jamie was over an hour late (he always was) and his immaculate, manicured appearance clashed horribly with the way Craig looked and felt.

It was as though he was looking at something he could never possess again and Jamie's self-confidence and posture made him feel so destroyed. They kissed but unfeelingly as he saw Jamie wince at his four-day beard growth and eye the messy flat with suspicion. Craig had always been very meticulous and clean.

"What the hell happened? This looks like the Third World War."

Craig sat down opposite and looked his boyfriend in the eye, knowing he must have seemed drawn and anxious.

"You look terrible," continued Jamie derisively, in his usual offhand manner.

"I'm ill," said Craig bluntly, and he could see in his boyfriend's face and in the way he edged slightly away from him that he knew. "I'm HIV positive."

Jamie started crying slowly at first but descended into uncontrollable sobs. Craig just felt numb as he moved from the armchair to the sofa and tried to comfort his boyfriend, but was nudged away. He tried again to put an arm around him but this time Jamie aggressively pushed him off. It was then Craig realised he was crying for himself. He'd always been totally selfish.

They were still nose to nose on the sofa but Craig felt all the intimacy had evaporated. He could sense that Jamie was consumed by rage and hatred. He'd stopped crying and just stared wildly at his boyfriend.

"How? We've always been safe!"

"I don't know," said Craig as he shrank from the outright aggression in Jamie's voice and felt the weight of his accusing gaze.

"What do you mean, you don't fucking know?" screamed Jamie. "How many have there been?"

"I don't know."

"You're pathetic," snorted Jamie hatefully as Craig just looked down at the floor longing to be held, disbelieving at how someone, this someone, his boyfriend, could be so utterly devoid of sympathy and so full of venom.

"What about me?" Jamie shouted. "Didn't you think of me when you were sleeping around?"

"It was nothing. It didn't mean anything," replied Craig, finding a voice from somewhere. "We agreed on an open relationship."

"Yeah, but we didn't agree that we'd be unsafe," said Jamie incredulously. "You've fucked everything up."

"I know."

"We're over," said Jamie without a shred of emotion — making it sound all the more cruel — failing to look his boyfriend in the eye and keeping his distance like he now regarded Craig as soiled goods.

Silence fell after the words that had cut him to his marrow. Even though Craig had seen it coming he'd held out hope that Jamie would take him in his arms and tell him not to worry, that everything would be all right. But as he closed his eyes and sank back into the sofa he listened to Jamie getting up and zipping his coat, preparing to leave. Preparing to desert him in his own private hell.

Even as he heard the front door slam that day and Jamie walking out of his life for good he still couldn't quite believe what had happened. He sat there and cried all afternoon, enveloped in darkness as the evening fell.

Drifting off to sleep on a Bangkok hotel bed with such bleak images in his mind, Craig felt a warming sense of triumph that he'd somehow survived.

He woke with a start, groggy and soaked in sweat, transfixed by the unfamiliar surroundings. Everything was out of place relative to his room in London and he felt totally bewildered, like all the certainties had been removed. But it wasn't a feeling he shrank from. He felt exhilarated by a totally new environment just outside his window and wanted to explore.

Craig flapped open the curtains he'd drawn on arriving and immediately covered his eyes as the sheer brightness dazzled him. It was clearly still daytime, even though he really didn't have a clue what time it was. The watch on his wrist was still stuck on London time.

As his eyes focused he saw through the white-hot sheen of the Bangkok afternoon and took in the view of the swimming pool below, a blue rectangle encased in concrete with a couple of palm trees the opposite end, presumably to give an impression of the exotic. Two tanned boys played languidly in the water, teenagers, maybe even twentysomethings, thought Craig; but they acted like kids as they splashed at one another, their bodies convulsed by giggles. They were being watched intently by a couple of elderly gentlemen at the side of the pool, he noticed, both lying like beached whales on loungers. Even from a distance they looked flushed and sweaty in the tropical sun, pot bellies spilling grotesquely onto their laps. When the boys began to splash the retirees it dawned on Craig that the foursome probably made up a very odd two couples. He let the curtain flap shut and sat back on the bed.

Not feeling particularly hungry, stomach still confused about what time of day it was, he opened the fridge door and grabbed a Kit-Kat and a Coke, like he could have done anywhere else in the world, needing the sugar buzz. Then he rummaged around in his bag for the Bangkok street map. As he laid it out he remembered looking at it in his Camden bed-sit and being disturbed by the enormity of streets and the number of indecipherable, alien place names.

As soon as he stepped from the icy, air-conditioned lobby of the hotel he was assaulted by the intensity of the light and heat. He put on his shades as the sun glinted fiercely from the surrounding concrete and off the constant metallic stream of cars, the belching traffic leaving him with a bitter, chemical taste in his mouth.

Sweat already pumped from his temples as he walked along the road looking to hail a cab. It didn't take long for a pale, blond figure to capture attention, an albino walking against a brilliant backdrop. The motorbike-taxi drivers sitting idly on the opposite side of the road in garish red-satin waistcoats collectively rose from their slumber and shouted over a chorus of "Hey you, where you go?"

He kept walking but felt uncomfortable, as though the eyes of the world were watching his every move, waiting for him to stumble. He liked London for its ability to lend an air of anonymity but it was already clear Bangkok wouldn't provide the same cover.

A *tuk-tuk* pulled up noisily beside him, its engine thrumming a strange tune. He looked at the driver who grinned easily over at him, his tan face impossibly dark.

"Where you go, mister?" he asked in broken, singsong English. "Good price."

"Er, Lumphini Park," Craig said hesitantly, wondering if he'd pronounced it right.

"One hundred *baht*," replied the driver, whose smile had disappeared like a light being snapped off. He held up ten fingers to emphasise the figure.

Craig, not knowing the scale of things, nodded meekly in agreement and climbed in the back of what he found to be a smoky, deafening but fascinating vehicle — almost a metaphor for the city itself.

They careered along, expertly zigzagging in and out the path of other vehicles that seemed slow and cumbersome in comparison. He saw the driver looking at him slyly in the mirror as he mischievously accelerated out of a sharp turn like he was operating some kind of fairground thrill. Craig smiled at the driver, enjoying his sense of fun, as he dropped him outside the gates of the park. He pocketed the money and sped off with a big grin on his face and it was then the English boy realised he'd been fleeced.

He was clearly in the central business district since above the treeline Craig could see the logos of Standard & Chartered and HSBC glinting like apparitions in the smog atop skyscrapers of glass and steel. Ground level was choked with the grime of the developing world as he stepped by people obviously scraping a living in the shadow of the monuments to the dollar and the yen.

Smoke curled from an ashen looking grill, tended by a comically skinny old man, some indescribable meat blistering on top. As Craig passed he couldn't help but put his hand to his nose as an intense smell crawled up his nostrils. He shook his head slightly and nodded in wonderment as the totally strange bombarded his senses.

Craig only stopped at the gates to the park itself as an old rotund gentleman, belly unselfconsciously flopping below his naked torso, stood watch over a polystyrene box filled with blocks of ice with cans of soft drink floating mysteriously beneath the surface like multi-coloured tropical fish. He pulled out a Coke.

"Twenty *baht*," said the man, not looking at him, as though totally disinterested.

Craig fiddled interminably in his wallet but the man stood patiently like he had all the time in the world. Eventually he located the green 20-*baht* note, handed it over and was on his way into the lush confines of the park and away from the concrete and noise.

As he walked around he came across a number of pagodas and gazebos that spoke of a genteel Oriental elegance, which also signalled another world, a different way of doing things. Siamese cats, dozens of them, wandered by and were a picture of studied indifference to people intruding on their turf.

It was a Saturday afternoon and even though it was the other side of the world people did Saturday things. Craig noticed the families, lovers and loners going about their weekend business.

He sat close to some old Thai men smoking and playing chess. They looked so content, like they'd been there forever. He felt relaxed just watching, the stress of a hectic flight eased from his shoulders as he enjoyed the lull of the late afternoon. Descending into a nap he only felt the electric thrill of being so far from home.

Craig was rudely awoken by a booming disco thud, though comfortingly the men playing chess next to him were still engrossed in their game and their cigarettes, oblivious. He spied the clocktower that read five o'clock and then looked in the direction of the sound, wiping the sleep from his eyes. On the manicured lawn was a straggly group, men and women of various ages in suitably sporty attire, swivelling their hips in time to the loud techno beat.

Craig laughed to himself as he watched the mass outbreak of fitness freaks. In the relative cool of the evening, he also noticed joggers going round and round. It was not the preserve of the young as in the West, but all ages, shapes and sizes. A colourful parade of a cross-section of city society sprinted or shuffled its way past his eyes.

As the clock struck six the trashy music gave way to the sombre tones of what he guessed to be the national anthem played over a crackly public address system. Craig saw that the old chess players had left, while the aerobics crowd stood dutifully to attention.

The light began to fade shortly after and people dispersed quickly but Craig was aware of an attractive young girl that had recently sat on a bench close to his. He caught her eye and she gave him a shy smile — crimson painted lips almost luminous in the dusk. She looked Thai but unusually had an outlandish bleached blonde shock of hair.

The distant sound of thunder from the traffic on Rama IV and Wireless roads made the park seem like an oasis of tranquillity amid the evening chaos. But Craig sensed they weren't the only ones loitering as the darkness gathered and the street lamps came on, an orange glow illuminating the comings and goings bathed in a deceptive silence. He watched, fascinated but wary, as a more sporadic procession replaced the joggers, not fitness freaks but fanatics of a different kind. And all the while the girl to the left sat, waiting.

A young Westerner in a business suit strolled past, looking to right and then left, looking for something. A middle-aged Thai man in a muddy-brown safari suit followed at a measured distance, obviously searching for company. A few minutes went by and a thin, nervous looking clerical type scurried past. Craig's eyes followed him as he headed towards one of the little open pavilions. Two Thai-Chinese septuagenarians wandered around for a bit, deep in conversation, before splitting up to sit on benches a few metres apart. A fashionably dressed guy in his early 20s, complete with *de rigueur* miniscule backpack, sat close by eyeing every passing man.

However, Craig was drawn to the girl sitting inches away. He felt he should have walked off and left half an hour before but was intrigued and he couldn't help glancing across. She finally met his insistent gaze with a beaming smile and covered the short distance between them. His heart began beating faster as she placed a hand ever so lightly on his thigh.

It was a short bench and they were almost touching as Craig looked into her unblemished, coffee-coloured face. She was remarkably beautiful, almost too perfect, he thought.

"Hi, my name is Natasha," she growled.

The voice was deep and rasping, so incongruous with the feminine vision in front of him he almost did a double take. And the name Natasha sounded like something out of a dated American porn movie. But he let her oversized hand continue to rest in his lap and focused on the blood-red lips beckoning him.

"Where you from?" she asked in pidgin English, hand still clamped to his thigh.

"England," he said, but was aware she wasn't really listening to his answers as she breathed her high, sweet whisky breath all over him.

Craig looked at the long legs and the skimpy shorts, the crop top and the pert breasts and felt intoxicated by her, by the heat and by Bangkok.

"Can I go your room?"

"Yeah," he said, after a pause.

"Where you stay baby?"

"The Malaysia Hotel," Craig replied, and Natasha let out a high, carefree laugh betraying the deep voice and the man inside.

"What's your name?"

"Craig, pleased to meet you," he said, holding out a hand for her to shake in a comical show of formality. She lifted the hand lightly and kissed it, at which they both giggled.

"Let's go," said Natasha, her tone hardening as though there was business to attend to.

"Don't you want to sit here and talk?" pleaded Craig, wary of what he'd agreed to even though he feared there was little else to say.

"Don't worry, I want to steal your heart, not your wallet," said Natasha, laughing again and seemingly desperate to put Craig at ease. "Let's go."

"Okay," he said, looking into her brown, doleful eyes but still not entirely convinced.

She locked her arm into his and hauled him from the bench with masculine strength. As they headed for the exit Craig felt eyes watching them and wondered whether the stares had been disapproving, warning or both.

He sighed inwardly as Natasha immediately hailed a cab but in a way he was relieved to have company. He didn't even know in which direction the hotel lay and darkness had fallen.

Natasha let him get into the taxi first and was right behind as he climbed onto the back seat. She said something in Thai to the driver. Craig, hearing "Malaysia Hotel," began to relax but became aware of the overwhelming smell of perfume in the enclosed space. Even the old driver up front began coughing and noticeably snapped up the air conditioning.

"Are you gay?" she asked, massaging his inner thigh.

"Yeah," said Craig. "Are you?"

"No, I'm all woman."

"I can see that," he replied, laughing.

"You know, whatever you like in Thailand you can get," Natasha said after a pause, looking at Craig seriously for the first time. "With this," she spat and waved a sheaf of money in his face.

Oddly her tone changed from aggressive to serene within seconds as she started to stroke the back of his neck. Craig sensed the storm rumbling beneath the surface had already passed.

"Where are you from in Thailand?"

"I stay in Samui but I came to Bangkok for short time with my boyfriend," Natasha said, voice full of angst again.

"Your boyfriend?"

"Yes, German man but him no good," she continued, looking on the verge of tears. "He met a younger boy."

Craig kept quiet but wondered whether the performance was for his benefit as thankfully they pulled up outside the hotel. It meant no more awkward silences or indelicate questions, he thought, at least until they reached the room.

He went to get his key from the woman at reception. Natasha stood next to him, all big hair and jangling bracelets like she was a Hollywood movie starlet. But in the harsh light of the hotel lobby he feared it looked like what it was, another cheap transaction, and Craig wanted it to end as soon as possible. The receptionist's face behind the counter was set in stone as she handed over the key, not even deeming to look at his guest.

The lift comprised the dimensions of a large coffin and was claustrophobic considering the number of newly acquainted strangers it likely held — maybe that was the point, Craig thought as he looked at Natasha. She looked back, expressionless. Neither had spoken since they'd entered the hotel, even though the English boy was racking his brain for something to say, anything.

As he unlocked his room the silence seemed to sheathe the pair with a new intensity. Craig regretted everything as he shut the door and locked it behind them with a finality that disturbed him.

"I take shower," said Natasha, all semblance of charm drained from her voice.

Craig slumped down on the bed, clicked on MTV, but listened to the unwelcome intrusion in his bathroom. He switched off the light and let the flickering images fill the room.

The Thai came out of the toilet, her body covered by a towel. She didn't look at Craig as she handed him a clean one, instead transfixed by the images on the television. She took the remote control, lay on the bed and turned the volume up as he walked resignedly to the shower.

When Craig returned to the bedroom with just a towel wrapped around his waist she was still staring at the TV and he didn't know where to start. He needn't have worried, for as soon as he hit the mattress Natasha was all over him, gnawing at his flesh, hands everywhere as her blonde hair fell irritatingly into his face.

It seemed like she was in a hurry when she bent down and breathed warmly into his ear: "Fuck me, baby." They hadn't even kissed.

She discarded the towel to reveal a small thong that barely concealed her manhood despite the lengths she'd obviously gone to. Natasha quickly turned over on her stomach and pulled the panties down to reveal her naked arse, handing a condom to him as if it had appeared by magic.

Craig thrust in hard and thought of Jamie briefly, the last time he'd had sex. He tried to lose himself, rapt by the TV, as he moved rhythmically on top of her, not looking down. He pushed harder and harder, more violently as the angst and tension burned away. Natasha groaned as she too stared open-mouthed at the TV. The shrill of her mobile phone in the background — "Can't Take My Eyes Off of You" — made Craig feel an irrational savagery towards her.

He pulled out as he came, walked to the bathroom and ditched the condom sadly in the toilet bowl. When he returned Natasha's face was illuminated by the strange blue glow of her mobile. On noticing Craig she smiled as if caught out, quickly ended the conversation — which he noted had been in English — and moved to the mini-bar where she pulled out a bottle of Sang Thip whisky and waved it at him.

"You like whisky?" she asked, all sweet smiles again as she began pouring two large glasses.

Grabbing the bag of ice from the freezer she smashed it violently on the linoleum floor with total disregard for the room below. Natasha then topped up the glasses with Coke, handing one to Craig.

They sat perched on the bed drinking, Natasha aimlessly flicking through channels. It had a kind of hypnotic effect for the English boy as he lay back and closed his eyes. He felt the sound of the TV getting more and more distant, then silence.

Craig woke feeling his temples throbbing with a hangover. It was still dark apart from the light from the TV flickering noiselessly in the corner. He looked at the indent next to him on the bed and it was clear the Thai had gone. His head ached more intensely as he looked over at the counter where he'd left his wallet. It took all his energy just to get up but he knew as he opened it that it would be empty.

"Shit," he said, holding his head as he calculated a loss of about 100 pounds.

The money had disappeared into the Bangkok night along with Natasha — all she'd left behind was the smell of her cheap perfume, he thought ruefully.

CHAPTER FIVE

Jamie headed for the gym. He was at least a three-times-a-week boy and an avid follower of *Attitude* magazine's "Fitness Guide" because he wanted the must-have item of the '90s, "disco tits."

He knew Oasis was hardly one of the opulent fitness emporiums as featured in the glossy pages of the style bibles, which were only accessible via a sugar daddy or an expense account, Jamie guessed. No, it was "all oxymoron and zero class, a tawdry affair run by Camden Council", according to one of the sneering gay rags.

More often than not the gym was deluged with boisterous school kids, the small high-pitched ones, not the cute teenagers, much to Jamie's annoyance. The place served its purpose though; it was cheap — like a lot of the clientele, he thought — and based on the fringes of Soho in Shaftesbury Avenue, just short sashaying distance from the Old Compton Street gay Mecca.

Jamie had chosen with care from his closet, as he did for every session, and had opted for the skintight shorts and Dolce & Gabbana vest after he'd showered, scrubbed and doused himself in his favourite perfume. He was hoping to lure the boy he'd had his eye on and was under the impression it wouldn't be difficult. According to *Attitude* if someone held your stare for over twelve seconds it meant they wanted you and Jamie calculated the guy had held his gaze for at least fifteen seconds last visit. He normally relied on such pop psychology as gospel and certainly hoped it was true as he was desperate for some "boy on boy action", as it was so charmingly termed in the pink press.

As he emerged from the changing room and strutted into the gym, Jamie was hit by a wall of house music and a number of shaved heads turned. He was constantly checking everyone out too, looking for something to break the monotony of gym, swim and clubbing interrupted by that dirty word ending in "k", work. And he knew the feeling was mutual.

It was early evening but the place was packed as Jamie hoped it would be, the gym obviously taking priority in many "busy, busy" schedules. Just like being in a club, the pumping music, the pumping muscles and the sickly narcissism coursed through the studio but he breathed in the mix of manly sweat masked by sweet cologne and smiled to himself.

Still Jamie pretended to ignore the looks, having caught a severe dose of London attitude, and was far too busy admiring himself in the mirrored walls anyway. He so enjoyed the rhythmic quality of weight lifting, like sex, and took pleasure in watching his muscles strain and bulge. He was already pretty hefty after a solid regime but Philippe had insisted steroids were the "new black" and he didn't think it'd be long before he indulged.

In the mirror Jamie spotted an old queen staring at his arse. He smiled sweetly but would have preferred to crack the man's skull open with the dumb-bell he so expertly wielded. He was just as impatient when queuing for equipment and had come close to violence several times.

The leers he got from the old Lycra-clad dinosaurs with their severe peroxide 'dos reminded him of the subservient role he was expected to play at work. The Saint may have been one of *The Face's* "Bars of the Year" but it still didn't mean any more than waiting tables for Jamie. Despite its edgy status the place had become so well known that it was filling up with pissed businessmen trying hard to be trendy. Of course they were the rudest customers too, though he wasn't averse to bitching back.

Jamie was a vision in D&G as he stalked back to the changing rooms, hardly a bead of sweat on his brow or a hair out of place. His act was all nonchalance but he was on the lookout for any cute guy with a high-maintenance haircut and modelling potential.

He showered down and again admired himself in the mirror as he headed for the outdoor pool that was framed under the darkening winter sky. Steam emanated from the surface and Jamie shivered in his skimpiest of bikini briefs as he dived into the "Fast Lane." There was a shoal of men in the roped off area of the pool, wet shaven heads and glistening, muscled biceps making them mostly indistinguishable from one another.

Jamie joined the parade in the race for the to-die-for abs he thought all gay men craved. He swam until his lungs ached, envisioning the picture of Tyson the supermodel he'd ripped out of the latest *GQ* — he'd kill for a body like that, literally.

He only stopped for breath when he noticed the guy he fancied walking towards the pool. His chest heaved with exertion as he watched the black boy with the fashionable buzz cut and identikit perfect body approach. Jamie glanced up right at him and saw the muscly, hairless legs and was entrapped by the sickly sweet cloud of CK One. Belying his size the boy delicately slid into the pool next to Jamie and started swimming, but not before offering a long sideways glance.

Jamie was beginning to get cold and wanted to get out but he made himself endure the shivers as he waited for the boy to finish the requisite number of lengths. He didn't want someone else to take what he now thought was rightfully his, they'd made eye contact for goodness sake, which he knew normally only occurred in central London when you came into contact with inquisitive policemen or drug-crazed muggers.

Finally the black boy exited from the pool just as elegantly as he'd entered and walked long-legged and panting to the changing room, his large upper body expanding and contracting. Jamie followed at a not too respectable distance.

They showered next to each other, both breathing hard after their endeavours. Jamie looked up into the jet of warm, refreshing water as he subconsciously felt the boy's eyes moving over him.

He lightly brushed Jamie's arm as he moved back out into the changing room, the human contact sending an electric surge through his body. He watched as the boy disappeared behind the lockers, a towel slung provocatively low about the small of his back.

He hurriedly finished showering but found his exit blocked by the guy who'd leered at him in the gym. He still had the stupid, hopeful expression on his face as he stood engulfed by white rolls of fat. Jamie gently nudged the old man out of the way, who gave a pathetic little yelp and strode to the lockers with a shiver. He didn't bother moisturizing or spraying, for once, as he was in such a rush to be done first.

He loitered just outside and was prepared as the boy came out of the changing room smiling a sweet smile. Jamie seized his chance. They exchanged smiles but more importantly mobile phone numbers and arranged to meet at Bar Code the next evening. His name was Jason and he was a dancer, which was not quite a model or an actor but it was close enough.

Despite the London chill, Jamie glowed orange from his recent sunbed visit, which he deemed essential since he couldn't afford that winter break in Morocco. Together with his lightened blond hair he looked at odds with the icy, dark January.

He was late for his date with Jason at Bar Code but felt it was his prerogative; he didn't want to appear too keen. It was a bar where macho was the fashion *du jour*, though most of those that walked the walk and talked the talk turned out to be window dressers from Croydon, he thought, laughing to himself.

Jason was also late, it appeared, as he scanned the bar, dismissing several glances as he did so. It was crowded, Friday night, yet there were still a lot of guys standing around on their own, immaculately turned out and obviously waiting to be picked up, even if some of them were unfashionably into their late thirties — there was something desperate about their perfectly groomed features and expensive clothes, straight out of the fashion pages of the glossies, and even Jamie felt it screamed contrived. He observed other men standing around in groups too, many sizing up those trying to brazen out being alone or laughing into their pints at friends' undoubtedly excruciating jokes.

Jamie stood propping up one of the chrome finished counters, sporting his very "in" Carhartt T-shirt, as worn by a cocaine snorting former children's TV presenter who had "moved on" to hosting some lifestyle show on Channel 4. He loved the shirt not only for its associations but also as it showed off his bulging chest.

He chose what he thought was a cool stance and idly flicked through a copy of the *Pink Paper*, stopping briefly at the contact ads, the only highlight. Jamie had a laugh at the desperados promising GSOH (good sense of humour) and offering VWE (very well endowed) but worried at the back of his mind that he was just as lonely as he checked his watch and began to fear that Jason wouldn't show.

He needn't have done. He was halfway down his pint when he spotted him, the same nervous grin on the boy's face. He pinched Jamie under his well-defined left pectoral, the contact sending a thrill through his body as though in anticipation of later.

"How are you doing?" asked Jamie, still slightly peeved that his companion was late but relieved he'd turned up at all.

"Sorry I'm late. You know what the Underground is like at this time of night."

"No problem," said Jamie, feigning total indifference, which he was absolutely great at. "Want a drink?"

"A pint of lager please."

Jamie excused himself to the bar as he quickly drained the remainder of his pint, racking his brains for a conversation starter as he pushed his way through the throng. He was pleased to have negotiated an awkward reintroduction but wondered how they were going to fill an evening. It would be easier if they got the small talk over with quickly and got straight down to it. There was a lot to be said for cyber-sex, he thought.

He walked back from the bar with the brimming glasses and really couldn't help spilling a little of the sticky lager over some bastard in an expensive jacket that didn't seem to understand the words "excuse me."

"Wanker," said Jamie, nodding over to indicate the guy who'd blocked his path.

"Yeah but he's quite cute."

"So how long have you been in England?" he asked, pointedly ignoring the last comment and taking a welcome slurp of his pint.

"Oh, a few months."

"And what are you doing?"

"I'm a dancer but at the moment I'm working in a pub. How about you?"

"I'm an actor and a part-time waiter."

"Acting in what?" asked Jason, somewhat sceptically in that kind of pissed off, arrogant way so perfected by Australians that Jamie despised.

"Well I did go to stage school and I've got a screen test next week to work in films."

"What kind of films?" Jason said insistently, a smirk playing at his lips.

"Well, I'm hoping it'll be a stepping stone to something else."

Jason offered a tight little laugh that implied he was totally superior, but Jamie ignored it and concentrated on the Australian's beautiful features and perfect body that was being advertised via a skimpy singlet.

"I was recently in *Cats*," said Jason as though an Andrew Lloyd Webber musical was actually *cool*.

"Funky," said Jamie, pretending he thought so too. "Did you have to dress up like a pussy?"

"Well, yeah, we had to wear a costume obviously," said Jason, gloriously unaware that Jamie was being facetious. "Want another drink?"

"Yeah, why not," he replied, smiling, but concerned at how fast he was drinking.

As Jason walked to the bar Jamie contemplated leaving. Nevertheless the alcohol had instilled nothing but lust in him and he stayed put even though he knew he'd regret it the next morning. He looked around, trying to convince himself the Australian was the cutest one there, which he supposed was all that mattered. Though he was also sadly aware it was becoming all that ever mattered.

"You look cute," he said, as Jason returned with the drinks.

"Thanks," replied the Australian with a grin.

"Do you like me?"

"We've just met," said Jason. "But I wouldn't be here otherwise, would I?"

Jamie, desperate to be liked, took some small solace from Jason's answer and began to feel more comfortable in his company even though he couldn't help feeling he was totally repulsive. *But he did have a great body.*

As the evening wore on and the DJ turned up the bass they drank more and talked less, which suited Jamie. Even the frequent silences became comfortable oases rather than the vacuous embarrassments they'd been. They relaxed in each other's company, though it was far more to do with the booze than anything they actually had in common, he thought. And, of course, the need to have his sexual appetite sated.

"Where do you want to go?" said Jamie, having to shout above the music as he finished his third pint. He'd run out of anything to say.

"Up to you."

Jamie realised there was a multitude of gay options, it being a Friday night, but he was anxious to get Jason home just in case someone else took the Australian's fancy. He couldn't bear to finish up the evening alone.

"I've got some pot back at my place. You just want to come back and chill?"

"Cool," said Jason looking totally unenthusiastic.

Jamie began rolling a joint as soon as they left the stuffy bar, smoking another substitute for conversation as all bonhomie foundered on the cold pavement. He was aware they must have looked a miserable and insular pair as the streets of Soho were alive with "Friday nighters" — office workers from suburbia having their big night out and drinking themselves into oblivion.

By the time they negotiated their way through the drunken throng to Embankment they were already on to the second joint and Jamie was beginning to feel the effects of the weed. They climbed the stairs to Hungerford Foot Bridge and he felt suddenly drawn to Jason as he glanced across at him. His companion seemed to feel the same way and they began kissing on the desolate bridge, hot, wet tongues entwined as the icy air encircled them.

For the briefest of moments something warm flickered in each of their glances but Jamie knew it wouldn't last as he hugged Jason and looked over his shoulder at the vastness of London blinking back, still a world of possibilities to him.

"Why didn't we get the Tube?" said the Australian accusingly as the cold wind began to bite as they headed onto the South Bank.

"It's romantic."

"Huh?" snorted Jason, obviously down from the brief cannabis high. "It's bloody freezing."

Jamie fumbled around, rolling another joint just to keep Jason sweet as they continued to walk in a heavy silence.

"Don't worry, it's not far now."

"It better not be," replied Jason, taking the dwindling joint from him and finding a smile from somewhere.

Jamie was always wary about taking guys back to his place because it wasn't exactly salubrious but he liked to stress "location, location, location." Though as they entered the dimly lit stairwell he groaned inwardly as he was hit by the familiar smell of urine, disinfectant and cheap cooking. "Home sweet home," he called out cheerfully as he put the key in the front door, Jason staying ominously silent.

He was too embarrassed to show him the living room that was littered with takeaway cartons and instead directed Jason straight to the bedroom as he went to the kitchen to fetch some whisky for both of them.

When he got back he was shocked to see the Australian already down to his Calvins and rifling through his frighteningly uncool CD collection.

"You hot?" Jamie said by way of announcing his entrance, though Jason failed to turn around, instead tossing various CDs aside, seemingly engrossed.

"Oh yeah, it's warm in here," he said, finally acknowledging that he was half-naked.

"That's the beauty of living in a council flat, central heating."

"Ah!" exclaimed Jason, oblivious amid the pile of CDs. "You've got Portishead."

"Of course," said Jamie, smiling, since among the boy bands and black divas was sprinkled the odd gem that he'd been instructed to buy courtesy of the style bibles. He'd never actually played the Portishead album *Dummy* but Jason stuck it straight on.

"The Bristol scene's totally hip right now."

"Yeah," he replied, thinking Jason probably didn't even know where Bristol was as he grabbed the Australian from behind.

The chilled lounge music played in the background as they wrestled with each other onto the bed. Jamie pulled Jason on top of him, still pretty much disorientated from the drink and drugs, but took the considerable black cock in his mouth, relieved to have a beautiful guy in his own bedroom.

Jason withdrew and came all over the duvet. Both giggled a cannabis laugh, though Jamie felt vaguely ridiculous as the Australian crawled under the covers as if to sleep while he still had all his clothes on, let alone having reached an orgasm. He sadly discarded his clothes one by one onto the floor and snapped the light off in a huff.

The light of morning seeped cruelly into Jamie's hangover as he squinted at the clock. It was already eleven. His headache began to throb even more acutely with the realisation he was meeting Liz for one of their awfully strained monthly lunches at one o'clock.

The optimism of the night before had vanished as he looked at the big lump next to him in the bed, a draughty gap yawning between them. The grimy stain on the duvet was a pathetic reminder for Jamie of what had passed for sex. He just felt totally numb as he watched Jason open his eyes.

"Hi," said the Australian, turning round to look at Jamie, but his smile appeared as meaningless and empty as his gaze.

"Do you want some breakfast?" queried Jamie, playing the perfect host.

"No, I've actually got an appointment. I better go," said Jason, pulling up the blanket around his naked torso in a ridiculous show of modesty.

A sad silence descended on the room that was as embarrassing as it was cloying. Jamie quickly got up and, still in his underwear, reached over to the closet, pulled out a towel and virtually threw it at Jason.

"Go and take a shower, it's just down the hall on the left."

Jason got up to use the bathroom. His flaccid penis betrayed the action of the night before and he quickly wrapped the towel around himself. Jamie lay back down on the bed and waited impatiently for the stranger to get out of his home. Despite the headache he turned on the radio to drown out the intrusion of another person in his flat.

When Jason returned to the bedroom Jamie was still in bed. The deafeningly loud radio made conversation impossible. The Australian sheepishly picked his clothes off the floor where they'd been discarded and Jamie watched in silence, just to compound the boy's awkwardness, as he hurriedly dressed.

"I'll walk you to the door," he said with bitter finality above the vibrating noise of the stereo.

They walked the few feet uncomfortably. Jason grabbed his coat from the hallway peg and trod on his incredibly fashionable and, no doubt, obscenely expensive trainers without bothering to untie the laces.

On the doorstep they kissed a sad, dry kiss. Jamie knew they were both playing out the script of gay etiquette that said you had to go through the motions right till the bitter end.

"Thanks for last night," said Jason, like he'd just completed some dodgy business transaction.

"I'll call you," Jamie replied flatly as he gave directions to the Underground station, like he'd done so many depressing times before to a battalion of one-night stands.

The Australian strode off without a second glance and Jamie quickly closed the front door but couldn't help watching from the window. He sighed as Jason disappeared out of sight, realising he'd just become someone else to avoid.

He walked into the living room and slumped on the sofa, flicking on daytime TV with the remote. Grinning out at him were Richard and Judy, whose bright faces he detested. Jamie couldn't understand the babbling and perfectly coiffured presenters set on a comfy sofa framed by pastel shades, but in watching avoided having to think about the world outside his door and what he was going to say to Liz at lunchtime.

"You still love me, don't you?" she had said the other day as another difficult conversation drew to a close when she'd phoned to set up the meeting.

"No, see you Saturday," was his reply as he cruelly clicked the receiver down, mouthing "fucking bitch" as he did so. And Jamie, standing forlornly in his hallway, wasn't really sure whether he did love her, whether he could love anyone. He always remembered just how pathetic she was in the face of his dad, how she'd never spoken out or protected him from Bob even when he was a kid. The scumbag who professed in his darkest moments that life was a "living hell" and ranted on about how "Hitler had the right idea" when Jamie came out as gay.

Bob had even insisted on buying a dishwasher when he'd found out about Jamie, so they wouldn't "catch anything" he'd said to Liz. Such was his level of neuroses even though he was a doctor.

Jamie had said in the latest phone call that he never wanted to see his father again "except in the grave" following the Christmas debacle. But in her worst school mistress tone, she'd replied, "That's okay, he says he doesn't have a son anymore."

Not daring to stand up to her husband meant Jamie had often borne the brunt, which was why he was no longer around. His main reason for the monthly lunches was not any particular desire to see the woman who'd given birth to him but to bug Liz for money, which she so easily parted with because she felt guilty, he guessed. Though to him, her biggest crime was staying with Bob.

They'd arranged to meet, as usual, at Harvey Nichols' fifth-floor bar and restaurant. Jamie's choice since Liz was paying.

By the time he was arriving at Knightsbridge he had carefully rehearsed his script. Naturally he was a few minutes fashionably late. Liz had already been shown to the table and was busily perusing the menu as Jamie approached. She looked up and he leaned across in order that she could give him the customary cold peck on the cheek, more for the sake of appearances than anything else.

It was always uncomfortably warm in the restaurant. Or maybe it was just the stuffy atmosphere between him and Liz, thought Jamie as he quickly discarded his fleece and sat himself down to the side of his mother — opposite was just far too intimate.

"How are you?"

"Why don't you leave him, Liz?" said Jamie, noticing her telltale heavy make up not so expertly disguising a bruised cheek, which he couldn't help staring at, betraying his father's sadist streak.

"I can't," she replied, lip wobbling as though she was going to burst into tears.

But she soon regained her composure as he'd seen her do so many times before through years of deceiving friends and family, who still thought Bob was a charming gentleman. Funny, thought Jamie, how she always left out the bit about the drunken, jealous rages.

"He's making an effort you know, he's been a lot better lately," she went on.

"Yeah, it looks like it," he said, again staring pointedly at her injured cheek and feeling disgusted as she sat nervously fiddling with her large diamond wedding ring. "He's never going to change."

"Look I don't want to talk about him."

"He's an evil bastard and you know it," he said, spitting the words out as Liz sat there like she always did, impassively, taking it.

"Would you like some drinks?" interrupted the camp waiter.

"Gin and tonic," said Liz, switching on a smile as though everything was just fine.

"I'll have the same."

"And to eat?" asked the waiter, sounding very interested.

"I'll have the club sandwich," she replied.

"Chicken Caesar salad," said Jamie.

"What dressing with that sir?"

Jamie took the "sir" to be a piss take so he made the waiter list all the numerous dressings, theatrically gave it a few moments thought and then said, "I'll go for the lite Italian."

"Very good," he replied, snatching up the fashionably oversized menus.

"So what are you doing for money these days?" said Liz, taking a big gulp of her drink.

Instead of saying, "I'm planning to work in soft porn movies and be fucked up the arse for a living", like a loyal son he fabricated: "I'm still working at the Saint."

Jamie knew she was probing just to keep the conversation focused on him. She excused herself to the bathroom to eat up some more time, he thought, or maybe to put another layer of blusher on that bruised cheek.

As Liz returned to the table the waiter plonked down their two plates and offered to refill their already finished drinks.

"Same again," said Jamie for both of them. He'd swallowed two painkillers for his hangover when she'd been in the bathroom but felt he couldn't get through the strained lunch without more alcohol.

Silence descended as they began eating. They'd already run out of things to say, even the important things they'd dodged and skirted around, and Jamie wanted to get the formality over with as quickly as possible. In a hush hardly disturbed by the scraping of cutlery on bone china, he realised he was bolting his salad not because he was hungry but because he wanted to be away from Liz, who'd brought the unwelcome aura of his father, and his childhood, along.

"Will you go on holiday this year?" he said between large mouthfuls of salad, scrambling for something to say.

"Yes, Bob's thinking about Thailand this year."

"Why Thailand?" replied Jamie, and sensed she was contemplating days of misery as she nervously brushed her bruised cheek under his unrelenting gaze. He knew she hated holidays because it meant being confined for two weeks with her husband. He could imagine how pent-up and anxious his dad would be after such a long flight, Liz a ready punch bag.

"Well Bob's always been keen on the Far East."

And he felt the hatred welling up inside again. It was "Bob this" and "Bob that" and of course he was interested in the Far East as it appealed to his neo-colonialism. He probably expected that people still wore linen suits and Panama hats and went around clicking their fingers for service, thought Jamie.

"Craig's in Thailand, he sent me a postcard recently. He's having a great time apparently," he said, even though he'd never even read the card.

"Oh, how is he?" asked Liz, feigning interest.

Jamie remembered they'd all shared a couple of excruciating lunches together.

"He's HIV positive."

"Oh dear," she said. "Well, he shouldn't be running around the world, he should be getting proper medical care."

This was typical, Jamie thought. It was as though Liz was saying Craig should just give up like she had done. She was never willing to take a risk, so why should anyone else?

"You're a trained doctor, you should know there are drugs that can keep you healthy even with HIV."

"As a retired doctor, I'm saying it's totally irresponsible," she replied.

Jamie could only hear his father's voice; they were one and the same. Liz no longer had any opinions apart from Bob's.

"Anyway, where would you like to go on holiday?" he said, changing the subject, exasperated.

"Another drink?" said the waiter, butting in condescendingly, as though scolding two alcoholics.

"Just the bill," snapped Liz.

"Sure," he said with a smile, making an unecessary fuss of cleaning away the plates.

"Where would I like to go?" she said, thinking aloud, as though it had never occurred to her before. "I've always wanted to visit India actually, I hear it's so colourful."

"Yeah?"

"Yeah," said Liz, a far away look in her eye. "I doubt I ever will mind you, your father hates Indians."

As was the custom she paid for lunch by credit card, the one small concession to freedom Bob had granted since insisting she give up work several years ago. She also handed over an envelope of cash for Jamie, just a few pounds to "help him out", as she did every month.

"You do look a bit tired and drawn, are you okay?" asked Liz, in an unusual moment of motherly tenderness.

"I'm fine," he said, blushing as he thought of the lifestyle that had brought a rather haggard look to his once fine features. "Shall we go?"

Liz, not needing much prompting, stood bolt upright and was already fastening her coat with trembling hands.

"What will you do for the rest of the day?" he said as they passed the manically grinning waiter on their way from the restaurant.

"Just some shopping but I've got to get home to cook your father's dinner."

"Yeah."

They went their separate ways at street level, though Jamie had leant across for the usual goodbye kiss and did feel something for Liz as she turned on her heels back to the prison of her life. But mostly he was consumed with a sense of hate for his own flesh and blood.

CHAPTER SIX

Craig headed down to breakfast and afforded a sheepish smile to the women on reception. They nodded back. He imagined Natasha already strutting majestically around the malls of Bangkok fingering new outfits and deciding what to buy on his money.

He walked into the 24-hour coffee shop where several people had their heads slumped on tables, looking like they'd been there all night and probably had. Craig noticed the obligatory couple of old Western tourists with young, garishly dressed Thai girls. The men chatted away while the women — probably the age of their daughters — stared blankly out of the window.

Then there were the Thai boys, most typically but totally implausibly sitting with white men in their forties, fifties, sixties and even seventies. Craig stared, with a mixture of fascination and disgust, at the men dressed like children in shorts and T-shirts sitting having breakfast with young companions. He saw some of the older gentlemen even snapping pictures of the boys, who were smiling through what he took to be their abject misery.

Craig ordered a pot of tea as he focused in on the many youths alone or in groups, all ready with an easy smile as they sat before a giant satellite television and watched the American garbage spew forth. He noticed that some of the teenagers huddled together were already sharing a bottle of whisky. Almost all were chain-smoking.

Several of the boys, dressed in cheap clothes and noticeably drenched in sickly perfume, continually turned around to stare as though eyeing his every move. Craig felt their allure but was also repulsed, as though the boys were something to be used up and then thrown away.

"Hi, do you mind if I sit here? All the other tables are full," said a swarthy, young, athletic-looking guy with an untended mass of dark curly hair, approaching his table. He spoke haltingly as though he wasn't fully proficient in English. Distracted, Craig looked around and every space was taken, leaving him with no choice, though the guy was looking at him so intently that he already felt wary.

"Go ahead," he replied.

The table was small and they sat directly opposite each other, making conversation almost obligatory. Craig wished he had a newspaper to hide behind and resolved to drink his tea quickly.

"I'm Israeli," the stranger said by way of an introduction, pointedly not looking Craig in the eye, his body exuding an obvious tension.

"Craig from England," he said, but watching disturbed as his breakfast companion ignored him to frequently turn fully 180 degrees to look at the boys set in front of the television.

"It's like being a kid in a candy store," he finally blurted out, the tendons in his wrist and forearm taut, clutching a glass of water just poured by the waiter, his eyes fixated on a pretty boy on the adjoining table.

"Pardon?"

"I'm addicted to these boys," said the Israeli with a mixture of self-loathing and desire, eventually facing Craig. "I can't help myself."

"Do you come to Bangkok often?" he replied, trying desperately to attract the waiter's attention in order to pay the bill.

"Yeah, many times," the Israeli said sadly, as though ashamed. "I'm resident in the US but I'm working in Korea as an English teacher and come here as often as I can."

"It's my first time."

"Oh," said his companion, clearly disinterested, as his eyes bore back into the boy on the adjoining table, who found he had to look away.

The waiter arrived with the bill as Craig fiddled in his wallet for the 100-*baht* note.

"See you around."

"Yeah man," the Israeli replied, not even breaking his stare but instead placing some money in front of the boy on the next table, making some kind of sordid down payment that the youngster couldn't afford to turn away, guessed Craig.

He moved back into the reception where he noticed more elderly white men sitting in armchairs reading newspapers or gently dozing off, untroubled by the bustle of people coming and going. There was a certain placidity about them compared to the frighteningly manic intensity of the Israeli, he thought.

Craig entered the pool from a side entrance and saw with some amusement that he was still being watched by the Thai boys in the dining room, which looked over the pool. He also noticed the pretty youngster now sitting with the Israeli, both engaged in some animated conversation.

A few youths were also sitting around the swimming area on loungers, either in the company of older men or obviously desiring company. Craig picked a chair in the shade out of the relentless sun, which others were already frying in. He watched as several sets of young eyes followed him.

One of the Thais from breakfast, who had been sitting alone, came and sat adjacent and waved a little wave and smiled a little smile as he did so. The guy looked very young, about sixteen, was slightly built and had an unattractive, pockmarked face. He was carrying a pen and paper and leaned over and thrust the pad at Craig.

He'd written in spidery handwriting: "Hi, my name is Oh."

Craig took Oh to be deaf and dumb, grabbed the offered pen and wrote down his name and where he was from.

Glances and little grins were exchanged between them as the idle chitchat continued for about five minutes. Oh's vocabulary seemed to be drying up when he wrote: "I come to your room, I like you!"

Craig couldn't help laughing and he did feel sorry for the not so attractive, handicapped boy who was seemingly shunned by his peers and the other foreigners alike but wrote back: "I like you too but just friends!"

Oh looked more resigned than disappointed as he nodded, lay back on his lounger and closed his eyes.

It was a tropical morning, the stillness only occasionally broken by a large palm leaf from the trees at the edge of the pool spiralling into the water. At this the attendant would scurry across and scoop it out. Craig relaxed and enjoyed the warmth and the calm after the hell of his last few months in London.

The sun beds began to fill up around lunchtime, while Craig noticed Oh had approached an older man with his pen and paper. He watched as they disappeared after the briefest of encounters into the hotel. He sadly imagined the two enveloped in silence, the boy taking his only solace in the comfort of the man's hotel room.

Another two guys came and sat next to Craig, sharing the lounger vacated by the deaf boy. One of them took his interest, a tall, slim Thai with great muscle tone and sporting the skimpiest pair of swimming shorts known to man. He also had one of the most beautifully exotic of faces, grimacing comically as he massaged suntan lotion into the back of a very white thirtysomething, inelegantly tattooed and overweight man. One of those men who'd started to give up, thought Craig, realising they'll never be beautiful in spite of moisturizer, but probably contemplating liposuction.

The guy caught Craig looking over and said unselfconsciously: "Hi, my name's Mike, where ya from?"

"Craig, from England, pleased to meet you," he replied.

Mike held out his hand to shake Craig's, oblivious to the Thai boy still pummeling his back.

"Hi my name is Kan," said the lad, not to be overshadowed, as he flashed a great white smile.

But before Craig had a chance to reply the Thai skipped off into the pool, all of eighteen, beautiful, and he clearly knew it. Mike and Craig briefly united in laughter at the boy's playfulness.

"I'm originally from Miami, Florida, but I'm working for the US Navy stationed in Manila," said his new chum, lowering his voice and already turning conspiratorial as Craig found Americans were wont to do.

"Wow," he replied, impressed. "So it's don't ask, don't tell?"

"Something like that," said Mike, looking more serious. "No one really knows about me in the Navy but as often as I can I come here to see Kan."

"How long have you known him?"

"We've been together about three years."

"Oh," said Craig, trying to calculate how old Kan was when they'd met.

"I'm in love and I like to look after him even when I'm not around. I pay him an allowance every month," he said, straining every sinew to appear sincere, though Craig sensed the American was probably one of the good guys. "Do you want to come out with us this afternoon?"

"Yeah, what will we do?"

"Just go shopping or something. Kan loves to shop," said Mike, rolling his eyes.

The American waved as a Thai guy in a sarong and bandana creation came towards them. He looked about thiry-five but was dressed like one of the boys who'd been in the coffee shop. On his arm was a very frail looking white man. Mike introduced the Thai to Craig as Tommy.

Tommy sat on Craig's lounger and said "hi" as he put a hand on his thigh, despite the elderly man looking on. He then did the same trick as Kan, discarding sarong and bandana and jumping into the pool with a hideous, high laugh.

"It's my last day today. I've given Tommy some money and no doubt he'll be going shopping this afternoon," said the older man in a very polished English accent as he sat down somewhat arthritically in a chair opposite Craig.

"Your boyfriend?"

"Oh no, not really," he sighed, a little too wistfully. "He's really a good boy though."

"Why don't you come shopping with us?" said Craig, already taking a liking to the genteel old Englishman.

"I'm far too ancient for all that kind of thing," he replied, smiling. "You go ahead and enjoy yourselves."

The four of them piled into the taxi, Mike in the front and Kan and Tommy in the back with Craig. The English boy noted that Kan had made a point of sitting next to him and already felt the Thai's spindly hand reaching for his inside leg, which he tried with little success to brush away, with Mike totally unaware in the front seat. The American was going in a couple of days and Kan was looking for another meal ticket, Craig realised.

On the journey they passed the familiar shiny towers of luxury hotels, corporations and shopping malls, some done in a fanciful pastiche of classical Thai architecture but all ultimately ugly and uniform. Craig found the endless cascade of concrete intimidating and depressing in the fierce glare of the sun as the boys nattered and giggled away excitedly in Thai like kids on an away day from school.

When the cab pulled to a stop he noticed a profusion of gaudy Western-style fast food outlets dwarfed on one side by an absolutely mammoth shopping mall. Both sides of the street, bisected by a four-lane road clogged with traffic, absolutely teemed with people.

"Welcome to Siam Square," said Mike, laughing. "A veritable shopping Mecca and nightmare for the sane."

They exited the taxi onto the pavement as people pushed past in both directions. There was a bus stop a short distance away and Craig saw even that had a television set fixed above it, blasting out MTV at full volume as people stood rooted to the spot, engrossed.

As they turned into an alley his attention was taken with a row of garishly painted boutique shops, which on closer inspection offered kitsch and outrageous clothing. Like with the coffee-shop boys of earlier Craig found himself both compelled and repelled. He guessed the sugarcoated, shiny consumerism served as the antidote to the grim realities and relentless poverty of the city and he saw Kan and Tommy smiling as though contemplating how they were going to spend the money they'd earned. Craig was aware he and Mike paled into obscurity next to their two flamboyant companions but he wasn't unduly concerned.

They sat down in some faux French café after Kan and Tommy were done, surrounded by shopping bags and exhausted by the heat and filth of a Bangkok afternoon. Craig lapped up the icy air-conditioning and wiped the sweat from his brow on a napkin handed to him by Tommy, who he sensed was already looking for a new sugar daddy following the imminent departure of the old Englishman.

"I'm so sad, my lover leave today," Tommy said laughing as he looked through his bags at what he'd bought, then back at Craig. "My heart is broken."

"But daddy will be back soon," said Kan, giggling at his friend's cruelty.

"Enough already," said Mike like he'd heard it all before and feared what his so-called boyfriend got up to when he was out of the picture.

Tommy was giving the English boy the eye but it was Kan he was entranced by, who now belied his effeminacy as he swigged greedily from a bottle of Heineken. The two Thais sat contentedly while the American looked fidgety and distracted, probably worried at what would happen once he'd left, Craig thought.

"He's a tough cookie, you know," Mike said to him, nodding at Kan.

"Yeah, I bet."

"A farmer's son and he's tough all right," said the American. "He once knocked out a guy who was coming on to me. He's a bit of a psycho."

"Yeah," Craig said uncertainly, sensing that Mike was gently warning him off his boyfriend.

As the American became more edgy and his conversation dried up Craig listened to the excited chatter of Tommy and Kan, who drank and smoked together as though united by their experiences. He felt hypnotized as he listened as their voices rose and fell, high and low, dark and light.

The beers flowed as the afternoon turned to evening and Mike eventually recovered from his funk.

"You fancy coming to Babylon tonight?" he said.

"What's that?" asked Craig.

"Just one of the best gay saunas in the world," said the American with a wink. "Why do you think I like it here so much?"

"You're a bad man," Kan butted in and slapped his boyfriend lightly around the head, though the expression on his face said he wasn't joking.

Craig, buoyed by the alcohol, glanced over and caught the boy's eye. Well Kan had been looking at him most of the afternoon using every opportunity he'd had. The Thai winked back nonchalantly as he continued drinking his bought-for beers like he was flavour of the month.

Craig had felt trapped in London because he was ill, but many Thai boys were completely hostage to the whim of the foreigners they courted, he thought. And despite everything as the American got up to the bathroom, he smiled across at Kan, a selfish smile of want and desire. In that moment Craig was as corrupt as all the other tourists that came to Thailand for just one thing and he knew it, but he also knew that wouldn't stop him.

He was grateful to get back to the calm of his hotel room following the afternoon's frolics with Kan, Tommy and Mike. His head hazy from the beer, he looked out of the window as night fell across the sprawling city and as the lights blinked back at him Craig wondered what else awaited him on his travels.

Exhausted, he flicked on the TV and finally lay on the bed. He let his thoughts about the frantic few hours he'd spent in Thailand whirl around. Now that he was travelling he'd never felt more alive. Contentedly Craig entered the black hole of sleep in the hot and sweaty night.

He woke with a start, being aroused by gunfire coming from the TV he hadn't switched off. He looked at the screen and watched as Al Pacino, with a smile playing at his lips, blew someone to pieces in *Scarface*. Craig laughed to himself, momentarily transfixed by the black comedy of the bloody scene. He stumbled across to the bathroom for a cold shower and prepared for his trip to the sauna.

Babylon was just a short walk from the hotel in the syrupy darkness and Craig felt relieved when he saw the discreet sign marking the entrance. Mike had something to "sort out" with Kan but promised they'd be along later in the evening.

As the English boy entered into a world of subdued lighting and water features the man behind the marble reception desk feigned surprise, even though Craig guessed he'd seen foreigners fall from grace a thousand times before. He laid down just a couple of hundred *baht* and with a curt nod the receptionist handed over a key and a crisp white towel in return and directed him upwards.

He pushed through a frosted glass door and up the spiral stairs as indicated to where he supposed the changing rooms to be, aware that the sauna was designed to disorientate with its faceless concrete walls and numerous unmarked entrances. Several smiling, towel-clad boys passed him in a narrow hallway. He had to squeeze by them and felt mildly intimidated at being so lost.

Eventually he tracked down a locker room that corresponded to his key number, aware that he was breathing hard in the odd silence, only broken by manic pop trash played over the PA system. There were others moving quietly around the changing room but they just looked and turned away again as if playing some kind of game to which Craig felt he didn't know the rules. Tentatively, he stripped and wrapped a towel around his waist as he'd seen several of the other boys do.

He wandered around the labyrinthine corridors barefoot and, as he climbed higher into the bowels of the building, into the darkness, Craig sensed the whole atmosphere become more predatory. Boys peered desperately out of the shadows, obviously looking for something. Often a large foreigner would stumble out of the gloom with a bovine awkwardness, making Craig recoil.

The smell of sweaty, young pumped bodies pervaded his nostrils and erotic images entered his mind as he felt his way along the hard black lacquered walls in the semi-darkness. All was a studied quiet apart from the occasional ecstatic gasp or growl against the infinite high-energy pop soundtrack. Silhouettes seemed to move sensually just beyond his reach but he finally found his way to a more brightly-lit stairwell.

Craig came to a rooftop bar where the charged atmosphere and silence was broken by the welcome sound of conversation. Many were sat in chattering groups in contrast to the selfish pursuits of below. He felt more relaxed, sat down and ordered a beer from a passing waiter.

The ice-cold liquid felt comforting as it slid down his throat in the soupy evening heat. He looked out over at the skyline, then up at the glowing full moon, a natural contrast to the twisted glass and steel towers of the central business district close by. But Craig's appreciation of the view of Bangkok by night was cut short as something far more alluring moved into his line of vision. On the adjoining table a Thai boy had sat down. He was quite short but very muscle-bound with a cute face under a harsh crew cut. The English boy noticed he had a tattoo of the devil above his left pectoral.

The verandah was virtually empty so he surmised that the boy must like him to sit in such close proximity. And sure enough as they sat in silence the glances from the little guy got gradually more intense as Craig took bigger gulps of his beer. When their eyes inevitably locked the boy smiled and got up and started heading towards the stairs slowly and deliberately.

Despite himself, Craig got up and followed, descending the stairs just behind the boy, close enough to touch him. The boy glanced back knowingly and he finally relaxed and smiled back as they entered a dark corridor.

Now right behind one another, the Thai boy caught his hand and led him through the silent, cloying darkness into what felt like a larger space. Craig could sense the presence of others, the hot breath on his face, the telltale whiff of cologne, but he couldn't see anybody, just vague outlines of shapes as his eyes struggled to adjust. And all the time he gripped the boy's hand tighter and tighter.

Somehow the Thai had backed him into a corner and Craig pictured the face of the boy, who was now expertly performing fellatio on him. He felt guilty about their totally unsafe sex but was selfishly too alive to his own pleasure to stop the boy.

His conscience finally prompted him to wrestle the boy away, though as they emerged from the darkness the Thai glanced at Craig and was still smiling. The English boy, too ashamed to look his brief encounter in the eye, felt momentarily saddened at what had amounted to a quick fumble that he knew his HIV status shouldn't have permitted, at least not without the inconvenience of a condom.

"My name's Eddie, you?" said the Thai, his grinning face rescuing Craig from the depths.

"Craig, I'm from England."

"Ah, my last boyfriend was from England."

Craig was a bit concerned that he was already being mentioned in the same breath as a former boyfriend but was beginning to realise the term meant little, or less than it did in the West. And as they walked back to the bar, he felt lifted by the light breeze and the chatter, so incongruous with the heat and heavy silence of below.

He ordered a beer for himself and his new friend.

"So what do you do here in Bangkok?" he asked, hoping their acquaintance would count for more than a two-minute grope in the dark. He was anxious to learn more about Eddie, more about Thailand.

"I work as a administrator for an English-language school."

"You live close by?"

"No, very far from here," laughed Eddie with regret. "Near the airport, very cheap there. I live with three other guys."

"Is it a big place?"

"Just one room," he said shrugging. "And two beds."

"Oh," Craig said thinking that despite his inquisitiveness he'd already uncovered more than he actually wanted to hear.

"They bring guys home sometimes and it's difficult to sleep," Eddie continued regardless, as though he didn't want Craig to have any illusions. "They always bitch at me in the mornings when I press my clothes."

"Sounds like a nightmare," Craig replied, imagining the Thai's roommates writhing around with various foreigners as he tried to get some rest in the stinking, hot night.

"I'm not worry, it's my day off tomorrow," Eddie said, smiling again, as though a day off made everything all right with the world. He reached across and held Craig's hand tightly as the muscles in his upper arm bulged attractively.

Both seemed more comfortable as the alcohol took effect and Craig quite enjoyed listening to Eddie's rising and falling broken English, which had seemed so foreign and indecipherable at first. He liked looking at the little man as his eyes, like two black pearls, danced around. He couldn't help feeling a sense of melancholy at the boy's story though, his placidity in the face of adversity.

"You want to come to DJ station?" said Eddie.

"Yes, I'd love to," replied Craig, smiling. He'd read in the *Rough Guide* that DJ was "Bangkok's gay disco".

Kan, Tommy and Mike passed by their table and the American winked over at Craig, though his boyfriend scowled across, obviously making his displeasure felt as the trio disappeared off into the shadows.

"Your friends?" asked Eddie, curious.

"Yeah, I just met them today."

"Oh."

"What's the tattoo?" Craig asked, just needing an excuse to brush his hand across the muscly chest set proudly above a rippling six-pack.

"It's the devil that's inside me," declared Eddie, laughing.

Craig already felt an attachment and laughed along, looking forward to his night with the devil.

"You want to go with him?" Eddie queried, screwing up his face in disgust as he caught the English boy glancing at a passing lithe young Thai.

"Of course not, I was only looking. I want to be with you," said Craig as he leaned across and kissed Eddie full on the lips. They didn't feel like strangers anymore.

CHAPTER SEVEN

Jamie took the electric razor and buzzed off the sprinkling of hairs on his chest. He looked at his arse admiringly in the mirror and plucked away a few straggly fair hairs. He thought hairless was better, more innocent.

He'd lost his job in the Saint after being caught snorting coke in the toilets. Not really a sacking offence since most of the customers were doing it too, he figured, but the manager had never liked him simply because Jamie turned down his lecherous advances one too many times. So he was intent on passing the screen test because he needed the money. It was as simple as that.

Jamie wasn't self-conscious about his body. He admired it but even so he wasn't sure how he'd perform in front of a camera. He was nervous and wary of George like he knew he should have been of Pete — there was something about the director that was plain intimidating.

He arrived at Adam Films, a small office space behind Oxford Street. The polished wooden floor and track lighting had smacks of interior design about it and photographs of naked men stared down from the walls, but all very tastefully done, Jamie noticed. It reminded him of a trendy gay bar. They always tried so hard to be the antithesis of sleaze but often ended up the opposite.

"Can I help you?" shrilled a very young and sickeningly pretty man from behind a black lacquer reception desk.

"I'm here to see George."

"Screen test?" said the receptionist, smirking disconcertingly.

"Yeah."

"He's still doing lunch, take a seat," said the boy, directing Jamie to a sexy low-slung leather sofa.

He did as instructed, sweating slightly despite the cold day. Jamie leafed through the artfully shot pornographic magazines scattered casually on the chrome and glass coffee table in front of him and listened as the receptionist detailed the minutiae of his sad little life to what he supposed was some bored friend. He wondered whether the pretty boy had been swallowed up by George and his camera lens too.

"Hi, got held up, you know how it is," said the director casually as he breezed in, camera equipment under his arm. The cloud of perfume still couldn't disguise the halitosis as he spoke directly into Jamie's face, invading his personal space.

"No problem."

"No calls please honey," George directed ominously to the receptionist as he led the boy to his office.

Jamie looked around the windowless room and was first taken by the array of pictures on the wall. The portraits were far raunchier than those outside, some violently so. A video camera stood in the centre of the office on a tripod.

"Like the pictures?" said George, looking pleased with himself as he sat behind a large black desk. "They're some of mine."

"Yeah," he lied, and felt himself slightly trembling, but the director sat coolly as though he had Jamie right where he wanted him.

"Okay, you got a pretty face, let's see what else you got," George said abruptly as he lit a cigar with surprisingly steady hands.

Jamie felt totally unnerved and all he could think about was a drink of icy cold water in the uncomfortably stuffy room. He tried to ignore George as he undressed but it felt so clinical, like stripping in a doctor's surgery. He rubbed himself as he got to his underwear and thanked God when he felt the stirrings of a hard-on. George continued to stare intently as though watching some art house movie with subtitles, totally expressionless, puffing out large clouds of distracting blue smoke.

"All off," he ordered.

Jamie removed his Calvins and triumphantly held the erection in his hand like he had passed the test. He started to pull himself up and down, caught sight of himself in a mirror and finally began to enjoy it.

"Very pretty but you can put it away now," said George almost derisively. "You're going to be incredibly marketable, marketable like a can of cola."

"Thanks," replied Jamie, letting out a nervous laugh and struggling to pull his trousers up.

"This game's like selling a piece of meat. If it's good people come back for more. Remember that," George continued dryly. "Always look as though you're having a fucking great time."

"Does that mean I've got the job?"

"Next week I'll call you with the details. So don't go wearing yourself out this weekend, if you know what I mean," said George, finally cracking something akin to a smile. He motioned as if the boy should leave.

He stood up to shake George's hand at the door but the director pulled him close and greedily stuck his tongue in the boy's mouth. Jamie fought the urge to punch him as he endured the filthy taste of the kiss and the groping, everywhere hands.

"Stay pretty," he said, winking cockily.

"See you," said Jamie, just wanting to spit the disgusting taste out of his mouth.

"Nice packet," said the receptionist.

"What?"

"You were being filmed," said the boy, laughing as he patted the TV screen in front of him. "Better get used to it."

Jamie felt like saying something but decided against it and was grateful as he opened the door onto the grim London backstreet. He just wanted to lose himself but felt in some ways he already had.

He felt the prickly heat of the lights on his body and blinked back the glare that helped shroud the assorted crew. Jamie lay on the hotel bed, half-naked and vulnerable, the cameras poring over his flesh in the brilliant, unforgiving light.

George had already run through the excuse for a plot. The piece was entitled "Room Service", another porn cliché, but the director assured Jamie it would be "classic Adam Films, bringing Europe's best boys to the small screen".

He had been curtly introduced to his Scottish co-star Aiden, who was to be the naughty hotel bellboy bringing Jamie his late-night snack and a little bit more. They formally shook hands and barely spoke two words to one another, Aiden not even proffering eye contact. George then offered up a selection of Class-A drugs to ease away any inhibitions. Jamie gratefully snorted up the white lines in the horribly uniform hotel room, with its grainy wallpaper and cheap fittings.

Now on the bed he fidgeted uncomfortably under the lights, in front of the all-seeing cameras. At a knock on the door he got up as instructed, dressed with just a towel around his waist, and let Aiden in, his flimsy bellboy uniform barely disguising the relentlessly pumped mass of muscle underneath. He claimed to be a "veteran" of the skin flick industry but didn't look particularly confident or even bored, just vacant.

As Jamie finally broke the blank stare of his co-star he watched, repulsed, as George licked his lips in anticipation with his discoloured, reptilian-like tongue. The director stood absorbed behind his camera, waiting, while Aiden put down the silver platter he was carrying and moved purposefully towards the bed.

"I know what you really want," he said in a breathy, low voice, slightly slurred from the drugs, and wrestled Jamie roughly back onto the bed.

He began ripping at Aiden's clothes just to keep the momentum going, already desperate to get the performance over with. Eventually his co-star was down to straining white briefs and Jamie, his towel now off, sensed George above them, saw the intrusion of the long camera lens just inches from him. It crawled all over his body as the magnesium arc of the white-hot lights dazzled his eyes and prickled across his skin. He noticed another member of the small crew in the corner of the room watching a monitor and simply nodding his head.

He writhed around on the bed as Aiden had him in a headlock, pulling him down closer to his crotch. Jamie ripped the underwear off and was mildly stimulated by the big dick. He lapped at it with eyes closed as the Scotsman roughly caressed his hair.

"Good, good," he could hear someone saying, not sure whether it was George, Aiden or one of the crew.

Jamie felt a finger massage his arse but he continued sucking. Tension wracked his prone body, the sweat poured from him, and he opened his eyes. His gaze caught George's, who was holding the camera just centimetres from him, an ugly expression of lust and concentration on his usually impassive face.

Aiden flipped him over like a rag doll and coarsely pushed lubricant inside Jamie. He felt the Scotsman enter him and gave unsteady gasps as the crew watched intently. His co-star wasn't wearing a condom because "bare backing" sold more copies according to George. Aiden had assured Jamie he was negative.

He athletically but mechanically eased himself in and out in any number of sexual positions as he pounded the boy into the bed, harder and harder. The rhythmic movement continued above Jamie, his face now flushed and sweaty, the make-up all but melted away as he stared out at the camera, resentful at its presence and close to tears. He watched helplessly as George zoomed in closer and closer, feeling more and more exposed. The camera lingered briefly on Aiden's blank eyes, then focused back on the vigorous pelvic thrusts that were relayed back to Jamie via the monitor opposite.

The Scotsman finally withdrew and Jamie, slightly disorientated by the coke and frantic to get the ordeal over with, took the penis in his mouth. Aiden rocked back and forth, still silent and expressionless. At last he moved violently and came. The camera loomed over Jamie as he watched his own distraught face staring back at him as it filled the monitor screen. Disgusted, the boy turned away from the image only to squint defencelessly back into the blinding lights.

Aiden slapped him on the back and went to take a shower as the crew gave a little round of applause. Someone threw Jamie a bathrobe, which he gratefully hugged around himself to cover his naked body. He felt cold, freezing, as he sat on the edge of the bed waiting for his co-star to finish, while George stood in front of a screen seemingly engrossed by the playback of what had just occurred.

Jamie was still blinking the brightness away, the unforgiving brightness that had searched every detail, as he entered the shower. He lost himself in the steam and revelled at being enveloped in the hot water. He stayed under the scalding jet a long time, anxious to feel clean again, but as he closed his eyes he could still see the glare.

The crew was packing up as he emerged fully clothed from the stall and he was thankful that there was no sign of Aiden.

"Oh, here's the star of the show," said George airily, raising a glass of champagne that he was guzzling with an associate. "Do have some champers dear, you earned it."

"Thanks," said Jamie, greedily swigging down a glass, angling to get away.

"Well done. Let's do it again in a few days. I'll call you," said George, absently handing him a thick brown envelope of money and a small wrap of coke.

"Bye then," replied Jamie, but his farewell went unanswered as the director continued poring over the flickering images on the monitor.

After being eyed with what he thought was something like suspicion in the lift by a bunch of Japanese tourists toting video cameras, Jamie enjoyed walking out into the buzz and anonymity of the West End with the wad of money enticingly in his pocket. He quickly located one of Westminster Council's convenient automated toilets and snorted up the rest of the cocaine. Hopefully he checked his mobile but the robotic voice informed him "no messages".

Darkness had fallen and he felt high and invincible as he pushed his way past office workers scuttling to get home in the rush hour to what he guessed was the certainty of their families. His nose was numb and his mouth dry from the coke but he was enthralled with himself as he skipped along preparing for another night out, alone.

Jamie ended up in a bar called CXR where he enjoyed the dimly lit interior and the obvious stares. He almost instinctively ordered Red Bull and vodka from the barman since it was recommended in *The Face*. The hallucinatory effects of the drink were supposedly legendary. Though he'd never experienced it he pretended he had.

He leaned against the wall, cocksure and confident of himself, just waiting to be approached from the shadows. Jamie knew in a place like CXR being young and cute made the offer of at least a drink an inevitability. He was aware many lads often spent the night being bought beers before disappearing to the toilets and never coming back, leaving some elderly and tearful desperado to foot the bill. He'd often done it himself with little guilt because he didn't really have a conscience.

He stood against a pillar enjoying the furtive glances and the drug high that still permeated his body. Sober, he convinced himself he wouldn't have been seen dead in a place like CXR, but Jamie was far from sober and didn't want to go back to another empty bed.

He became aware of a handsome-ish guy in a suit who had moved to within touching distance beside him. The man kept glancing around, then would nervously look back into his pint glass if Jamie happened to catch his eye. He rarely liked to do the chasing and was content to let the guy either make a move or disappear off home, though he'd be pretty upset if he just upped and left.

"Hi, I'm Gary," his admirer said finally as some kind of opening gambit. "I work in a bank."

"Sorry, I'm a bit tired," said Jamie as he yawned rudely, but he wasn't totally disinterested since he noted Gary wasn't bad looking and his London accent concealed any sign of a lisp. "I'm Jamie."

"What do you do?" Gary asked over-enthusiastically, way too eager.

"I don't."

"But I think you're really cute," said Gary, undeterred and still looking shyly into his glass.

"Oh bless," replied Jamie with scorn, but quite turned on by Gary's seemingly bashful nature.

"You have a boyfriend?"

"Er, no," he said, slightly disconcerted that things had turned so serious so suddenly.

"You want another drink?" asked Gary, seeming to sense Jamie's unease.

"Yeah, Red Bull and vodka please."

Gary returned with the drinks and stared at Jamie as he handed over the vodka mix.

"Yeah?" said Jamie in response to the rather worrying glare, sensing that his brief encounter had gone from a shrinking violet to a psycho in the space of two drinks.

"Oh nothing, I just like you."

"You've known me for about ten minutes," he replied scathingly.

"So?"

"You like me?" repeated Jamie. "Well I suppose I'm a nice guy, great in bed too."

They both laughed, breaking the tension, and Jamie realised they were probably going home with each other. The vodka and drugs had already limited his ability to make rational decisions and want and desire had taken over in spite of his drinking partner's freaky intensity.

"I really like you," Gary said, staring at him closely.

"Hey, I like you too," he replied, leaning into his companion's ear because he liked lapping up the adoration, but he knew Gary's earnestness should have set alarm bells ringing.

"Really?"

"Sure," said Jamie, trying to play things down and swigging back the remainder of his drink with a finality that suggested he wanted to leave.

"Did I say something wrong?"

"No, I just want to go home," said Jamie as casually as he could, sensing he'd got Gary hook, line and sinker. "You coming with me?"

"Yeah," he replied, leaving half his pint on the counter and trying desperately to keep up with Jamie as he strode out of the bar.

He showed Gary immediately into the bedroom, not interested in the usual etiquette of coffee and yet more small talk.

"What?" questioned Jamie, returning from the bathroom to find his guest rifling through his scattered collection of books and CDs. But he didn't see the Stereolab album Gary had already slipped into his inside suit pocket as some kind of bizarre trophy.

"Just looking," he replied, holding his hands up defensively.

Jamie, clad in only a towel after a quick shower, just snorted and was beginning to regret the intrusion as he watched Gary making a big deal of getting undressed.

"Shy?"

"Can you turn the light off?" he said, now clumsily down to his briefs.

"Jesus," said Jamie, exasperated, but complying with his guest's wishes.

He took the lead in what was fairly uninspiring and awkward sex. It felt almost like Gary had never been close to another human being as they writhed around pointlessly but he held onto Jamie as if not wanting to let go.

"Okay, I'm tired," said Jamie, unfulfilled, as he cruelly prized off Gary's grip from his shoulders. "Let's sleep."

Neither of them had come but Gary didn't argue. Jamie at least felt mildly comforted by the presence of another as the anaesthetic of drugs and alcohol wore off and sleep mercifully approached.

The light flooding in from the window hit Jamie like a collision and he pulled the duvet up over his head as Gary busied around, getting ready for work. He directed him to the shower and hoped he'd be quick.

Reluctantly he got up to show his guest out as they both exchanged phone numbers on scraps of paper as ritual demanded, though Jamie was careful to write down a fake number.

"I'll call you," said Gary, gazing lovingly into Jamie's eyes on the doorstep.

"Sure," he replied as disinterestedly as possible, looking away as he rudely slammed the front door on Gary and the outside world.

He watched his one-night stand leave from the window and ripped the carefully penned phone number into little pieces that he let scatter to the floor. Jamie then checked the post, all junk, apart from a postcard from Craig. He read the first couple of lines about what a good time he was having in Thailand and then chucked it in the bin. He went back to bed and hopelessly buried himself under the duvet.

"*Guyz* magazine want to do a supposed exposé of the British skin flick industry," said George, excitedly puffing a large cigar behind his gargantuan desk. "You know more than anyone that sex sells and it would be good publicity for you too."

"Really?" replied Jamie, not entirely convinced he wanted to be depicted as a porn star in a national magazine.

"You're an excellent cover story, babe."

"I'm not sure."

"Well, you know what?" said George, his pale skin flaring pink as he finally lost his carefully cultivated cool. "If you want to continue working for me you don't have a choice."

"Okay," replied Jamie meekly.

There was a journalist assigned to cover the story and Jamie had been informed of his credentials, though he wasn't sure "experienced tabloid hack" meant he'd get a fair portrayal.

He was briefly introduced and watched the reporter skulking around the fringes as filming began. Jamie saw him taking particular note of the various drug paraphernalia that littered the set, but George stalked about with the camera, all business as usual.

Aiden was his co-star again but it could have been anyone. The director had bullied Jamie into taking copious amounts of coke beforehand and now he didn't really know where he was. The Scotsman just pawed at him as they thrashed around dispassionately.

"Look interested!" bellowed George at an increasingly resentful and slovenly performance from his stars.

The photographer from *Guyz* was busy taking stills and Jamie blinked as the flashbulbs popped but otherwise remained expressionless. He was left feeling numb by the drugs and the mechanical sex as the magnesium flare of the flash continued remorselessly.

The lights and amount of people in the small studio made it positively suffocating. Jamie felt the sweat running off him and sensed the camera scouring his every pore. When he caught George smiling over at the journalist his stomach cramped but he continued pulling himself off like the script demanded. As he finally came he experienced only relief, while Aiden withdrew and ejaculated pathetically over his prostrate body.

Jamie averted his gaze from the several sets of prying eyes as George eventually lowered the camera, then dashed into the bathroom, bolting the door. He turned on the shower burning hot and stepped under, only dislodged from his solitude by an impatient knocking. It was Aiden, who gave him a short hug, but he knew whatever shred of connection had been between them had been destroyed by the camera lens. He nonchalantly brushed the Scotsman away but his co-star simply shrugged.

"Have another line," said George as Jamie came back into the room, nodding at a mound of white powder on the coffee table.

He walked over and cut himself two large lines without a word and snorted hard, hoping to take the pain away as the photographer and journalist continued to hover at an uncomfortably close distance.

After some coercion from George Jamie sat opposite the reporter, his shirt undone provocatively to the navel as though he'd become one of the director's commodities.

"What are your ambitions?"

"I want to be an actor," replied Jamie, totally without irony.

"Do you think this will look good on your CV?"

"Yeah, I see this as a leg up," he lied, when all he was really interested in was the money and the drugs. Honestly he couldn't see a way out.

"If you could star in any TV programme what would it be?"

"*Baywatch*," he replied, deadpan.

"Why?" asked the journalist, laughing uncontrollably.

"The muscle boys and the sunshine," said Jamie, just playing along, almost oblivious that his nonsensical quotes would appear in a national magazine.

"What about unprotected sex?"

"I have regular HIV tests and I'm negative," Jamie replied breezily with a fake grin, knowing he was totally ignorant of his status.

"What about drugs?"

"They help me to relax," he said, breaking out into nervous laughter as he got up and walked out of the room, not wanting to be part of the circus any more.

He got a thrill from seeing himself staring out of the cover of *Guyz* until he read the mocking strapline: "Is this the next *Baywatch* babe? Sex and drug revelations of a porn star."

Jamie took it down off the shelf and avidly read the article, but was sickened at how his words had been twisted. Drugs were a prominent feature when he felt he'd hardly mentioned them, and he was portrayed as a one-dimensional, vacuous addict playing "Russian roulette" with unsafe sex.

In his last line the reporter cuttingly concluded that: "These films are made by the corrupt for the desperate in an industry that consumes new bodies every day."

Jamie, with tears rolling down his cheeks as he finished the piece, felt, not for the first time, totally betrayed and violated.

CHAPTER EIGHT

Jimmy, Eddie's conspicuously wealthy Thai friend, gunned the engine of his sexy blue convertible and coolly flipped up the concealed headlights as they sped away from Babylon. The Thai boy, sitting snugly on Craig's lap in the cramped two-seater, held a big fat joint to the lips of his new acquaintance.

Craig felt the fingers against his mouth as he breathed in and watched the tip flare an explosive orange. He was thrust back in his bucket seat as Jimmy accelerated onto the expressway and felt the satisfying weight of Eddie on his thighs.

Jimmy glanced over every now and then at Craig and offered a smile, the kind of self-assured look the English boy guessed money bought in a jungle of a city like Bangkok. He realised already that most weren't so lucky.

Craig ran his fingers across the thick, muscly neck in front of him and brushed the prickly, shaved hairline. Eddie turned around and flashed a smile but his eyes were as dark as the night sky above them. Still, the English boy felt exhilarated at the pumping music in his ears, the wind through his hair and the relentless heat emanating off of the tarmac. The extravagant Thai script on the road signs that flashed by was a reminder of how much a stranger he was.

They came to a halt at a traffic light and Craig noticed other drivers staring over at them. The convertible stood out among the cheap Japanese cars and weathered pick-up trucks, but then that was the whole point he guessed, in a land where he'd already witnessed the god they'd made of conspicuous consumption, as it was in the West.

Craig took another hit from the joint and tossed it spinning into the air as they raced away from the lights. The dope made him relaxed and he slipped into the mood of the night, pushing his hand under Eddie's singlet and feeling the warm, velvety skin. The boy's nipple ring felt strangely cold and alien against his fingers.

He was unprepared as they took a sudden sharp turn off the road and into a murky underground car park. Craig looked across at

Jimmy for reassurance but the driver stared ahead as they came to a stop at the far end, furthest from the entrance. He touched Eddie's arm for an explanation but he was fiddling with his mobile. The luminous green read-out reflected off his face gave him a sinister look as he spoke a deluge of Thai into the mouthpiece.

Craig looked away, momentarily mesmerised by the glow of the headlights arcing against the concrete bunker of the car park. Jimmy ominously cut the engine and Eddie stopped talking as they sat in a tense silence. The English boy opened his mouth to speak but shut it again as the noise of another car engine filled the void. The vehicle drew up beside them.

"Have you got 1,000 *baht*?" said Eddie to Craig with a look that forbade the English boy to refuse.

He unquestioningly handed over the cash for what he guessed to be some kind of drug deal. Eddie thrust the money at the now open window of the other car, from which a shadowy figure returned a brown envelope almost instantaneously. The Thai deviously shoved the package down the side of the seat and with a squeal of tyres the other car reversed and boomed back off into the darkness.

The three waited in silence for another couple of minutes, after which Jimmy hit reverse and then jerked the car forward.

"For later," said Eddie, turning around and smiling at Craig mischievously as he tapped the brown envelope.

Totally in the boy's thrall, he just nodded back dumbly, but was relieved the palpable tension had lifted as they came above ground.

Jimmy drove just the right side of recklessly until they reached a four-lane road clogged with taxis and *tuk-tuks* disgorging bright-eyed foreigners. The driver perceptibly slowed the car as they became part of the view.

"This is the world famous Silom Road," said Eddie, laughing. "Where all the tourists come looking for bargains."

"And prostitutes," chimed in Jimmy, rolling his eyes.

They turned off Silom and came to another car park but this one had a guard at the entrance and was lit with harsh fluorescent lights. The swept tarmac was scattered with Mercedes and Lexus, which gleamed and glistened in contrast to the Third World street above. Again Jimmy drove to a far, deserted corner.

As they stopped Eddie keenly brought out a clear plastic container from the envelope. It was filled with powder that looked yellow and discoloured against the bright white lights above. Eddie held the receptacle to Craig's nose.

"Harder," he said as the English boy sniffed up the drug. "It's 'Special K', ketamine."

They greedily shared the drug between the three of them. Eddie held the plastic, which was still spotted with powder, up to the light. He wet his finger, ran it around the remnants and thrust it into Craig's mouth, massaging the powder into his gums as he stared blankly into his eyes.

Eddie opened the car door and got out. Craig followed but had to hold onto the door to steady himself as he stood. The Thai grabbed him and pulled him close with such force that they were nose to nose. Craig tasted the bitter amphetamine on the boy's swollen lips and ran his tongue across the full mouth. He closed his eyes and let the moment take him to another place but the Thai boy bit down with his teeth, his eyes flashed wickedly as he pushed Craig away playfully and smiled. The Englishman smiled back, wide.

They pushed through the nightly crowds of Patpong, which Craig knew to be the city's infamous red-light district. Eddie expertly negotiated through the throng but the English boy held onto his friend as he felt dazed. The sweat oozed from his brow, while the pulsating neon dazzled his vision and a cacophony of voices assaulted his ears:

"You want sex show?"

"You like boy?"

"Sexy girl?"

"You like fucky, fucky?"

"Live sex show inside, very cheap."

Craig hastened his step as another hand came across to grab him, another face leered into his, offering another beckoning, crooked smile. Pimps emerged from the shadows and disappeared just as quickly, like lights being flicked on and off. But inside, behind the blinding neon and the cheap façades, he couldn't help but wonder what was going on — so-called entertainment that some came thousands of miles to see.

The tourists stood around the tacky market stalls like moths attracted to a flame, captivated by the brightness. Craig blinked away the light as he watched a big black rat scuttle off into the sewers, and shuddered. The bright lights and smiles couldn't put a gloss on everything, he thought.

Craig felt more comfortable when Eddie and Jimmy pulled him inside a dimly-lit bar because, despite the thundering house music and the flashing smiles of the bar boys, it was air-conditioned cool inside.

"I'm just going to talk with my friends for a few minutes," said Eddie, nodding over to a muscle-bound group of shaven headed clones as he sat Craig on a barstool like some kind of naughty child.

He couldn't contemplate negotiating his way through a conversation with strangers when he wasn't even able to stand upright properly on account of the elephant tranquilizer he was regretting having shoved up his nose. But Craig was aggrieved at being so alone in a strange city on the other side of the world as he watched the guy he'd bought drugs for hold court with his Thai friends.

"Would you like a drink?" asked the barman, somewhat rhetorically, through a smile.

"Yeah, one Singha," Craig replied like an automaton as he stared at the boiling lava lamps set pointlessly in the bar.

Eddie did look over now and again while Craig sucked on his ice-cold beer, concentrating hard on looking cool. But he felt anything but. He so didn't want to be the stoned guy in the corner who passed out and no one ever saw again.

His mood turned when Eddie's friends suddenly left the bar in a tangle of hugs and air kissing. The Thai approached Craig with a sheepish smile and hugged him.

"Do you wanna do E?"

Craig felt the hot breath on his neck and simply nodded in agreement. Anything it took for them to be together he was stupidly willing to do.

As Eddie dragged him to the bathroom he noticed Oh, the deaf and dumb boy, at the other end of the bar with the old man from earlier. He waved. Oh smiled back, then returned his empty gaze to the chubby companion old enough to be his dad — and old enough to know better, thought Craig.

"Who was that?" snarled Eddie.

"Just some guy I chatted to at the hotel."

They entered the toilet cubicle, squinting under the harsh lights, as Eddie locked the door. Craig looked around at the small, filthy space and put his hand to his nose at the smell. The Thai seemed oblivious as he fiddled around in his pocket and brought out a small plastic bag. He revealed two round, crumbly pills and held one to the English boy's lips, then pushed the green lump of chemical onto his tongue, which he gratefully swallowed back. Eddie popped the other pill in his own mouth, grabbed Craig around the neck and stuck his tongue lasciviously down his throat.

They reentered the comforting darkness and noise of the bar. Eddie led Craig back to his stool and then went and courted several more of his friends who had come in. The English boy sat down resignedly and watched the group as their pumped torsos vied with each other for width, huge arms ballooning out of high-cut vests — vests that tapered away to reveal the tautest of stomachs and skinny little waists. This was their life, ruled by the iron of the gym, Craig thought bitterly and, if honest, a little jealously. Steroids and anorexic diets all so they could stand posing in a bar or club flashing their rehearsed smiles.

He ran his eye over each body and gauged they were almost identical in their perfection; only the faces differed. Craig felt sickened as he watched the boys admire themselves in the mirrored walls. He was fit but he felt shrivelled and inadequate next to these fine specimens, all laughing so confidently at the bar.

"Hey big man, you on your own?" said Mike, interrupting Craig's thoughts as he bounded into the bar.

"Kind of."

"I was walking by with Kan and Tommy and thought I'd just drop in to say hi," he said, winking. "We're on our way to DJ, will you join us?"

"No, I'm coming along later with Eddie."

"Oh yeah, the muscle man," said Mike, looking across at the Thai boy whom he'd obviously had some intimacy with, thought Craig.

"I've gone AWOL, trying to sort things out here."

"What?"

"I told the Navy I'd been beaten up and robbed. I need a week to deal with Kan. I love the kid."

"Oh," he replied vacantly, because even though he could see the tears in Mike's eyes, he didn't care.

"You all right, buddy?" said the American, patting him on the back.

"Just a bit drunk."

"Okay, let's meet up later at DJ."

"Sure," said Craig, forcing a smile and relieved as the annoyingly affable Mike turned on his heels.

He was beginning to feel less and less self-conscious as the cocktail of drugs took a grip. Craig zoned out and watched the people's mouths in the bar open and close like goldfish. Eddie still occasionally looked over, piercing through the glaze of his world, but he could only look back and smile almost helplessly.

"Want another drink?" bullied the barman.

Craig nodded because he'd nursed his beer for almost an hour and had a paranoid fear he would be thrown out on the street into the darkness to fend for himself if he refused.

"You okay?" asked Eddie as he came over belatedly, looking concerned and presumably not wanting the responsibility of a casualty on his hands.

"Yeah, I'm okay, just a bit wasted."

"Wanna go to DJ now?"

"Yeah, I want to dance," replied Craig, but not sure whether he could actually get to his feet.

When he rose from the stool he felt unsteady again and saw Eddie grimace as he lurched ungracefully from side to side as they moved through the crowded bar.

"Water!" shouted the Thai at the barman and threw a banknote impatiently down on the counter.

Eddie frantically wiped the cold bottle across Craig's sweaty forehead and then unscrewed it and held the water to the boy's parched lips. Craig gratefully sucked at the icy liquid as his friend motioned for him to follow out of the door. He did faithfully because he was terrified of being alone, feeling like he did.

The heat of outside crawled all around him as people thronged the narrow alleyway, but Craig felt totally disconnected from their world. Instinctively he grabbed Eddie's outstretched hand and was pulled into DJ Station opposite. The Thai boy pointed to a raised platform full of writhing, half-naked bodies but all Craig could see was a daunting sea of people he'd have to negotiate.

At least the air-conditioning felt refreshingly cool on his greasy face as the elated crowd jumped up and all around them. It was frantic; sweat shimmered off brows and bare, toned bodies, while glazed eyes were picked out by coloured points of laser light. Craig mercifully felt the tautness and uncertainty that had dogged him melt away almost immediately as the music lifted him up.

The light and sound of DJ Station raced through his mind, the remnants of his hell of a year finally slipping away. He danced as though he was free. The feeling of exhilaration that arrived so suddenly and seemingly from nowhere was all-consuming, like riding a giant crested wave. Craig bobbed around in the drenched, glistening crowd, saw the hope in their eyes and the happiness in their smiles. He was smiling too and for the first time in a long while felt it deep down inside.

*   *   *

The English boy looked around as he glided downwards from the steep high of Ecstasy. He had caught Eddie's glance several times and the Thai would come and dance almost provocatively in front of him, then move off into the crowd again. This time he came and clasped his hand powerfully around Craig's wrist and motioned for them to leave.

"My American friends have a party in their hotel suite," slurred Eddie into his ear. "Let's go."

Craig mutely allowed himself to be led through the crowd and was uncomplaining as he was pulled roughly into a toilet cubicle. They stood facing one another in silence for a few seconds, the air charged with cigarette smoke and a muggy dampness. In the background the satisfying thud of the music continued, but somehow more distant and less intense. Eddie pushed Craig against the wall, concrete spotted with condensation. He held his two hands up to the English boy's face and pushed his tongue violently into his mouth.

Craig hitched up Eddie's vest and moved his mouth down to the hard, round nipples — he caressed them with his tongue, first the left then the pierced right. He bit into the meaty, solid pectoral muscles and the Thai gave grunts of appreciation. He desired so much and as he moved his tongue down to Eddie's dick he felt euphoric. The impatient knocking on the toilet door only made things more urgent and vital.

Eddie came furiously and dragged the English boy up to face him. They were both breathing hard and smiling as they looked into each other's eyes. So elegantly wasted it could have made the cover of a magazine, thought Craig. The Thai grinned again as he brought out another pill, like a magician revealing his latest trick.

"Mitsubishi, it's very strong," he said, holding it up to the light, examining it as though it was a precious stone, then crudely biting off half and handing a segment to Craig. "Let's party."

Outside DJ five of them clambered into a cab, though the only one Craig was familiar with was Eddie. He was wedged up in the back seat against another foreigner.

"Hi, my name's Devon," he said, offering a hand to shake in an unnecessary show of formality.

"Craig," he replied in a vague, stoned way, hoping it would prevent the guy from elaborating.

"I've arranged this party. My friend Stefan and I are over from Hong Kong and he's trawling the boy bars as we speak looking for suitable guests, or 'fuck toys' as I think he calls them," he said, face creased up as though in laughter, but no sound was emanating. "We're holding it at our place in the Sheraton but we don't want cigarette burns in the Oriental rugs."

Craig just nodded, thinking he was meant to look impressed, but going along with it anyway.

"What do you do here?"

"I'm on holiday," Craig replied flatly.

"Oh, another tourist," gasped Devon. "How wonderful."

The English boy shifted uncomfortably in his seat but resisted the urge to lash out at the supercilious American. Besides, there was an audience; four of them were crammed in the back and another guy nervously chain-smoked out of the open window up front. As an edgy silence descended the smoker turned on the radio. The cabbie stared stoically ahead as the passenger tuned in a dance station and yanked the volume up deafeningly loud.

The music rattled around Craig's brain and he felt totally adrift, surrounded by strangers as he looked out of the window at the grey streaked sky against the backdrop of a totally alien city. He was despondent that the brittle light of early morning had caught up with his long night.

Incongruously, they pulled up outside the imposing entrance of the Sheraton as a uniformed flunky rushed to open the cab doors. Craig noticed the loyal staff member not batting an eyelid as the dishevelled, drug-fucked mob stumbled out and into the hotel lobby.

"I feel a bit underdressed," he giggled nervously in his sweaty T-shirt and jeans ensemble as the five of them made a mockery of the polished marble façades.

A couple of staff at reception looked over dubiously but nodded the group wearily to the lifts. Excited chatter followed as they arrived on the pristine, brightly-lit corridors of the penthouse floor. The spacious, luxurious rooms undoubtedly cost more per night than most of the party guests earned in a year, but Craig suspected it was mere pocket money for the ostentatiously wealthy Americans.

After they'd done one noisy circuit of the corridor Devon finally located the room and knocked on the door. A guy with a Gaultier shirt unbuttoned to the navel answered, fake smile already in place. Craig thought he looked a little too immaculate considering the hour and how supposedly wasted everyone was. Not a hair was out of place on his gelled to perfection, high-maintenance haircut.

"Hi, my name's Stefan," he said, addressing Craig with a steely gaze and an educated American accent inflected just too far the wrong side of ironic for the English boy's liking.

"My name's Craig," he replied, turning away, already having seen enough to register a thirtysomething WASP, slightly balding, going to fat *and* with a point to prove.

"Come in, come in," he said, looking pleased to see Eddie but then ruining the sincerity with the worthless gesture of a Continental-style kiss on both cheeks.

Craig guessed the American had already been there and done that and was the type to use up and discard young boys with smooth, brown skin when they ceased to be entertaining to him.

He wasn't disappointed, for as they moved through the hallway and into the large suite Craig was confronted with several badly dressed, skinny boys shivering in the icy air-conditioned room. They looked so timid and out of place with the bold and extravagant furnishings and fittings. The huddle nervously slurped beer and tried to blend into the background, their chatter obliterated by MTV blasting away on a huge stereo TV dragged to the centre of the room.

Devon launched himself onto the empty sofa ignoring everyone as he lay down and stared up at the ceiling.

"And these are our friends," said Stefan, sweeping a hand in front of the Thai boys as though he was unveiling a work of art, and let out a bellicose laugh that made Craig wince. "A little young, I know, but we're paying, goddammit."

"Okay, it's over to you, Devon darling, you're the host with the most," the American continued as though trying to belittle his apparently comatose friend.

"Help yourself to drinks. Time to get the K going, club kids," Devon replied, but still fixated on the ceiling.

Most of the Thai boys looked impressed and intimidated by Stefan's strutting performance and the opulence of the penthouse but Craig despised it already. He left the room with Eddie and they found two beers in the well-stocked fridge.

"These guys are very rich," the Thai said reverently, but Craig pointedly refused to comment.

"I need a microwave ... an oven," said Devon, sitting up and barking into the phone as they reentered the uncomfortably well-lit room, his voice getting louder and louder and more agitated. "Read my fucking lips, a microwave, that's M-I-C-R-O..."

"Now darling, you don't want to get us all thrown out onto the Third World pavement, do you?" said Stefan, aggressively snatching the receiver and slamming it down. "Room service isn't going to bring us a microwave to cook Special K."

"Why don't we just send it down on a plate and get the kitchen to cook it?" Devon asked, and sounded disturbingly serious.

"And how would you like your K, sir? Medium rare or well done?" said Stefan, accompanied by another grotesque belly laugh. "But how *are* we going to cook it?"

"We need some candles," said one of the boys who'd come in the cab with Craig.

Stefan snapped his fingers and dispatched two of the boys to fetch candles from the 7-Eleven thirty-two floors below. "Well you gotta delegate," he said, winking at Craig as the couple obediently left the room.

"Fuck, fuck," shouted Devon as he lay back on the sofa, now fondling one of the boys who'd come and sat next to him. "I forgot to ask them to get ice, how can I fucking drink JD & Coke without ice?"

"What's a girl to do?" said Stefan, cruelly mocking his friend.

"Look, forget the microwave. Just bring me a bucket of ice," Devon shouted into the phone again.

"So when were you posted to Asia, Craig, may I ask?" said Stefan.

"I'm actually on holiday."

"Oh, I see," said his interrogator, mouth forming into a pout as though "holiday" was a dirty word. "We've been in Asia, well HK for ten years. It's still so conservative there but we're constantly pushing the boundaries. Isn't that right, Devon, darling?"

"Yeah."

"We just have to get away as often as we can. Weekends in Bangkok, or KL, or Singapore, or Sydney," Stefan said, sighing, as though it was all such a drag. "It is hard work in Hong Kong but I'm damn good at what I do. They ask me how this or that stock is going to perform and I say 'this baby's going up' or 'this little sucker's going down' and they buy and sell on my say so. What do you do?" he continued disdainfully, like nothing could possibly come close.

"I'm a nurse."

"Oh darling that's so worthy ... did you hear that Devon? He's a nurse."

"Fuck you!" spat out Craig.

"No, I think you got me all wrong," said Stefan blushing, obviously intimidated by the outburst. "I think you do a great job."

The doorbell rang, breaking the tension, and Stefan nodded at one of the Thai boys like nothing had happened. The boy got up and answered the door as instructed.

"Perfectly house trained. He lives with me in Hong Kong. My house boy," the American said, still addressing Craig.

"Whatever," said the English boy, turning away.

The perfectly attired waiter came flapping in and acted as though there was nothing unusual about the scene he was met by. Craig felt embarrassed but also realised he was very much part of the whole mess and party to some of its worst excesses. He was among professional guys with lives yet they still craved boys who were little more than skin and bone. Most of them present were underage, he guessed, but he couldn't help feeling an unwelcome spark of attraction. Disgusted, he excused himself to the bathroom so he could have a cigarette.

"May I join you?" Stefan asked, still refusing to let go.

"If you like," Craig replied as unenthusiastically as possible as he padded to the toilet with Eddie by his side.

"See my *raison d'être* is making money for my clients and myself, shitloads of it," said Stefan in the cavernous bathroom. "And I'm bloody good at it."

Craig and Eddie blew out smoke from their cigarettes and just stood in silence, looking totally disinterested.

"We're doing these Thai boys a favour," the American continued, ploughing on regardless as though he just wished someone, anyone, would listen. "We give them a good time and pay them big bucks. I mean some arseholes come over here and pay them 1,000 *baht* for a night."

"Let's get this party started," bellowed Devon, poking his head around the bathroom door with a manic smile. "K's ready."

There was a big silver tray on the coffee table, almost dwarfed by the mound of ketamine that had a gold card tossed casually on top. The tray was passed around with reverence as each took his turn. Some of the boys were noticeably hesitant, as they'd obviously never indulged before, but were egged on by the Americans, who knew the power of drugs on the vulnerable, guessed Craig. Stefan stood over everyone's shoulder just to make sure they got a good dose.

"Take one more hit," bullied Devon to the boy on the sofa next to him.

The kid still dallied so the American, who seemed to be coming more and more unhinged, took the card and shoved it under the boy's nose himself.

"That's a good boy," he cackled as the Thai hoovered it up like he was told.

The Englishman revelled for a few moments in the rush, climbing higher as he became entangled with Eddie, but he couldn't help but watch as the other boys huddled closer together, presumably to blot out the cold from the air-conditioning or maybe to protect against their American aggressors.

"Craig, have you met Devon yet? He is actually the host of this party so it would be appropriate for you to talk to him," said Stefan.

"What?" he replied, incredulous that the American just wouldn't shut up even though Devon, the so-called host, was now passed out on the sofa.

"Well Craig I'd feel a lot better if you and Devon got acquainted, he is your host after all," continued Stefan as his voice rose hysterically.

Suddenly the boy who had been cuddling on the couch with Devon got up and started jabbering something in Thai. He pointed to the American, whose body was convulsing like it had been given an electric shock, his face had turned an unreal pale, beads of sweat popping from his forehead. Green bile was flowing copiously out of his mouth, his eyes an ominous blank.

CHAPTER NINE

He was jolted out of his apathy by the phone, its shrill tone unusual in the typical silence of his flat. Jamie picked it up, briefly expectant, but sighed inwardly when he realised it was his mother Liz.

"Hi," he said, hoping to hide the fatigue and depression in his voice. He'd been moping around his home for days since the exposé in *Guyz*.

"How are you?"

"Fine," he lied.

"It's our thirtieth wedding anniversary this weekend and we'd like to invite you along."

"You mean *you'd* like to invite me."

"Your father said you should be there."

"What, so he can give me those disapproving looks?"

"Well, it's up to you," Liz said, trying to be casual but sounding flustered.

"Okay," Jamie finally replied after a long pause designed only to keep his mother in suspense.

He looked in the mirror once he'd put the phone down, resentful of another call that had made him feel awkward and uncomfortable. The image staring back at him had dark rings under the eyes and he brushed a hand through the untended, straggly beard growth wondering what the future held, but not really seeing beyond a weekend with his parents in a wintry Brighton that he was actually dreading.

He'd agreed to the anniversary dinner because he didn't know how to excuse himself without repercussions. Jamie knew his family was all about appearances and that Bob probably *did* expect him there. He also believed in karma and thought by doing something supposedly good he could balance out the debit column in his hemorrhaging account. Most crucially he wanted to keep on Liz's good side so he could continue priming her for money.

He dressed soberly and unenthusiastically in shirt, trousers and sensible shoes. He wasn't travelling to the South Coast to enjoy himself or to flirt and wanted to look as conventional as possible for Bob's sake, though he bitterly regretted the fact the evil bastard still had some kind of hold over him.

Jamie had scotched the idea of the whole family travelling by car together. Liz said "it would be just like old times" but he remembered the fearful rows his parents had had when he was a kid. They'd be driving somewhere and he'd have to cower on the back seat, covering his ears, trying to block out Bob's sick taunts. No, he'd take the train and meet them in the allotted seafront pub.

He had happy childhood memories of Brighton since the passing of time softened the rough edges. Jamie remembered the blue skies, the gleaming pier and the big ice creams handed over by men always flashing bright smiles. Even to a kid the town possessed something seedy yet alluring with its penny arcades and whiff of fish 'n' chips on the breeze.

But when he arrived he discovered the romance and blue skies had long gone. It wasn't the Brighton he remembered; it was February and the town looked grey and lonely, totally threadbare. As he walked from the dreary station, past the gaudy hotels and junk shops disguised as antique emporiums selling the trash of those long since dead, the chilling wind gusted around him, filling in the empty spaces. He smiled to himself bitterly as he recalled the Morrissey song about the "seaside town they'd forgot to close down".

When he reached the front he edged forlornly along the gum-stained promenade, viewing the colourful kiosks with their garish Brighton rock and candyfloss pathetically trying to brighten the dullness. Jamie put his collar up to the breeze as he stepped onto the pier and watched as the gulls screeched overhead and the lime-green sea raked over the harsh pebbles. He breathed the cool, salty air and looked back at the front, fearing that his parents were already waiting in one of the cheerless pubs.

Liz had given him directions with typical neurotic precision and warned him "not to be late", obviously on account of his tyrant of a father. And as he approached the dreary façade of the Red Lion, a place that the concept of theme pubs and renovations had obviously missed, he hoped by some miracle that they'd got their wires crossed and he was at the wrong place.

Jamie opened the door with some trepidation and was hit by a smell of stale beer and cigarettes. Sure enough he saw his parents at the bar, stood almost to attention. His mum hadn't even noticed him, nervously eyeing her watch, no doubt, because he was slightly late. Bob had seen his son and nodded over trying to look relaxed in a stuffy sports jacket. When Jamie approached resignedly Liz finally looked up and offered a tepid smile.

They self-consciously exchanged "hellos" and offered each other weak grins on what was supposedly a joyous family celebration, the only three customers in what appeared to be a cavernous pub. They could have been the only three people left in the world, thought Jamie, but still they had embarrassingly little to say to one another.

He watched as the barman, possibly sensing their awkwardness, moved around behind the counter and switched on a stereo. Jamie saw Bob wince as the Spice Girls began to boom from the speakers, while a fruit machine winking sadly in the corner offered up the only sign of life.

"Want a drink?" Bob said to his son, not even offering the warmth of eye contact.

"Lager please," said Jamie, going for the most masculine drink he could think of, though he looked at his dad's pint and of course it was a manly, dour-coloured bitter.

"Half or pint?" he questioned, almost mockingly.

"Pint," Jamie replied as he watched Bob grimacing at the camp and affected barman waiting to pour his drink.

"This used to be our favourite pub, me and your dad's," said Liz.

"Sometimes you should leave the past behind," he whispered harshly as silence fell again.

They stood at the freezing bar like three cardboard cutouts, the bubble-gum pop of the Spice Girls the only sound reverberating in their ears. Jamie saw the barman watching in rapt silence too, feigning indifference and pretending to polish the glasses above their heads.

"I hear you might be going to Thailand," he said to Bob, finally breaking the terrible silence.

"Yeah, looking forward to it," his dad said morosely, staring straight ahead from the bar as Liz nervously sipped her drink to the other side of him as though waiting for the coming explosion.

Jamie sensed his mother knew that the day had been too stressful to avoid cracking Bob's veneer of near civility. There was a familiar tension in the air that he just wanted to escape from. Yeah, just like old times, he thought.

"Are you all right?" said Liz as she timidly looked across Bob at Jamie.

"I'm fine," he said, swigging back his drink and looking into his pint glass.

"I hadn't heard from you for a while..."

"Oh don't bloody fuss woman," said Bob, butting in and ominously flexing his shoulders in the restrictive sports jacket.

"Yeah, sorry I've been busy," Jamie lied, addressing Liz in a bid to further rile his dad. He sipped at the remainder of his drink and fingered nervously at the cigarette packet in his pocket but not daring to light up.

"Happy anniversary," Jamie said eventually, beaming ridiculously at his parents and holding up a virtually empty glass.

"Thanks," said Liz, turning to Bob with only tears in her eyes as her husband of thirty abusive years raised his hand as if to ward off any shred of sentimentality.

"Cheers," he said finally, turning to Jamie and clinking his glass with the merest hint of a smile on his face, but recoiling just as quickly as they each went back to seeking solace in the bottom of their drinks.

"Want another?" shrilled the barman effeminately from behind the counter at them, noticeably perking up as another group entered the bar.

"No," said Bob, whirling around with what Jamie noticed was something close to hatred in his eyes, something he'd seen far too much of.

He excused himself to the bathroom and laughed ironically as he saw the semi-naked pictures of men staring down at him above the urinal. Obviously the Red Lion, Bob and Liz's favourite, had become a gay bar.

"Ready?" asked his mother as Jamie came back and they prepared to leave.

"I better use the loo first," said Bob gruffly.

Liz threw her hands up as if to say, "Why didn't you just go with Jamie?" but instead kept her usual counsel.

"Where are we off to next?" said Jamie, just willing the nightmare to end as quickly as possible.

"English's Fish Restaurant," replied Liz, smiling. "Your dad and I had our first date there."

"Romantic," said Jamie, not being able to resist a dig as he smiled back at the barman glancing at him longingly from the bar.

"He was once," said Liz, sighing like she'd been transported back to all those years before, when she'd been so full of hope.

"Some bloke made a pass at me in there," said Bob at the top of his voice as he came back from the toilet, flushed and shaking with anger and embarrassment, barely able to contain his fury.

"What?" queried Jamie, incredulous, as the barman and the group of men who'd recently come in stared across at the ugly commotion, while Liz as ever stood dumb and impotent at her husband's side.

"I should've bloody clocked him one," he shouted wildly. "They're all the same, that lot, bloody disgusting. Sick, that's what they are."

The barman and the group of men erupted in piercing laughter as Bob's voice rose to a shriek, while Jamie stood momentarily dumbfounded. But there was nothing left for him to say — his father's hateful words and the bar's laughter ringing in his ears, he turned his back and walked away.

He exited the pub feeling totally desolate but hoped they wouldn't come after him. Some line had been crossed, a divide that could never be reconciled, and Jamie knew he was on his own, though really he'd always been alone.

He wandered and wandered the streets until the grey sky darkened in sad relief to the orange glow of the street lamps, blending effortlessly into Brighton's shadow of waifs and strays. He finally walked into a faceless pub with a rainbow flag fluttering conspicuously outside. Jamie sighed inwardly at the interior of track lighting, chrome finishes and a sea of shaved heads but ordered a pint from a barman defaced by piercings and sporting the automatic smile.

For some reason the barman had reminded him of Craig and as he settled back onto an aluminium stall he thought briefly of his ex and of the promise of sunny Thailand, but then he thought HIV and didn't want to think any more. Craig and he were long over and a succession of men had followed with another battalion waiting in the wings.

The shrill of his mobile jolted him out of his thoughts. He knew instinctively it would be Liz trying to defend the indefensible and he angrily snapped the phone off. He hoped they'd be involved in a car crash on their way home, one of those accidents featured on TV where the car's so crumpled it's unrecognisable. He imagined the broken glass, tangled metal and scattered limbs and it actually soothed his troubled mind.

The pub began to fill up with the after-work crowd as Jamie leafed aimlessly through one of the free gay newspapers, which was nothing more than an excuse for contact ads. He knew one of the designer-lager sipping locals with little to go home to would be intent on taking him back to upset an immaculately minimalist loft apartment. Even though he felt like wallowing in his own misery, he could think of nothing worse than going home alone, as he didn't even have anywhere to stay for the night.

"Hi, you're cute," said a guy, breathing into his ear.

Jamie cringed at the terrible chat-up line but turned to face his admirer. He smiled at a stocky black guy, muscles bursting from a tight Adidas T-shirt that screamed retro, vintage jeans and a pair of "old skool" trainers.

"Hi, my name's Jamie," he said, bracing himself for the worst, since the guy's outfit may have looked as though it had been thrown together but there was a certain contrived cool about it set off by the thick-rimmed NHS style glasses.

"Pleased to meet you, Jamie," his admirer replied with a broad smile and stuck out a big hand for him to shake.

"How come you get to go out during the week?" Jamie said irrelevantly.

"I'm Steve, by the way," he said, eyeing Jamie a little oddly, presumably because he hadn't even asked for his name.

"Hello."

"I'm a fashion student, that's why I don't have to get up every day," he said in a pronounced way that failed to disguise his south London accent. "What do you do?"

"I'm working for a film company. Just down from London for the day," he replied, but guessed Steve was far more interested in talking about himself. His heart had already sunk at the words "fashion" and "student".

"Oh," said Steve, his mouth forming into an ugly pout. "What kind of films?"

"Drama," said Jamie, laughing, but only to himself.

"Great."

"And what will you do when you graduate?"

"I'm going to be the next big thing, well, according to the *Evening Standard*," he said, giggling, but Jamie could tell this guy was totally enthralled with himself. "Some of the big fashion houses have already been sniffing around."

"Oh, so you're going to be the next Alexander McQueen then?"

"Mate, I like to think of myself more like Versace but with a twenty-first century twist," he said without a hint of self-deprecation.

"Oh," said Jamie, nonplussed. Maybe if he'd been feeling more secure he would have told him to fuck off but when Steve put his arm around him he didn't protest; in fact he felt strangely comforted.

"Mine was *the* killer show at the last Student Fashion Week in Shoreditch. I pissed on most of the other collections. Not literally of course."

He stared at Steve, almost disbelieving of his arrogance, but the black guy just winked back and cockily stuck out his pierced tongue. He guessed the bravado was all part of the act (and a bit of a turn on) but Jamie also knew he'd despise him the morning after.

"You have a boyfriend?"

"Girlfriend," said Steve, rolling his eyes. "I'm bi."

Of course you are, thought Jamie, repulsed again.

"And you?"

"I don't believe in boyfriends," he replied, trying hard to sound blasé.

"But you're gay, yeah?" asked Steve.

Jamie felt like saying, "What do you think, arsehole? I've got my arms around some big black guy," but he just nodded.

"I don't believe in labels," said Steve, as Jamie felt the black guy's hand move from the small of his back and onto his butt.

"You want to come home with me?"

"For coffee?" laughed Steve. "Sure, why not?"

Jamie wondered whether his admirer had taken anything and whether he had any left. Bound to be a line or two of coke, or that's what he'd say.

"Where are you staying?" asked Steve.

"With you," said Jamie smiling.

"You didn't book into a hotel?"

"Come on, shall we go?" replied Jamie, draining his drink, anxious to avoid any more awkward questions.

"Okay," said Steve, but still looking dubious. "Did you come alone?"

"Oh, my friend's already pulled."

"Like you then," said Steve, letting out an unnecessary belly laugh as he took Jamie by the arm and led him through the crowded bar and onto the street.

They walked in silence until they approached a couple of beggars holding their hands out.

"You know my concept for the Student Fashion Week collection?"

"No."

"Beggars," Steve said, embarrassingly sweeping his arm before him and indicating the two poor bastards crumpled up on the floor and looking pathetically up at them. "Just *so* street."

As they walked on Jamie turned to face his companion to see if he was taking the piss but his expression remained deadpan.

"We all have to get our inspiration from somewhere and I look to the streets for mine," he continued.

By this time Jamie had switched off completely and was plotting his escape. He felt bullied into submission by how great this guy said he was but the last thing he wanted to do now was sleep with him.

"Hey, I'm gonna get some food from McDonald's, want anything?" Steve said cheerily.

"No, I'll just wait for you outside," said Jamie, smirking to himself.

As Steve went in to order his Big Mac and fries or whatever, Jamie bolted across to a clump of telephone boxes on the opposite side of the road. He got inside one of the unlit cubicles that, thanks to vandalism and British Telecom's ineptitude, now obviously served as a public toilet for the town's winos. Despite the smell he waited, shivering and expectant in the dark.

Eventually Steve came out with the telltale brown bag and looked at the spot where Jamie should have been. He peered desperately from left to right and then threw his long arms up into the air and let his shoulders slump as though he was going to sob.

Jamie was shaking with laughter in the phone box as he watched Steve frantically looking all around himself once again. After a few seconds of contemplation he then strode purposefully off, probably cursing under his breath, fragile ego shattered and his sole consolation a Big Mac that would undoubtedly taste bitter in his mouth.

"You want fries with that?" said Jamie to himself and began laughing hysterically again as he left the phone box, though it was beginning to dawn on him that he was alone and had nowhere to stay.

He hugged himself against the cold night and set off blindly, finally accepting the tariff at the Sea View Guesthouse, a B&B that quite patently didn't have a sea view as it was nowhere near the front, though it was cheap.

Jamie was ushered to a box room with yellowing walls. He fell on the bed, which miraculously had clean sheets, but damp hung sadly in the air. Still groggy with drink he looked up at the nicotine-stained ceiling and listened to the rain that now battered against the windowpane and the shouts of the resident mentally ill. Jamie fantasised about suicide but thought what a grim way to go and actually laughed, laughed hysterically before crumpling into tears.

CHAPTER TEN

"For fuck's sake somebody do something," wailed Stefan, standing helplessly over his friend.

When no one else moved he started to slap Devon's face harder and harder but the American had stopped shaking, as if frozen.

"Why the fuck did you take so much?" shouted Stefan at the now immobile body, falling to his knees.

Stefan's houseboy jumped to his feet, shoved aside his employer and leaned over Devon, feeling frantically for a pulse. The placid look on his face turned to something like panic as he checked again *and* again, then sadly shook his head.

"Call an ambulance!" he shouted.

"We can't call an ambulance, I'll be finished — what about my career, my family? My dad's a United States congressman for fuck's sake," Stefan said, simpering. "This stupid bastard has ruined everything. I warned him to slow down."

"Call an ambulance," Craig ordered Eddie as he rushed over to the body, ripped off Devon's shirt and began pumping the sunken chest and expertly administering mouth-to-mouth.

Stefan remained totally impotent and sobbed deeply into the arm of the sofa, the kept boy his only comfort.

After a few minutes Craig turned away in sorry defeat, sweat dripping from his forehead and his shirt soaked. He looked around the disordered room, the faces etched with a kind of stoned indifference.

"We're going to have to go," he said, taking charge as one of the boys cleared the remainder of the K from the coffee table. "If the authorities get here we'll all be fucked."

"You're just going to leave us," sobbed Stefan disbelieving as he clung to his boy and nodded pathetically at Devon's prostrate body. "You're gonna leave us here all alone."

"I'm sorry," said Craig, getting up and urging the rest of the room to follow. "The ambulance will be here soon."

Everyone hurriedly filed out, most transfixed by the glassy eyes of the body on the sofa that stared back accusingly. As the English boy passed the pathetic and tragic sight, Stefan collapsed next to his dead friend and clung hopelessly to someone he'd bought, but Craig didn't feel anything akin to remorse.

He had a terribly depressing comedown following Devon's death at the Sheraton. But it didn't stop him going to Babylon the following day after getting out of bed in the late afternoon, when the sun had satisfyingly dipped behind the concrete edifice of the Malaysia Hotel.

At the "Disneyland of sex", as Mike called it, Craig disappeared into one of the rooms with yet another one of the willing boys, but his heart wasn't really in it and he didn't bother listening to the Thai's familiar patter. Every experience seemed to be merging into one, leaving the meaningless pattern of something not even as significant as a one-night stand.

The brief fumble in the darkness certainly hadn't appeared to make either of them any happier and as Craig stumbled back into the dimly-lit corridor he saw the Thai's childlike, scrawny body and felt ashamed of himself. His companion walked close behind but Craig quickly managed to lose him in the labyrinth of corridors.

He had a shower and left because he wasn't interested in any complications or disappointments. Craig was averse to facing the consequences of his actions but he knew, too, that the freedom his trip allowed was turning him into someone he liked less and less.

He tried calling Eddie when he got back from the sauna but his phone was switched off, meaning he was with the guy from Switzerland who he said he'd had to meet. On first glance, Craig hadn't been able to fathom the Thai fascination with older men but once he discovered the economics of the situation it answered most of his questions. It didn't stop him being jealous when Eddie had told him about the Swiss boyfriend though. It was an indication of how much he liked him.

In the darkness of the room he briefly wondered about Stefan's state of mind. He'd probably fled to Hong Kong just after they'd left the hotel room, thought Craig, who couldn't imagine a guy like that taking the rap for anything. Not when he could buy his way out of trouble.

The ringing of the phone interrupted his train of thought and he picked up the receiver with anticipation.

"Hi, is that Craig?"

"Course it is. How are you?" he replied, immediately recognizing Eddie's voice at the other end.

"Fine thank you. Are you alone?"

"Er, yeah," said Craig, marvelling that it was okay for Eddie to be off with some Swiss guy all weekend while at the same time being concerned that Craig may have taken the liberty of inviting someone to his room.

"Sure?" said Eddie, laughing too, at least seeing the funny side of his double standard.

"And you?"

"I'm on the bus, on the way to Samet Island."

"How about Mr Switzerland?" he pressed.

"Huh?"

"Your Swiss boyfriend, where is he?"

"Not boyfriend, just friends. We'll just spend a few days in Samet," he said, protesting too much. "I think you'll have good time tonight."

"Yes, I'll probably go out later," said Craig, sighing as he tired of the probing questions and replacing the receiver of the phone.

He got in the taxi and asked for Surawong Road. It was just behind the strip of joints that made up Patpong. Craig was headed for the appropriately named Soi Twilight and the even more appropriately named Dick's Café to watch some of the street life walk by, as recommended by Mike.

According to the American, Dick's was the perfect vantage point to witness the comings and goings of Twilight's sweaty den of go-go bars. Craig had given up pretending he wasn't interested but he was still having a hard time admitting what he really liked. Nevertheless, he was taken by the usual array of lovelies and not-so lovelies at the mouth of the *soi*. A motley crew of young boys gathered for the sole purpose, he guessed, of grabbing the attention of any passing foreigner, particularly a *farang* with a big bank account and a weakness for something he almost certainly couldn't get at home. Craig knew it was as easy here to pick up as walking into 7-Eleven and taking an item off the shelf, being careful to pay on the way out of course.

He walked past the straggly bunch and was immediately overpowered by their wide smiles and pungent perfume. He was followed down the *soi* by their catcalls:

"Where you go mister?"

"I make you happy."

"You want go with me?"

Vaguely aroused he turned back and smiled, knowing they'd smile in return. As his eyes ran over them he was aware they may have been too young and too bony but he wasn't entirely convinced.

Craig had only been in Bangkok a short while but he was no longer under any illusions, and he observed most of the foreigners that flocked to Twilight were doing so very much with their eyes open — they knew what they wanted, how to get it and most importantly, how much it was going to cost them. He saw tourists not into the scene watch the parade of ladyboys and rent with a studied expression of fascination and disgust, which he supposed was out of nothing other than fear and possibly to hide their own desires.

He sat down outside Dick's and watched as the night unfolded before his eyes, the brightly clad boys so desperate to catch any type of attention.

"Quite a show, isn't it?" said someone on the table adjoining his.

"Yeah," he replied as disinterestedly as possible because he feared they might have too much in common.

It was not that his neighbour was the stereotypical-looking dishevelled sex tourist — he was thirtysomething, svelte, tanned and immaculately dressed in shirt, chinos and deck shoes. But opposite him on the table smoking furiously and fiddling with a mobile phone, probably out of a mixture of nerves and boredom, was a young, skinny, tanned Thai boy.

"The name's Jacques, from Canada," the Westerner said, offering Craig a long, slender hand. With the other he was smoking a thin cigar.

"Craig, pleased to meet you."

Jacques didn't bother to introduce the boy, who was self-consciously sipping his beer and staring off into space. Craig sensed the Thai had the whiff of poverty about him; his clothing was trashy and mismatched and the way he held his cigarette was uncultured and ugly on one so young. Jacques, on the other hand, with his horribly inflected but educated North American accent, fine clothes and poise, looked every inch the rich heir.

"Wonderful isn't it?" said Jacques spreading his arms wide, indicating a group of boys out in the street and laughing aloud.

Craig was sorry for the Canadian's companion but felt partly responsible in some way as he sat impotently and listened to the North American.

"What do you do here then?"

"What do I do?" Jacques replied as though it was the most stupid question he'd ever been asked, as if he'd actually *do* anything.

"Well?"

"Actually, I'm a university lecturer, part-time," he said, lowering his voice and laughing as though he couldn't quite believe it either.

"And my real name's not Jacques ," he said, fixing Craig with an unforgiving stare as the Thai boy jabbered away on his mobile.

"I think your friend's bored."

"Oh, don't worry about him," said Jacques, rolling his eyes. "He cleans my toilet."

"So you work in Bangkok?"

"At the moment, but I've just been to Jakarta and I'm thinking of moving there," he said with a wide smile, revealing a film-star perfect set of teeth. "The boys there are just so darling and so young."

"Oh?"

"Well let's put it this way dear. If I start seeing anyone younger I'll be fucking fetuses," he said, creasing up with laughter again. "Hey, I'm so rude, would you like a drink?"

"Yeah, that would be nice thanks," said Craig in spite of himself, his fear and dislike of the Canadian morphing into some kind of crude fascination.

Jacques waved over the waiter as though he was a dog and ordered two Mai Tais and a beer.

"I hope you don't mind me ordering for you but the cocktails are great here."

"What's your friend's name, by the way?"

"Oh darling he doesn't have a name, he's a houseboy," said Jacques, letting out another ear-splitting laugh as the Thai looked shamefacedly down at the table. "No, I'm being silly. This is Tong One."

"*Sawasdee krub*," said the boy as he looked up and smiled sheepishly at Craig.

"Hello."

"He's quite happy," said Jacques. "He's always a bit quiet in the company of foreigners."

"I'm sure."

"Oh do be a darling and get daddy some more cigars, would you?" the Canadian said, addressing Tong, who almost jumped to attention as though he couldn't wait to get away as he quickly headed up the street on his errand.

"I call him Tong One because there's another Tong who stays over with me, Tong Two of course," he said, cackling at his own wit.

"How did you end up here?" asked Craig, again disregarding the flippant comment about boys.

"You shouldn't ask personal questions about how people ended up here. You might not like the answers."

"Where will you go after Dick's?"

"We're going to Dream Boys of course," Jacques said, slurring his words, obviously drunk. "And believe me they are a dream, well most of them anyway. I 'offed' one the other week. I really had to make sure I got my money's worth though."

Craig wasn't sure whether he wanted to hear another twisted story, but only because he could now invariably see himself as the protagonist. Taking the role of voyeur he nodded for Jacques to proceed with his tale.

"I took the boy to a hotel because I really don't like taking them to my house. I didn't spend all that on interior design just to have it ruined by some excited puppy you know.

"Anyway, we got into the room and he said he was going to take a shower and insisted I take one too. I said 'no' and he got all huffy. Then he just said 'make the sex quick' because he was going to go to DJ with his friends, but I replied I might want him to stay all night," he said, shrugging as though the boy was being simply impossible.

"I started to screw him and he kept crying out and I was getting a real kick of making the little shit pay and just went harder and harder. Then I pulled out and he asked me to come over his back but I shot in his face.

"Then I told him to get changed, gave him 500 *baht*, which is well below the going rate, and asked him to leave. Of course I complained to the bar's manager the next night and got a free drink," Jacques concluded victoriously, like he was recounting the tale of a bad meal or purchase that he'd just received compensation for.

These stories were becoming all too familiar to Craig as he sat finishing the drink the obnoxious Canadian had bought, ready to make his excuses and leave, but he could picture himself going to Dream Boys. He didn't have a lot else to do, he mused, though he knew it was the poorest of excuses.

As they reached the go-go bar's tacky façade that announced "Dream Boys", Craig wondered whether any of the boys outside trying to hook in passers-by had actually dreamed they'd end up selling themselves and their friends. Not that Jacques seemed overly concerned; he was engaged in a jokey rapport with the staff on the way in, indicating that he was a regular visitor. Tong followed a short distance behind like an obedient pet.

A few of the boys inside flocked around the Canadian and, though he waved them away laughing, Craig noticed the smug look on his face. Clearly wanting to be somewhere else, Tong ignored the attention Jacques was getting and nervously smoked another cigarette as he looked down at his shoes.

Craig observed some kind of demarcation between boys in garish orange uniforms — the waiters — and the actual prostitutes in nothing but Lycra shorts, though "everyone's for sale" Jacques noted helpfully.

One of the help led them to a counter adjoining the stage. Craig sat on a stool, flanked either side by Jacques and Tong. The Canadian didn't seem to mind that his boy had deserted him since he was already absorbed by the youths wearing the skimpiest of briefs parading around in an infinite circle.

"Ringside seats," he said, presumably to Craig, but failing to take his eyes off of the stage as he simultaneously lit another cigar and ordered a bottle of Johnnie Walker from the over-attentive waiter.

"The view's great from here," replied the English boy, guiltily contemplating more free drink and the touch of another dark, spindly youth.

"I'm working my way through the numbers," Jacques said, blowing a cloud of smoke towards the show, pointing out the numbered discs on the boys' underwear and letting out another unwarranted, throaty laugh.

As a variation on a theme, in the corner of the bar was a workout area where a number of boys were showing off on gym equipment before they took to the floor. Craig was quite captivated as he watched the youths' newly developed muscles strain and bulge. How many glasses of whisky and Coke, he wondered, would it take him to part with the few hundred *baht* required to take someone back to his hotel room?

"Hey, which one do you like? We're going to have a party tonight," shouted Jacques as he leaned over to address Tong.

Craig could see the boy wasn't interested; his failure to answer said so much more than the garrulous Canadian ever would, he thought.

"Well, I think they're all darling," he continued undeterred. "But let's not be greedy, a couple will do."

It was clear to Craig that Jacques saw such transactions almost as his right — the right that deemed if you paid enough you could do whatever you wanted with whomever, provided they were consenting of course. Though he suspected the definition of consent became a little muddied by the involvement of money, particularly lots and lots of it.

Nevertheless the English boy enjoyed his whisky, almost permanently topped up by the fussy waiter, and the trashy dance music. He was even more captivated by Number Seven — a skinny boy who looked the youngest on show. And what was great in such a fantasy land, Craig found, was that whatever you wanted you got, provided someone didn't get to him first. Whoever you winked at, they'd wink back, and probably wiggle their little butt at you for good measure or do something equally provocative.

Craig knew by the fourth or fifth time they'd held eye contact he was taking Number Seven home. Though his heart sank at how blasé he'd become about such a deal it only took another cheeky wink from the stage to banish any lingering doubt.

"Number Seven is a cutie pie," said Jacques, nudging him.

"Fuck off, he's mine," replied Craig, laughing but far from joking.

"Which one you like sir?" said an eagle-eyed Thai waiter as he approached Craig, even though he'd obviously witnessed the exchange between punter and prostitute.

"My lucky number," he shouted above the pumping music. "Number Seven."

"You want me to bring him over?"

"Okay."

"Good choice," said Jacques, and as he put his hand on Craig's knee, struck the all-knowing, suggestive expression reminiscent of a saucy seaside postcard.

But the English boy wasn't really listening because Number Seven was walking towards him dressed in tight Lycra shorts with a flimsy vest making a lame attempt to cover his torso. A torso that had been tanned under the tropical sun — probably on some bought-for holiday, Craig surmised — an upper body that had the faint outline of musculature but was essentially that of a boy, though the devilish, know-it-all smile said otherwise.

He incongruously held out a hand for Craig to shake, a tan hand that, he guessed, was used to intimate contact with pudgy white men and their greasy money. But the boy smiled through it all.

"What's your name?" he asked as the boy took a little notepad tentatively out of his pants, which Jacques rudely swiped.

"I like you. Where you come from? I go with you to your hotel room!" he bellowed, reading from the pocket-sized book in between mouthfuls of laughter as the boy frantically tried to retrieve it.

"I've been listening to your shit all night," shouted the Englishman, grabbing Jacques by the collar of his dress shirt. "I don't want to hear it any more, now piss off!"

They were nose to nose and tears quickly sprang to the Canadian's eyes. Odd how he felt it was his right to treat boys like slaves but crumpled at the merest hint of confrontation with an equal, thought Craig. Getting up theatrically, Jacques thrust two 1,000-*baht* notes into the hands of a waiter, handed the notebook back to the go-go boy and strode to the door. Craig was disheartened to see Tong hurriedly follow but was really glad to see the back of them both.

"Thank you," said Number Seven, giving Craig a *wai*, a sign of respect — respect certainly a rare commodity in a place like Dream Boys. Far more in keeping he then placed himself on the Englishman's lap.

His insignificant weight, slight arms and the deference in his voice already suggested to Craig that there was more to his story than a phrase book and a winning smile. But instead of asking any questions, he swigged back some more whisky and felt the warming contours on his thighs.

The weight shifted in his lap as Number Seven turned around again to face him with dark brown, almost black almond-shaped eyes, but there was something so pleading about his gaze that Craig was afraid to learn more about the boy.

"Can I go with you?" said Number Seven, unleashing a practised smile.

"I'm sorry," he replied, discreetly pulling 200 *baht* from his wallet and sticking it in the boy's shorts. "You're not my type."

There was a look of bemusement on Number Seven's face but he got up without a word and walked over to another, much older guy, who Craig had already seen undress the boy with his greedy eyes.

His conscience still nagged uncomfortably at him for rejecting the lad but he found himself transfixed by the group of young guys now jerking themselves off on stage — a bizarre, titillating competition to see who could come first.

Craig noticed the vacant space next to him and smiled; at least he'd done something right by telling Jacques where to go. Then he looked across at the old *farang* with a flabby arm firmly locked around Number Seven. He was negotiating with the waiter in the blue blazer, haggling over his prize like he was literally a piece of meat.

Not that Craig could afford to be holier-than-thou. He already had an eye on Number Sixty-nine, who was working out topless in the gym. He looked slightly older than the rest and there was something about his expression that was cocksure. Craig couldn't stomach any more uncomfortable brushes with Third World realities and hoped if he did choose Sixty-nine that the boy would keep his mouth shut, other than to whisper the requisite sweet nothings. He'd left London precisely to escape the "real world" and, as he watched the boys come one after another on stage, as though it were choreographed, it really was like being in a dream.

What followed was some terrible lip-synching to chart hits by a number of garishly dressed, horsey *kathoeys* so he reverted to watching Number Sixty-nine who, naturally, returned his attention. The go-go dancer didn't need any encouragement as he walked nonchalantly over, though there was a certain bored familiarity about the walk, about the whole routine.

"Hello darling, how are you?" he said in passable English, without reference to a notebook of prompts.

He was smiling, friendly and over familiar, but jaded as he barely bothered hiding a yawn behind his expensively bejewelled hand. Number Seven in two or three years' time, thought Craig.

"Ahn at your service," he continued, laughing in a self-deprecating but quite sexy manner. "Why you not go with my friend?"

"Not my type."

"Am I your type?" said Ahn, seizing the first opportunity that came his way.

"Maybe."

"Up to you," he said, making as if to walk away, then turning around and smiling confidently.

Craig glanced away from Ahn momentarily as he watched Number Seven walk out of the bar in gaudy, boyish clothes, hand in hand with someone old enough to be his grandfather — it was a pathetic sight.

"Hey, I thought you said he wasn't your type?" said Ahn, putting his hands to his heart as though aggrieved.

"He's not. Come and sit on my lap."

"You have to pay 200 *baht* to the bar..."

"I know the charges," said Craig, cutting him short.

"Sorry baby, you look young and I thought this might be your first time."

"No, I'm not a Bangkok virgin," he replied, and they both laughed.

For Craig it was the first time he'd laughed genuinely all night and it was dawning on him fast that he should have made good on his plan to leave Bangkok sooner rather than later.

"Hey, what are you thinking about?" said the boy, with a prostitute's sixth sense.

"Nothing. I'm going to Samui tomorrow. I need some time at the beach."

"I go with you honey," said Ahn, but laughed it off like he really didn't care.

They rapidly drained the whisky bottle, though Ahn seemed thirstier than Craig, who was quickly tiring of the show.

"Let's go soon."

"I go get changed then we go," said Ahn, ever eager to please.

"Okay."

"Stay here," he whispered sensually into Craig's ear as he left to dress.

Craig was embarrassed when Ahn returned because he looked so cheap in platforms, skinny-rib top and figure hugging jeans. But he dutifully handed over two crumpled 100-*baht* notes to the waiter as they left the bar. He felt even more sordid as they exited the dim cover of Dream Boys and out into the crowded reality of Surawong Road. He pathetically looked down at his shoes in case he caught the withering stares of any passing, middle-aged tourists when he knew he should have been addressing his Thai companion. Craig was grateful as Ahn hurriedly hailed a cab and they headed back to the Malaysia.

He found the light in the hotel's lobby particularly unforgiving, as the immaculately coiffured night manager always seemed to have a scowl on his face and looked even more pained when there was a boy in tow. Ahn timidly hung back as Craig approached the reception but the manager kept his eyes fixedly on the Thai as he handed over the key and dubiously took the boy's ID card, scouring it like he was an immigration officer. Finally the concierge issued an almost imperceptible nod to signal his approval.

"I'm hungry," said Ahn.

"Okay let's eat," Craig replied, leading him to the coffee shop.

Again it was too bright and probing for Craig's liking and the place was already full of older men either with younger Thai men or women, or looking hungrily for a companion. He was comforted slightly when Ahn sat in front of the big-screen TV that would negate the need for any forced conversation. He noticed other couples sitting around watching the American trash, seemingly transfixed for the want of anything better to say or do.

The waiter, leaning lazily on the counter, finally spotted the pair and sauntered over. Ahn ordered *tom yum* soup, while Craig just went for a pot of tea. The boy laid his forever blinking mobile phone on the table like it was the latest fashion accessory.

"Why don't you just switch the bloody thing off?" asked Craig irritably, wishing they'd gone straight to the room.

"I need to check my messages," said Ahn, giving him a bemused shrug and a sideways glance.

They sat in silence for the rest of the meal, both supposedly engrossed in some made-for-TV movie on Cinemax. Craig couldn't be bothered trying to recapture the waiter's attention so he paid at the counter as Ahn followed.

In the claustrophobic lift the Thai shot Craig a professional little smile but the English boy couldn't help feeling all sincerity had drained away since they'd left Dream Boys; now there was just a deed to be done — it was as though the clock was ticking.

Ahn snapped on the TV as soon as they got in the room, which made Craig bristle for its sheer audacity. He was boiling up inside and the fact he had to pay for the whole charade made him doubly angry. He just wanted the boy, who was now lounging on his bed watching MTV, out of the room. But rather than confronting Ahn he left him to it as he shut and pointedly locked the bathroom door. He felt better as soon as the hot water of the shower hit him, even though he was slightly concerned at leaving his wallet alone with the boy.

After a longer shower than usual Craig reentered the room, but to his dismay Ahn was still lying disinterestedly on the bed and hurriedly ending a conversation in English on his mobile.

"I go take a shower," was all he said as he ambled to the bathroom.

Thankfully it was a quick wash and the Thai did look sexy when he marched back into the room with a towel wrapped lazily around his little waist, showing off his dark torso. Craig, who had changed into shorts and T-shirt, grabbed at the boy and pulled him onto the bed.

Finally, after much coaxing, he got an erection and they had penetrative sex. Craig enjoyed the boy being face down on the bed and being in total control but as he came he felt a wave of revulsion course through his body. Immediately he ran to the bathroom, slid the condom off and watched it bobbing sadly in the toilet bowl.

When he came back into the room Ahn was already half dressed. He should have been pleased but felt worse that the boy was actually going because ever since he'd been diagnosed he hated spending nights alone, though it was all he ever seemed to do.

"Got to see a friend," said the Thai coldly as a cocky smile played at his lips, the smile that had attracted Craig in the first place but was now mocking him.

He didn't reply but instead just reached for his wallet, pulled out 500 *baht* and threw it down on the bed even though he knew the going rate was double the amount.

Ahn looked at the money questioningly, then back at Craig, but maybe experience had taught him it was better to say nothing because he simply folded the cash and carefully put it into his pocket. He then pulled on his shirt and quickly turned for the exit, calling out "goodbye" as he did so, which went stonily unanswered. Craig listened as the door clicked shut and felt a mixture of anger, disillusion and relief.

CHAPTER ELEVEN

The winter darkness had already descended and Jamie increased his pace as he entered Soho Square, where someone he knew had recently been robbed and assaulted. The number of parked cars casting shadows at the perimeter of the dimly-lit space made an excellent hiding place for muggers and he certainly didn't want his throat slashed for the fake Rolex he was wearing, though he knew his friends may have found it ironic.

He'd read in the newspaper that the streets were becoming more and more violent and he always suppressed a tinge of fear every time he went out late at night. Though, obviously, queer bashing was never mentioned in the mainstream press, Jamie knew the "pink" metropolis was not all aerodynamic bars, designer beers and liberalism, but he guessed he was safer in the Soho ghetto than almost anywhere else in the UK.

He entered The Edge, a three-storey Continental-style bar, which he secretly admired for its incidental lighting, glass surrounds, polished wooden floors and pastel colouring set off by supposed works of art hanging on the walls.

Not intimidated by the attendant throng of media types discussing advertising budgets or, more likely he thought, the latest episode of *Eastenders*, he pushed his way through to the bar and ordered a Red Bull and vodka from the flawless, film-star like Mediterranean-looking barman. The server glared as though Jamie was the enemy but offered just the hint of a smile as he handed back his change on the regulation silver platter.

He was lucky to grab a seat at the end of the crowded bar, which gave him a good sidelong view of the space. Jamie relaxed properly for the first time that day, for several days in fact, as he sipped his expensive drink and listened to the "handbag house" or whatever they called it, though he felt he should know, just in case anyone tried to strike up a conversation about the innumerable variations of house music.

It was a Friday so the bar filled up quickly, buzzing with an atmosphere of those with high hopes for the weekend, though he felt every weekend was becoming the same. It was like some bad movie on a permanent loop — go to a bar; get drunk; go to a club; get high; pick up; maybe have sex; throw them out at lunchtime; nap all afternoon and prepare for Saturday night where he'd maybe take two pills instead of one; home Sunday morning and sleep all day. Or if he was really short of cash he'd stay home on Saturday evening mesmerised in front of the TV with a supply of cheap wine.

There was always the lure of the Internet too where sex with anyone, anywhere in the world, was just a couple of clicks away. Jamie had even met a few of his cyber conquests but they'd all been a disappointment. Some were downright freaky, like the sicko who'd asked him to leave a turd in his bed, or the one who'd been dressed from head to toe in rubber and the guy who said he was a Bruce Willis lookalike but turned out to be a dead ringer for a geriatric Marlon Brando. He was addicted to the Web while being aware it never really bore fruit and, like a bad habit, it had become detrimental.

However, cyberspace negated the need for small talk and allowed him to get straight to the point, because as he looked around the bar at the yapping, Barcadi-Breezer sipping brigade posing like too many peacocks, he felt a hatred well up inside. Jamie could just imagine their banal conversations about the latest mobile phone they'd bought or what Third World beach resort they were going to fuck their way round this winter. But more than anything he was disgusted because he recognised his own image staring straight back at him.

Two or three drinks and "you end up going home with any old white trash" according to Philippe, though Jamie would be happy for company since he noticed he was the only guy in the bar alone. In a place full of people it made him feel desolate but he wasn't about to walk out. He checked his voice mail and his text messages — both nil — then ordered another drink, which he clung to for some kind of comfort.

He was a captive audience as the obsessively fashionable crowd talked at one another but his heart almost stopped when he saw Gary walking through the sea of Diesel T-shirts and G-Star jeans like a blot on the landscape. He stood still and maniacally scanned the bar as if desperately looking for something, while Jamie knew all he could do was wait to be noticed.

He sensed the sweat prickle under his armpits as he sat poised with an increasing urge to run but felt Gary's eyes finally settle on him with a horrible inevitability. He was headed straight over, literally elbowing people out of the way. Jamie feared for his personal safety but above all else was terrified at how any confrontation would look, that he'd lose his carefully contrived street credibility in the coolest bar in town. Though he knew the style bibles claimed you were nothing these days without the ultimate status symbol — the stalker.

Gary was still a few feet away as the bar was so deep in people, but Jamie could see words spilling out of his mouth, his face set in a scary glassy-eyed stare. Behind him, however, was a burly doorman who'd obviously seen the commotion and was closing fast. The music was loud and as the stalker moved closer still, with the bouncer in hot pursuit, all Jamie could see was his mouth moving up and down like a manic goldfish.

As he reached his target Gary was simultaneously caught in the doorman's grip. He thrashed around like a hooked fish as Jamie's ears were bombarded by the stream of swearwords coming out of the foaming mouth just inches from him, punctuated by pathetic "I love yous".

"You know this guy?" panted the doorman as he struggled to hold Gary back.

"Never seen him before in my life," Jamie replied smugly as he stared directly at Gary. "Keep taking the tablets."

He looked so gutted by the putdown that his body went limp and he gave up struggling. Jamie saw the tears well up in Gary's eyes as he dropped the frothing psycho routine and suddenly focused on the humiliation of everyone staring at him. He looked so pathetic with one arm ripped and dangling off of his cheap suit and offered no resistance as the bouncer spun him around and pushed him flailing to the exit.

Jamie was quaking inside but had managed to keep a façade of cool throughout and breathed easier once the bar had gone back to ignoring him. He guessed they'd moved on to discussing far more important issues, like where to go next, and he found the courage to order another much-needed drink despite the condescending stare of the barman.

"Hi," said some squat, chubby middle-aged black guy who'd nudged up to Jamie. "I saw you had a bit of trouble earlier, you all right now?"

"I'm fine and whatever you want old man I'm not selling," he replied almost wanting to retch as his nostrils filled with the fetid body odour emanating from the man's leather jacket. "Why don't you look elsewhere?"

"Look, we could have dinner or something," the man said as he ploughed on regardless, a hopeful smile lighting up his face.

"Which part of no don't you understand?" he replied. "Now fuck off."

Not waiting for a comeback he snatched up a copy of one of the weekly gay magazines from the bar but couldn't resist the satisfaction of peeking over the garish pages as the black guy turned and walked away like a scolded child.

As he scoured the myriad thumbnail pictures of guys' nether regions his mind turned to the upcoming week away to Spain with George. He had a horrible feeling the director would expect to sleep with him since he was paying for the trip. Still, that was the cost of a week in the spring Mediterranean sunshine, Jamie mused.

Almost done with his drink, he decided he wouldn't go clubbing because he still feared a psychotic Gary lurking in the shadows. He knew he could probably pick somebody up and take him home. The sex part was still fun but Jamie was so tired of the afterwards. It was the having someone cluttering up his flat, the not knowing what to say and the sad etiquette of swapping phone numbers the next morning that really turned him off. No, he thought, finishing his drink, he was going to go back home and get online. The Internet was a much more efficient way of having fun and any unwanted guests could be extinguished at the press of a button.

Jamie pushed his way out of the bar and sensed people were smirking cruelly at him after the earlier commotion.

"We had to move your boyfriend on," said the doorman into his ear, wielding a final indignity.

"He's not my fucking boyfriend," Jamie spat back, but he was so preoccupied scanning the horizon for Gary that he failed to even look at his grinning tormentor.

He felt safer when he entered the light and warmth of Tottenham Court Road Underground station, though the high drunken shouts of England's youth reverberated around the corridors like some ominous warning. London could seem so lonely and intimidating at times, thought Jamie, as he scurried down the escalators and through the achingly bright tunnels, studiously avoiding eye contact with the onrushing army of suburbanites.

Lads ambled by boisterous and drunk, while their girlfriends followed wide-eyed and shrieking. Jamie felt like he was from a different world and, despite all the stuff in magazines and on Channel 4 and BBC2 about how cool gays were, he was of the general opinion that a majority not only didn't accept gays but hated them, him. The taunting he had received in the school playground — and from his own father for goodness' sake — as a kid still haunted him. He knew one gay-friendly series on Channel 4 wasn't going to change all that.

There was a burst of air as the train roared into the platform. He could see the driver and wondered whether he was part of the "one under club." He'd heard the drivers who'd run over some poor suicidal wretch had formed a club and they met for a drink every month. Jamie had teetered on the edge once too, when he was being bullied so savagely at school. He remembered being consumed with bitterness as he stood at the very precipice of the platform at Oxford Circus, waiting. But he hadn't had the courage, or wasn't desperate enough, and marvelled then, as now, at how bad it must be to actually throw yourself in the way of a moving train with all that cold steel and darkness waiting to envelop you forever.

The Tube pulled into Tower Hill. It was only a short walk home and he was going to miss chucking out time at the pubs so he wouldn't have to sidestep the drunken hoards mouthing off about football and the like, which was a different language to him. He pulled his coat tightly around himself and raised his collar as he stepped from the Underground and into the dark amber-lit street.

As Jamie rounded the corner of the corridor to his flat with door key in hand he was confronted by a bundle on his doorstep and in a flash recognised Gary. But it was too late. He was immediately up on his feet, arms outstretched. Still wearing the suit, which now ridiculously had one arm completely ripped off, he looked pathetic with his head bowed and his eyes swollen, as though he'd been crying all evening.

"I'm sorry, I'm so sorry."

"Okay, you can come in and clean yourself up but you can't fucking stay," he said coldly, waving away a sobbing Gary's attempts to hug him. "Okay?"

"Okay."

He slid the key in the lock and quickly flicked the light switch on, sensing Gary's burly frame looming behind him in the narrow hallway. Jamie pushed open the door to the living room, turned the light on and ushered his visitor inside.

"I'll fix us a drink, sit yourself down."

"Right."

As he busily fussed around the kitchen making two whisky and Cokes he could picture Gary in his lounge observing the overflowing ashtrays, the pile of newspapers on the floor, the discarded takeaway cartons and the pornographic screensaver on the cheap PC in the corner.

"Just a minute," called Jamie from the kitchen, catching the fear in his own voice.

He entered the room somewhat concerned as he watched Gary walking around the room picking things up and putting them down like they were precious artefacts. He seemed oblivious to Jamie, standing watching him with drinks in hand.

"Oh, sorry," he said finally, putting down a gilt-framed picture of his scantily-clad host and a friend in the Canaries, and moved back to the armchair.

Jamie handed him the whisky with a thin smile but wondered how he was going to get the unwelcome intrusion out of his space.

"You look like you had a bad day, what happened?" said Gary, playing the concerned lover, as though what had happened was all perfectly normal.

"Really, Gary, I don't want to discuss this with you," he replied, leaning over for the TV remote control. Jamie would rather watch some after-pub television featuring comedian Graham Norton than confront the problem in his living room, the six-foot tall problem in a suit with one arm.

They both sat engrossed by the stupidity of "entertainment TV", or they *looked* engrossed, though Jamie was too on edge to be thinking of anything other than his unwanted guest. Even Norton's interview with a one-legged, one-eyed transsexual porn star couldn't take his mind off of the non post-ironic statement just inches away and he watched in horror as Gary cradled his drink and eased back in the armchair like he wasn't going anywhere. The empty laughter of Graham Norton filled the room but neither of them were laughing.

"Okay Gary, I want to go to bed soon, you're going to have to leave," Jamie said as though addressing a recalcitrant child, while Gary obliged by sitting in a sulky silence.

"Gary? Did you hear me?"

"Okay, I'm going. I know you don't love me anymore," said Gary in a feeble voice as he miraculously swigged back his drink and stood up.

He silently headed for the hall as Jamie followed just a couple of paces behind, willing him on. Gary opened the front door but then stopped, his six-foot frame forming an intimidating silhouette in the doorway.

"Why did you give me a fake number?" he said, whirling around on the threshold to face Jamie, his mood switching from hurt to confrontational in the blink of an eye.

"Sorry, I've just got a new mobile and that was my old number."

"So can I have your new number and your home number?" said Gary, expressionless, as he continued standing menacingly in the doorway.

Frightened and exasperated Jamie lunged for a pen and paper on the hall table, cautiously not conceding the position he'd maneuvered Gary into. Bitterly he wrote down both genuine numbers and resolved to change them if things got too bad, though he knew the heat would be off next week as he was going to Spain.

"Call me in a couple of days," he said mock cheerily, thrusting the scrap of paper into Gary's large open palm.

"I will," said Gary, Jamie's heart skipping a beat as he moved onto the step and then into the corridor. "Bye."

He slammed the door and nervously fiddled with the chain and the deadlock. He then unplugged the phone and switched off his mobile as he moved into the living room and watched Graham Norton cavort with some grade-B soap star on his sofa.

The second phone line was hooked up to the Internet and he logged on. It was now past midnight and the time Jamie acknowledged when the desperate, including himself, sought solace in the electronic chat rooms of cyberspace, a last refuge after returning empty handed again from the pubs and bars. What a fucked up place he inhabited, too, where no one was who they said they were and every click was your next fantasy.

Jamie (aka JayJay69) clicked into one of the several London chat rooms on the gargantuan Gay.com site, which covered the whole world from Athens to Zimbabwe and everything in between. The blue screen had a soothing, hypnotic effect and time paled into insignificance as he stopped worrying about Gary and concentrated on the statistics of Fireman25.

Fireman was twenty-five and had a "GSOH and was VWE", which Jamie knew meant he had a great sense of humour and was very well endowed. He laughed to himself at how the two descriptions always went together but played the game.

"Hi, why do they call you Fireman?"

"Because I put out fires with my big hose," he replied.

Jamie was unable to suppress a giggle at yet another cliché and he guessed Fireman25 was probably a balding, lily-white and podgy 60-year old with halitosis and a smaller than average penis hidden beneath rolls of fat, rather than being some muscled hunk that was good with his hose.

"I'd like to take your cute butt with my uncut, 10-inch throbbing dick. It's so hot it feels like it'll explode."

"My arse is yours, do what you like," Jamie typed back, feeling the swelling of a hard-on but unable to dispel the image of some tub of lard at the other end sweating through his fat.

"You're not really 21, are you? You're just a teenager," admonished Fireman.

"Yeah, I was scared to tell you, just keep fucking me baby," typed Jamie more frantically, trousers undone and wanting to get off.

"Oh baby I'm pounding you hard now."

But Jamie saw the alias suddenly disappear from the screen and felt total anti-climax since Fireman had obviously doused his inferno and then pulled the plug.

"You asshole," he shouted aggressively at the vacuous blue screen.

Undeterred he left the now empty chat room and went back into one of the main London rooms, relieved to see a long list of names. Without hesitation he checked out GymInstructor9, who was "VWE, uncut nine-inch dick and hot, gym-toned body".

They entered a private room and though Jamie imagined GymInstructor to be a muscular, active gay man what he couldn't see was the disgustingly obese woman, who'd never seen the inside of a gym, attacking the keyboard with big doughy fingers, a half-finished tub of ice cream atop her monitor.

"Virgin huh? We'll see about that. Ready for the ride of your life?"

"Oh please, you've got to do better than that," typed Jamie, already numbed by the detachment of cyberspace.

And before GymInstructor could direct what he guessed would be a stream of foul abuse his way Jamie decided enough was enough. He signed out and pulled his trousers back up as a mixture of guilt, shame and hatred clouded his mind.

He got up and looked tentatively out of his lounge window. It took a worrying while for Jamie's eyes to focus but he was briefly cheered to see the passageway was as empty as he felt.

CHAPTER TWELVE

He was having a cold shower, which felt refreshing first thing in the morning in the city heat. Eddie came into the bathroom wearing his large grin and nothing else. Craig returned the smile, drinking in the petite muscle man who was back in his life now the Swiss guy had flown, no doubt tearfully, back to Zurich. They'd celebrated their reunion the night before.

"Good night?" queried Craig, attempting to shrug off an intense hangover.

"Yeah, very good but work today," said Eddie mournfully as he proceeded to soap himself under the rejuvenating jet of water.

The cold water didn't even seem to register as he caressed Craig, looked into his eyes as he drew him close and kissed him gently. The English boy couldn't help wondering how often and with how many Eddie had been so tender but he passed on the questions and just enjoyed the moment.

They both dressed hurriedly after the distractions of the shower and the night before. Craig gave Eddie his claret and blue Fred Perry polo shirt and laughed to himself thinking how he wouldn't look out of place in Old Compton Street, though the thought of London briefly reminded him of what he'd left behind and why, dampening his enthusiasm.

"I see you tonight. I want you to come watch Thai boxing with me," said Eddie, combing his short, short hair in an absurd show of vanity.

"Oh yeah, I'd really like that."

"What do you do today?" said Eddie, fixing him with a sincere look. "Be good."

"I'm going to Siam Square for shopping, cinema and McDonald's," replied Craig, craving the trappings of the West.

He handed his key to the receptionist as they left the Malaysia for the metallic glare of the city. The streets were clogged with dusty, belching traffic and their sweaty but terminally patient drivers.

They joined the commuter crawl on Rama IV Road where a pall

of smog hung over the city's financial district. Their bus was full of workers that Craig felt viewed him with a mix of amusement and studied disinterest. The English boy watched as Eddie stared out of the window and guessed he was probably miles away from the clogged streets, maybe dreaming of another weekend getting high — looking for another chance to escape.

He finally raised himself from his stupor and squeezed Craig's arm to indicate they'd reached Siam Square. They said their discreet goodbyes and arranged to meet that night as the Englishman pushed his way off of the bus.

Craig felt a deep affection when he watched the crowded vehicle pull away with Eddie framed in one of the windows, though he also felt a deep longing for a break from him and the destructive "paradise" that Bangkok had so quickly become. At the back of his mind were the men in lab coats pointing accusing fingers; he knew the doctors were right, too, that his current lifestyle would see a quicker descent into illness. But when that soulless man in surgical white told him he might not reach thirty there existed the screaming need to block everything out and he was still running.

Eddie had looked understanding when Craig said he wanted to spend a few days at the beach down south on the island of Samui, though he could see behind the smiling façade that he'd hurt his Thai friend. Craig felt selfish at planning to leave him behind but his need for a break was also part of the depressing realisation that he couldn't actually do much to help the Thai's plight. Poverty and hopelessness couldn't be conquered with a few drinks here and there and a couple of pleasant dinners; he knew that and he knew that Eddie knew. He might have earned more in a month than the Thai did in a year but it still didn't equip him to cope with the depth of the problem. He had enough of his own.

"You meet many boys there," Eddie said when Craig had told him of his planned trip, which was about all he could manage by way of confrontation.

The English boy had declined to answer because he knew that statement was probably true; he *would* meet boys there. In spite of his liberal upbringing and his politically correct utterings, Craig was exploiting his privileged position as a relatively wealthy Westerner because he could. He knew he was able to wrap boys around his finger just on the promise of a couple of drinks and he was finding the power addictive.

Craig turned his attention back to Siam Square, which was alive with garishly dressed Thai youths and dominated by huge advertising hoardings featuring frighteningly pale local models wearing Levi's and draining cans of Coke and Pepsi. He was careful to throw his change to a twisted beggar and was glad of refuge from the cloying tropical heat on entering one of the gleaming glass and chrome malls, sweat running messily down his face.

Craig felt he could have been anywhere as he sat in the fiercely air-conditioned McDonald's slurping a Coke. He took out his second-hand copy of the *Rough Guide to Thailand* and turned to the chapter on Bangkok where he saw a number of things underlined by the book's previous owner. He smirked at the blue biro marks next to Khao San Road, the backpackers' haven, Wat Po, the temple of the reclining Buddha, and the Grand Palace. He felt like some kind of anti-tourist sitting in a fast-food joint after a night out in Patpong.

Temples were the last things on his list, though he escaped the heat of the day aimlessly wandering Siam Square's very own temples to consumerism. He window shopped like the majority of the population, who peered into retail outlets and looked at items behind plate glass windows that he supposed would often have taken more than their annual salaries to even contemplate buying. Craig found something oddly hypnotic about the malls, in sharp contrast to the chaos they held back outside, as he was taken in by the cool comfort of the air-conditioning, the softly scented atmosphere and the polished surrounds.

He was stunned back into reality as he stepped outside into an afternoon that seemed to bow under the impact of heat and noise with the dazzlingly bright sunlight reflected off of the scores of vehicles edging by below. He quickly hailed a *tuk-tuk* and they dodged and weaved back to the hotel.

There was a knock on the door. Craig's heart jumped with anticipation because he knew he liked Eddie more than he should. He opened it and sure enough the Thai was there grinning cheekily at him.

"Good day at the office?"

"What?" Eddie replied, wrinkling up his face as though he didn't understand.

"Good day at work?"

"It was okay. I take a shower and then we go," he said as he casually discarded his clothes and walked stark naked to the bathroom, blowing a kiss nonchalantly over his shoulder.

When Eddie returned from the shower he sported just a towel slung provocatively below his little waist. He sat next to Craig on the bed, put his hand on the English boy's thigh and leaned lovingly into his shoulder.

"How long you stay in Bangkok?"

"Only a couple more days. I've just booked my trip to Samui," Craig replied bluntly.

"You'll meet many boys there," said Eddie, repeating his mantra as he spat the words out.

"I just want to get out of the city."

Craig's bold statement went unanswered as the television chattered away in the corner and a silence fell between the two of them. The Englishman felt the gulf between East and West yawn open again.

They stood together under the hotel's canopy and waved down a cab. A taxi stopped almost immediately, its windows obscured by the warm monsoon rain cascading out of the dark sky and bouncing off the black road as they jumped into the back seat, laughing. The dark mood of earlier had lightened.

"I used to box," said Eddie, running his fingers across the scars on his face. "But it takes away your beauty."

"You're still beautiful."

"No, not beautiful," said Eddie, though admiring himself in the rearview mirror and obviously pleased with the compliment he'd been fishing for.

Craig felt his friend's taut, muscly arm and could quite picture him snarling at an opponent in the boxing ring, his svelte body ready for anything.

They ran through the greasy rain into the stadium, which was alive with an excited buzz.

Eddie purchased the tickets from a small kiosk and led Craig to their hard wooden seats, quite close to the ring. The English boy looked around at the variety of Thai men of all ages, the majority puffing away on cigarettes awaiting the action and no doubt trying to forget another day's toil.

Craig felt very comfortable as the vocal crowd reminded him of home and Saturday afternoons with his dad watching Crystal Palace Football Club. At Selhurst Park they'd dissected every move and misplaced pass, though it was really all they had in common. It was safe ground. Maybe boxing was the only thing these men had to talk about, he thought sadly.

A band struck up and there was a reverential hush as people stood. Craig sat where he was but felt a tap on his shoulder from the man behind, who was motioning for him to stand. He looked around at the whole stadium on its feet and thought he better comply as Eddie was laughing silently next to him.

"It's national anthem," he whispered.

The fighters — one in red shorts, the other in a blue pair — entered the ring as the anthem stopped. They swung their arms and stretched their muscles as they strutted to their corners. Like regular boxing it felt very tribal and base but Craig could already feel the game evoked great passion; he could see it in the spectators' faces.

He gazed across at Eddie, who had his eyes firmly fixed on the ring too, as the barefoot fighters finished limbering up and began a sacred dance as the band struck up again. In the brief interlude that followed the Thai relayed the strengths and weaknesses of each fighter and Craig recognised a fan's fervour.

The band trailed off and the pitch of the crowd rose measurably as the rivals eyed and sniffed one another like two nervous animals. Sweat already glistened from highly toned bodies that were trained to inflict pain.

Red Shorts landed the first punch and kick with a palpable impact before being headbutted, which knocked him slightly off balance. Craig was shocked but enthralled by the violence as he listened to the fans baying in his ear and watched the two agile young men trade blows.

The initial exchanges were followed by a more rhythmic sequence. The fighters danced gracefully around one another waiting for an opening but such pauses were followed by violence of often feline savagery. And at the end of round three Craig could see Blue Shorts was cut around the eye; blood seeped out of a swelling wound.

Round four saw the injured fighter slower out of the blocks. Red Shorts tellingly sensed indecision and the taste of victory as he landed a flurry of blows. His violent body was slippery with sweat, straining muscles caught under the floodlights, and as he pummeled his victim the crowd roared him on. Finally Blue Shorts lost his footing and slumped to the deck, clearly not getting back up.

The winner turned away from the prostrate figure and saluted the stadium, holding an awesome fist aloft as the blue corner rushed to administer first aid to their fighter. Craig was cheering for the victor too, caught up in the excitement, the blood, the muscles and the violence, all brought to life under the bright, bright lights.

Eddie looped his arm through Craig's as he guided him through the maelstrom of Hualamphong Station. There was always something romantic about railway stations, he found, with people scuttling every which way and the destination board promising far-flung places.

Craig would take the thirteen-hour train ride to Sura Thani in the south, then by boat to Samui for what Eddie disparagingly described as "sun, sea and sex". But he was sad to be leaving the Thai, who was edgily smoking and drinking coffee as they sat in the station café.

"What are you doing tonight, then?"

"Maybe DJ Station," said Eddie, expertly swatting a mosquito as it landed on his arm.

Craig rolled his eyes, realising that life would very much go on despite his absence, and it reinforced his decision to move on. A vital part of the travellers' armoury was the ability to up and leave, as it meant not hanging around and dealing with consequences, but he knew he couldn't run forever. A day didn't go by without him thinking of HIV, but the black clouds had rolled away since Thailand. Reminders of home only seemed to bring with them a dawning of his own mortality and he was dreading the day he'd have to board a plane for Heathrow. He didn't want to give up his current lifestyle until it was exhausted.

He waved from the window of the train but Eddie, after leaving him at the carriage, had already turned back to the heaving crowds of Bangkok. Craig felt a pang, watching him disappear into the distance, as the train lurched away from the platform.

He relaxed again while the tropical panorama of Thailand unfolded through the train window. Picking up the can of Singha beer he'd ordered he toasted his reflection in the glass.

The night fell fast as the train rattled on and the beaches of Koh Samui flickered comfortingly in his mind. It had been winter when Craig left England but that now seemed part of another world. He had taken the sleeper and climbed into his bunk as the gentle, rhythmic movement gradually lulled him to a more peaceful place.

*　　　　　*　　　　　*

He awoke to the sound of excited voices, Thai voices. The pitch rose and fell with the shifting of the luggage. They were obviously aware that the final destination was close. Craig climbed from his bunk and was immediately lifted as he looked out of the window and saw the sparkling Gulf of Thailand, silvery blue in the sunshine. They'd left the smoggy hue of Bangkok far behind.

The sights were soon obscured by the shacks of Sura Thani and as the train pulled in Craig looked out at the sea of expectant faces. Sad that none were expectant for him, he joined the clamour to disembark all the same. He approached a man holding a "Koh Samui" sign aloft and boarded a bus that finally disgorged him at a rickety old ferry moored in an oily harbour.

It was only morning but the heat and light were already fierce and Craig wiped the sweat from his brow as he entered the boat along with the crowd of other travellers. Excited voices seemingly from all corners of the world filled the air. He was ushered to the top deck by a Thai kid, no more than twelve, though his face was weathered by sun and sea.

Craig slung his bag down with the growing mountain of backpacks and grabbed a place by the prow. He watched the Thai boy expertly untie the boat's moorings like he had undoubtedly done a thousand times before. The Englishman laughed to himself as the boy pushed the vessel off with a crooked smile, a cigarette dangling from his young lips.

The breeze felt good as the boat cut through the gulf to Samui. Craig drew heavily on a thick joint he'd been offered by a charitable fellow passenger. He was glad to have left Bangkok as he felt the spray of the sea cool his face.

He watched the ragged shoreline of Nathon, the nominal capital of Samui, come into view. As the boat docked, Craig grabbed his bag and approached the plethora of *songthaew* drivers eagerly awaiting the latest influx. He climbed in the truck that offered the best price to Chaweng beach with a band of other travellers.

Craig glimpsed the lure of white sands and azure seas as they careered around hairpin bends and rocketed up and down palm-tree clad hills.

"Matlang," the driver called from the cab, indicating Craig's stop.

Left at the side of the dusty road he followed the vague directions he'd received, walking down a gravel path. He eventually approached a somewhat ramshackle reception area below a sign that proclaimed "Matlang."

"Yes, very cheap room, may I help you?" said a young woman behind the desk, eyeing Craig.

"How much?"

"How long you stay?"

"Probably a couple of weeks."

"Five hundred *baht* per night," she replied with an unyielding smile.

"Excellent."

The woman showed him to his little thatched wooden bungalow under the shady coconut trees. As Craig entered he threw his bag on the floor and fell exhausted onto the double bed.

As he woke from a fitful sleep and listened to the excited shouts outside his bungalow, Craig wondered about the beach. He dragged himself to his feet and followed a little path that, within yards, led him to a white, sandy strip. A group of Thais were playing football, sticks for goalposts. He watched them run up and down as they flicked and juggled the ball. The sea had gone out, leaving a broad expanse of beach that stretched almost to the horizon. Dusk was falling but the sun seemed to have left some lingering brightness, and heat still emanated from the powdery floor between Craig's toes. He felt the warm, tropical breeze on his face and smiled.

He tracked the mosquito bites down his leg, red and ugly. After surveying the dusky scene the previous night he'd gone to bed and fallen asleep almost immediately. Craig had awoken naturally, raised from his slumber by the heat, the wind sashaying through the palms and, more practically, the need to eat.

He retraced his steps down the path to the beach and marvelled at the light, putting his hands up to shade his eyes. The island had looked different in the evening melting away into the darkness; in the morning there was a luminous, windswept quality.

"Massage sir, very good," said an approaching Thai woman, jolting him out of his appreciation of the dawn.

"Maybe later."

"How long you stay?"

"About two weeks."

Craig walked back up to the Matlang and chose a dining table on the terrace, away from a group of gap-year travellers so urgently trying to broaden their minds. He was glad at such moments that he was alone instead of having to make conversation with some eighteen-year-old from the English Home Counties.

After breakfast he walked down the beach, kicking up sand in big powdery clouds. The surf was rough, seemingly swollen by a mid ocean storm. Craig strolled along contentedly, dodging the odd sunbather staked out by early morning and still pink from the day before. The beach was fairly empty though, an emptiness that stretched into the far distance. Backpackers were obviously still sleeping off hangovers and bad trips, he thought.

Chaweng seemed to get more congested with bungalows and hotels the further Craig walked. Empty white sand gave way to the intrusion of parasols and sun loungers, soon to be filled by travellers and honeymoon couples, he supposed.

He cut off the beach and into the dusty, haphazard concrete of Chaweng town. Thais sped by on scooters or sat minding their market stalls, idly waiting for another customer. He passed a bar and recognised a blonde busily sweeping up the debris of the night before. Natasha obviously knew there was nowhere to hide so she waved and beckoned him over instead.

"You follow me?" she said, laughing, but looking sheepish.

"No I just wanted the sun and sea."

"And sex. You know anything you want in Thailand you can get."

"I know," he replied, blushing.

"You go with me again?"

"No, I can't afford it," he said sarcastically.

Natasha laughed but for the first time Craig noticed she looked embarrassed and there was something hollow about her laughter.

"See you later?" she said questioningly after him, but he didn't answer as he walked back towards the beach. Natasha didn't pursue it.

The speedboat's engines roared as it cut through the dark, still waters to Koh Pan Ghan, a neighbouring island, where the infamous Full Moon Party was about to go off. Surrounded by young, virile travellers all intent on having a good time, Craig felt full of anticipation.

He jumped off the boat and followed the other partygoers down a rough dirt track. The dull thump of music that had been barely audible as they docked became louder and more discernible. When they finally reached Rin beach Craig was gripped by the swirl of sound and colour framed under the most amazing starlit sky. Rocky cliffs rose in silhouette at either end of the curving beach and in the distance the sea cascaded onto the shore. All around people danced joyfully, as though delighted to have momentarily escaped the monotony of their lives.

There was a vigorous tumult of revellers as he trailed the length of the beach to a cliff path. A beacon of blue neon nestled at the top, which Craig followed. The Bar of Tranquillity was the source of the light. He'd heard it was the place to get hallucinogenic magic mushrooms and he ordered some from the smiling girl behind the bar. For 500 *baht* she handed him back a mushroom shake that he sat and sipped as he watched the beach far below, where people teemed like ants in the moonlight.

As he left the bar he was still lucid but felt a surge of joy course through his body. He was drawn back to the light and sound of the beach where boys and girls darted by laughing, smoking, drinking and cavorting in the waves but Craig wondered, with a tinge of melancholy, whether it would get better than the moment.

He spun around in front of one of the large speakers. He'd kicked off his shoes and was dancing barefoot in the sand. He looked at the other faces, lit by the moon, infused with hope. The light resonated off of the skin of a beautifully tan Thai boy. He looked into his exotically brown eyes and the boy grinned back. They danced closer and closer together and eventually he brushed the boy's shoulder. He took it as his cue and grabbed Craig's arm.

"What your name?" he asked in halting English.

"Craig, what's yours?" he replied, observing the boy's lithe body dressed provocatively in all white.

"Leo."

They walked in what he felt was a contented, stoned kind of silence and headed down the beach as the music and light faded into the background. Craig and Leo fooled around in the surf and the English boy sensed lust rising like the ocean swell.

Walking back to the party Craig held Leo's hand. The Thai finally jumped on his back and they ambled along the sand like carefree school kids.

Looking up at the stars as he lay on his back with Leo resting on his chest — the sky had turned from dark velvet blue to mauve — he stroked the boy's thick black hair and wondered how many times he'd felt this good in the last year and how many times he'd have to look forward to in the future.

The fast approaching morning light seemed not to offer hope, but underlined something already past. As the new day dawned he looked around at the beach that was grey, somber and littered with bodies like a scene from a great battle. Craig woke Leo and they trudged back with the other walking wounded through a sea of beer cans to the waiting boats in an all-encompassing hush.

He was thankful to get back to his bungalow and pleased he was still with Leo. They both fell onto the bed and instinctively cuddled one another, being too tired for anything else. Craig watched the boy as he fell asleep and admired his smooth, brown, athletic body. He lay back contentedly and thought he was in love again, in love with life at least.

He felt drained by the drugs as he lay motionless on the bed, entrapped by the heat. Leo had left an hour ago for his afternoon shift — he was a barman at the local cabaret joint, the Kitty Bar. He had failed to smile when Craig said goodbye and barely acknowledged that last night happened. The Thai had asked for the "taxi fare" back to Chaweng and the English boy was unsettled by the way he'd demanded it, grabbing the sheaf of notes out of his hand without a word, face etched with melancholy and shame.

As he moved outside onto the porch he watched as a storm built around the island. The wind rustled through the palms as the dark, heavy clouds visibly rolled in. Blinding flashes of lightning periodically split the horizon into jagged shards, followed by explosive claps of thunder. As the first fat drops of rain fell Craig opened his mouth and tasted the warm water and sat rapt by nature's *son et lumière*.

He fitfully dozed as the storm gradually subsided, leaving another oasis of calm in its wake. The blue skies lifted him and he walked the few yards to the shoreline where the sea had been whipped up fiercely. Brown bodies, a mix of locals and tourists, were sent tumbling in the white, foamy surf. Craig jumped in and felt his greasy body cleansed. The current pushed and pulled around him and a huge breaker unexpectedly pitched him forward. He coughed up salt water as he finally bobbed to the surface and laughed at being tossed around like a cork.

Craig dried off and walked down the beach as some bar played Bob Marley's "Buffalo Soldier", the fat, languid rhythm seemed apt for the day, perfect for his lazy saunter. He already found the somnolent atmosphere of the island infectious and the thought of leaving affected him.

At a beachside bar he ordered a beer and watched the daily volleyball match take shape. He knew most of the bar boys came down late afternoon before their evening shift to keep lean and tan for nightly admirers. Craig stared at Leo, who eventually cracked a smile and came running over. He took a swig out of the English boy's beer and then went skipping back to serve the ball, much to the amusement of his giggling friends.

The game ended as the sunlight began to fade. Craig had enjoyed watching Leo athletically stretch for the ball but felt a little guilty, even embarrassed at his voyeurism. He was taken unawares as the Thai came running over and kissed him roughly on the cheek, the dark mood of earlier having evaporated as quickly as the morning's passing shower.

"You miss me?" asked Leo, theatrically clapping the sand from his hands.

"Of course."

When darkness fell they jogged up the beach together, the only sound their feet splashing in the surf as they moved further and further away from the bars. Craig finally turned to Leo and pulled him close. He pushed his tongue into the boy's mouth and felt an intensity of passion that was reciprocated as they kissed and kissed.

Following their *al-fresco* embrace they took a shortcut through some beach bungalows to Chaweng, laughing as they stumbled about in the darkness. The long strip of shops and bars seemed to have woken up after the heat of the day. The pair stopped at a rudimentary kitchen at the side of the dusty road as a procession of motorcycles buzzed by. Craig ordered chicken fried rice and watched while the woman threw the ingredients into a sizzling black pan, cracking an egg over the top as she tossed the mixture in oil.

The food assaulted the taste buds and he enjoyed the different sensations as he shovelled in the rice with his fork and spoon. They both sat together on a low brick wall by the road as they ate, Leo engrossed in his food too.

"Can I meet you tonight?"

"You meet me but you must pay bar," Leo replied, shifting uncomfortably as he failed to look Craig in the eye.

He felt for the boy but he was also angry with himself for getting involved again — the so-called "Land of Smiles" was becoming one big illusion. They sat in an uncomfortable silence as a tourist approached Leo, an aged fat man, face seared red by the sun and with a horrible desire in his eyes as he nodded and leered. The Thai smiled back but was careful to touch Craig's leg and the man moved on.

"Who was that?" Craig bristled.

"He's been here long time, used to be my boyfriend."

"I'm sorry."

"You don't want to see me again?"

Craig just stared into Leo's eyes and saw his sadness. He desperately wanted him and wanted to make him feel better but other than give him a few hundred *baht* there was little he could really do. For many, the boys and their pearly grins were little more than commodities and Craig knew he'd become part of that.

They walked in silence back to the Thai's room and Craig felt upset by the squalor of it all as they entered an ugly concrete building. Leo unlocked his cell-like room, where there was a small bed perched on a concrete floor. There was no furniture but bright, cheerless clothes hung from a harsh metal rack in one corner, the whole grim scene illuminated by a bare light bulb.

"Don't worry, my friends are out," said Leo sullenly as he switched on a small electric fan above the bed in a pathetic attempt to regulate the stifling temperature.

"You don't live alone?" replied Craig, barely able to conceive that more than one person could live in such a cramped space, rolling a joint as they sat on the little bed.

"No, I live with my two friends."

They smoked as if it could make everything better, though Leo no longer looked at Craig when they spoke, as if some guilty secret had been revealed.

"You want shower?"

"Yeah," said Craig, wiping the beads of sweat from his brow.

Leo pointed Craig to a rickety wooden door opposite the bed and thrust a towel in his hand. He opened the door to be confronted by a tiny space partially taken up by an industrial looking plastic barrel filled with water, a ladle beside it. It wasn't what he'd expected but he undressed and gratefully poured the cool water over his sticky body. The joint seemed to have at least eased the tension between them and Leo joined him as they splashed around, having fun and trying to forget.

He walked his friend to the bar for his evening shift and they promised to meet later that night. The cabaret show at Kitty Bar didn't start till late so Craig continued on to The Club. Unusually for Samui it had style and he liked the music and the chilled atmosphere. The acid jazz and whisky helped take the edge off a difficult evening as the Englishman sat and watched a game of pool.

He moved back to the cabaret bar after a couple of shaky games of pool and a couple more drinks. Leo didn't spot him immediately so he sat anonymously at the counter. Incongruously Manchester United were playing on a bank of TV screens but all eyes were focused on a naked ladyboy sliding up and down a pole behind the bar.

Craig enjoyed watching the clientele as much as the performance. A mostly white, middle-aged crowd were seemingly entranced by this girl who'd been a man. He noticed they'd wince and fuss with their hands if she came too close, while the ladyboy stared out beyond the men as she writhed around and looked off into the distance like she wasn't really there.

The show began and the various ladyboys trawled out their laughably amateurish act as they did every night for the tourists, Craig guessed, like they were little more than trained circus animals. He clapped and laughed along as the girls mimicked everyone from Judy Garland to Whitney Houston but was distracted as the tourists' cameras flashed constantly, capturing the gaudy costumes, fixed smiles and vacant eyes, all evidence of exotic holidays for friends back home.

"You want to pay bar and go with me?" said Leo hopefully after the show had finished.

"I'm tired," replied Craig as he put an arm consolingly around the boy.

The Thai made to get away but the Englishman saw the tears rolling down his cheeks. He hated himself for making the boy so upset but he didn't have any answers, at least not the right one.

He reached his bungalow and realised that despite all the fun he'd had he was in a very foreign country that often played by indecipherable rules. Craig felt very alone. All the miles away from home impacted on him for the first time as he lay on his bed, enveloped by the darkness and the relentless heat, thinking about the boy who he'd let down, who he couldn't help.

Thoughts of Leo still hung over him like a black cloud in contrast to the sun-bathed verandah of the Matlang, where he ate his breakfast with little enthusiasm. Craig looked out to sea beyond the island and it dawned on him it could already be time to move on again.

"May I join you, young fellow?" said an older man, so at odds with the backpacker fraternity, approaching his table.

"Yes, if you like," he replied, looking up, slightly startled but not overly interested.

He sat down gently, smiled and then perused the menu. The English boy guessed his companion was in his fifties but he looked healthy, he was particularly slender and his skin was leathery and well tanned. He wore cheap beach clothes, though the dignified way he held himself told Craig the man was probably comfortably off.

"I'm John," he said in his very deliberate English accent as he held out a greeting hand.

"Craig."

"You probably think I'm a bit old for all this," he said, laughing.

"No."

"I was head of the history department at the University of Kent but I just had to take time out," said John, sighing contentedly. "I wanted to see the great big world and here I am."

"How long will you be away?"

"Until I get bored, or until I run out of money. I hope it's the former."

"Yeah."

"I hope you don't mind but I saw you with a Thai boy on your balcony the other morning," said John, lowering his voice conspiratorially.

"Yes, I'm gay if that's what you're asking," said Craig, laughing at John's quaint attempt at discretion and already enjoying his new companion's gentle self-deprecation.

"You want breakfast sir?" said a waiter, interrupting their conversation, addressing John.

"Er, just toast and jam and a pot of tea."

"And you?" probed Craig.

"Yes, well that's one of the reasons I ran away I suppose. I've been married for years and my wife couldn't cope any more," he said, colouring like a naughty schoolboy. "It was for the sake of the university really, the sake of appearances, but she knew all about my affairs with men."

"Oh."

"Sorry. I didn't mean to make this a confessional," John said sensitively. "It's just that I feel so free now. Craig, it's taken me thirty years to recapture this feeling, one I had when I was a young lecturer on a sabbatical in the United States. I just feel it's my duty to let people know not to live life the way I've done."

"What do you mean?"

"Don't deny yourself, do what makes you feel happy as long as you're not hurting others," John said, smiling. "I've finally woken up to that."

"What about your wife then?"

"She realises it's for the best. In fact it's a relief to her."

"Your breakfast sir," said the waiter, reappearing with tea and toast.

While John concentrated on his meal, Craig looked out to sea and pondered what he'd just heard. While it was nothing he didn't already know he found the academic's philosophy strangely comforting. He knew he didn't have time to let life run away from him either.

After breakfast they walked down the beach, allowing the cool surf to wash over their feet. John had moved slightly ahead and Craig enjoyed his almost feminine gracefulness. He'd obviously worked in academia all his life and it seemed to have protected him from life's rough edges; he still possessed the infectious enthusiasm of a kid, thought the English boy.

They found a secluded spot where they planned to spend the day lazily sunbathing. John asked Craig to apply suntan lotion, which he did, and was surprised at the firmness of his old body. When it came to Craig's turn he enjoyed the sensation of having the cream massaged into his back by those slender and experienced hands.

At lunchtime he left his companion on the pretext of getting them something to eat but instead he headed for the cabaret bar in Chaweng. He still couldn't stop thinking about Leo and the look on the boy's face when he'd left him the night before.

Behind the bar was a ladyboy who actually looked quite sinister by daylight and Craig approached tentatively.

"Where's Leo?"

"Leo gone," she replied, expressionless.

"Where?"

"Koh Pan Ghan with new boyfriend," she said, cackling cruelly, probably having seen it all before.

Craig left with the sound of laughter ringing in his ears, just thankful that he had the means to move on.

He brought back some papaya salad and two Singha beers for their lunch. John had vacated the spot on the sand but Craig saw him waving furiously from the water. He waved back, hurriedly undressed and dashed into the sea to join his new friend.

They sat and dried in the sun, ate their salad and drank their beers. Craig lay back on the sand and tried to forget about Leo, though he wondered whether it was as easy for Leo to forget.

In late afternoon, as the heat of the day began to subside, the pair walked to Craig's regular beachside bar where a halfhearted game of volleyball was in progress. Some of the boys called out his name and he was already beginning to feel like a local.

"Someone's popular," said John, laughing, as Craig shrugged modestly.

"Where's Leo? This your new boyfriend?" said the barman, giggling as he came over to take their order.

"This is John," said Craig, introducing his companion.

"Pleased to meet you sir," said the barman, bowing reverently.

"The pleasure's all mine," replied John, joining in the fun.

A group of local youths turned up knocking a football around and one diligently set up goals out of clumps of seaweed. Craig left John at a nearby table with his beer and ambled over along with a disparate bunch of Europeans, Israelis, Americans and Australians set to face Thailand. They kicked and rushed around against the backdrop of a setting sun, which turned the scene a golden orange.

Craig scored a good goal and cheered with the surge of adrenaline. He looked over at John — old John who he guessed would have loved to join in — sitting transfixed on the sidelines. Craig waved and his friend saluted back.

They played on until they were finally beaten by the fading light. The players patted each other on the back, shook hands and exchanged smiles by way of a common language. It was acknowledged that most would be back the following day. Craig dunked himself in the sea and trotted back to the bar, breathless and high after his exertions.

"Good game?" asked John.

"Yeah, brilliant," replied Craig as he chugged down an ice-cold beer.

He eased back in his chair and looked up as the first stars began to twinkle in a seemingly airbrushed sky. The activity of the afternoon had ebbed away and it was just the pair of them sat quietly at the beachside bar.

"Will you have dinner with me tonight?" ventured Craig.

"I thought you'd never ask," replied his companion, giggling like a schoolgirl.

They ordered more drinks as they clearly both appreciated the company.

"It must be wonderful to have your whole life ahead of you," said John wistfully, looking out to the dark expanse of ocean. "So many possibilities."

"What do you mean?" said Craig a little too aggressively, stung by the reminder of his own mortality.

"Sorry," replied John, taken aback. "I mean I just wish I was young again like you..."

"John, I'm HIV positive."

"Oh, I'm so sorry," replied John, flushing almost imperceptibly under his deep tan as he fiddled uncomfortably with the wedding ring still on his finger.

In the ensuing silence he reached his hand across to Craig's and held it tight.

"Let's go," said the English boy stoically once they'd drained their beers.

"I'm really sorry."

"Don't be sorry," replied Craig. "It's something I have to live with."

"Do you want to talk about it?" said John, putting his arm around the boy's shoulders as they began walking down the beach.

"All I've done for the past year is talk," said Craig, laughing wryly. "There's not much left to say. Let's just enjoy ourselves while we can."

"That's been my motto for the last few months."

They sat in the restaurant but it was difficult to return to the polite chitchat of before. It was as though John's idealism had foundered on life's harsh realities and Craig felt guilty for disarming him of his boundless enthusiasm and hope, but couldn't help resenting the sharp, though unintended, reminder of his own status too.

They managed to get through the meal, though the expensive food tasted bitter and felt uncomfortable in his mouth. It sat even more uneasily in his stomach as John paid the bill on his credit card.

The pair walked back along the beach in the darkness to the bungalows. In the distance, the incessant beat of music could be heard from the Chaweng clubs. Any other night Craig would have been lured by the neon honey traps but he just didn't have any desire left. They continued grimly on to Matlang, passed frequently by young travellers simply bounding with energy.

"Fancy a nightcap?" said John as they reached the resort.

"Why not?"

They ordered a whisky set from the bar that never seemed to close and took it back to John's porch. His host lit some candles and the pair sat looking out to sea, though Craig noticed he was topping up their drinks unhealthily fast. It was almost as if he'd taken it upon himself to ensure they both forgot the darkness of earlier.

Even though he knew he could never forget, he felt soothed by John's old-fashioned courtesy and finally reached out to him. They awkwardly embraced and Craig wouldn't let go because he just couldn't face the night alone. As he kissed the professor he knew bitterly it was a mistake but remained silent and let his companion gently guide him inside and onto the bed.

Craig listened to John breathing hard and felt paralysed as the elderly man trembled uninvitingly in the darkness. He closed his eyes and willed himself to sleep, though he at least allowed his friend the consolation of holding him.

As the day's first light flooded into the bungalow Craig awoke, still fully clothed, and quietly disentangled himself from a dozing John. Shooting one last look back at the sleeping figure as he crept out of the bungalow he knew there could be no going back. He'd decided to leave the island that morning because he sensed the night had marked the passing of something for both of them. Craig knew it had been an aberration and he also guessed that John wished he was thirty years younger, though fleeting youth had really come and gone for them both, he thought sadly.

CHAPTER THIRTEEN

February had turned to March but as he looked out of his bedroom window it could have been any month, indeterminate year. It was a drab, grey morning that followed an uninspiring few days but he was lifted by the fact he was going to Spain. Gary the stalker had called several times but Jamie had totally changed tack and was offhand and rude, which seemed to work.

His mum, Liz, had also begun to deluge him with calls and messages since the debacle on the South Coast and he eventually deigned to grant her an audience, but only after he'd returned from Spain. Rather than referring to Brighton, when he finally spoke to her she'd been full of meaningless pleasantries. When she'd asked him how he was, Jamie thought he could hardly tell her he was being screwed on camera for money, but he did contemplate sending his dad a video of his bravura performance in "Room Service."

He was meeting George at the relevant British Airways counter at Gatwick at midday for the 2pm flight to Barcelona. The porn director had already called Jamie twice that morning to make sure he was coming, since he probably knew how unreliable such boys could be with their nocturnal habits and their drug cravings. George had been up since six because, as he admitted to his young companion, he enjoyed the discipline of an early start and couldn't function without an hour's meditation and yoga, even recommending that Jamie try it.

The last thing George had said on the phone in his intentionally difficult to place accent, somewhere between public school and Estuary English, was, "Dress slutty darling."

Jamie was concerned about the trip, concerned about another film shoot to the point of being neurotic. But he was also looking forward to Spain, the spring sunshine, and he knew George would have access to a mountain of coke, though he thought it odd he'd hardly ever seen the director touch the stuff.

It was gone ten o'clock and he hadn't packed; it hadn't even crossed his mind. Dirty laundry cluttered the floor of his room, indicative of the chaos that was his life. Jamie grabbed some clean clothes from the closet and placed them in a Louis Vuitton suitcase. It was a fake of course but he knew appearances were everything, because that was the one important lesson Liz had taught him.

He chose a singlet from his wardrobe, pulled on a pair of fake snakeskin trousers and stuck sunglasses on the top of his immaculately gelled hair. In the bathroom Jamie applied some foundation around his eyes to disguise the rings and looking in the mirror he was pleased to note he still liked what he saw. The phone rang just as he moved out of the front door but he didn't bother turning back because he had a horrible feeling who it might be.

George was already at the check-in and surveying his chunky, ostentatiously expensive Rolex when Jamie arrived at 12.20pm. Even from a distance he was the usual mish-mash, a mix of cool and eccentric. As the boy approached he could see the bald dome shining pink under the bright airport lights. The director had on the cravat and a terribly mismatched stripy shirt offset with tweed trousers and a pricey looking pair of loafers. George was flanked either side by two funky aluminium cases that Jamie guessed housed the heavy camera equipment which he'd once disparagingly remarked were "antiques" only to be told they were "old school".

"Where the fuck have you been," the filmmaker said aggressively, totally devoid of humour as his eyes bore into Jamie.

"Yeah, sorry, I didn't pack till this morning," he replied, blushing as other people in the queue turned round to look at the commotion.

"Well, you're here now I suppose."

"Yeah."

"You look cute today," he said, breathing into the boy's ear after eyeing him up and down.

"Thanks," said Jamie, almost recoiling from George's halitosis-tainted breath, barely concealed by the overpowering smell of perfume.

Still he was impressed to notice they were business class and consequently didn't have to wait long to be attended to. Indeed, the girl behind the desk of the "World's Favourite Airline" was all cool efficiency but couldn't help breaking into a condescending smile as George and Jamie approached. Bitch, thought the boy, as he too smiled before handing across his passport.

She took the luggage from them and punched some numbers into the computer as Jamie nervously drummed his fingers on the desk. She looked up from the screen and handed them their boarding cards.

"Boarding at one-thirty, have a nice flight," she said, offering up another fake smile.

George swiped the tickets without a thank you — he wasn't big on pleasantries — as they moved away from the check-in and into, hoped Jamie, the bar.

"We're staying at the Hotel Romantic in Sitges," said George with a chuckle. "I should've been waiting at the airport with roses."

Even though he didn't find the joke remotely funny Jamie laughed along as George roughly guided him by the arm and into the "Sky Lounge." The boy was pleased to note it was a bar but thought it ironic that a place so obviously full of nervous passengers overlooked the runway and the big tin hulks taking off. Maybe it encouraged the troubled to drink more, he mused, craving a snifter himself.

A waitress eventually arrived at the "Please wait here to be seated" sign and showed them to a table. Jamie, not knowing what to say to George, put his head in the drinks menu.

When she returned the boy put the tariff down and was confronted by the director's unblinking gaze. He shifted uncomfortably in his seat.

"What are you drinking, honey?" George asked him, presumably for effect.

"Gin and tonic please, a double," Jamie replied.

"Just orange juice for me."

"Sure, gentlemen," said the waitress with a lopsided smile and, as she turned, Jamie noticed the skirt way too high up her knee.

"Classy this place, isn't it?" said George with an unwarranted belly laugh that made other people in the bar turn around.

At least he thought he was hilarious but Jamie cringed as the director lit one of his large cigars. When George blew out the first thick cloud of smoke the waitress, who was preparing their drinks behind the polished chrome bar, looked aghast.

"Sorry sir, this is a no smoking area," she said as she came rushing over, batting away the smoke in front of her face.

"Look love, just mix us our drinks and stop acting like a traffic warden. You're a waitress."

The young woman refused to respond to the put-down and

turned on her heels.

"Silly cow," said Jamie, siding with George but secretly sympathising with the waitress.

As the director leaned back contentedly, puffing away, a suited midget with greasy hair and a squint approached their table with the girl in tow. His jacket bore a large gold nameplate that announced: "Bar Manager."

"Look, I know what you're gonna say but we're not moving," said George.

"Sir, I'd prefer it if you moved to the smoking area," replied the manager in a grating, nasal voice.

"Call the fucking cops then, 'cause we're not going till we get our drinks!"

"Just this once then," the airport employee replied, rather deflated. "Get the gentlemen their drinks."

The waitress let out a huge child-like sigh but did as she was told and roughly plonked down their orders on her return as George simultaneously blew out a huge blue cloud of smoke.

"Was it something we said?" he laughed as the girl haughtily turned away, while Jamie gratefully swallowed back his drink.

"So how have you been?"

"Do you want the edited version or wide-screen in 3D?" said Jamie, finding a sense of humour from somewhere.

"Well, you should know I always prefer wide-screen."

"I've got a stalker."

"A stalker, is he cute?"

"No, he isn't cute and I think he's bordering on psycho," said Jamie, not expecting any sympathy from his companion who he knew, like any good tabloid reader, was titillated by others' foibles and misfortunes.

"Could be a possible storyline, stalkers are very *in* these days. What's he done so far?"

"Well I came home recently and he was sitting on my doorstep."

"Did you let him in?"

"I didn't have a choice, did I?" said Jamie, ashamed.

They'd finished their drinks but George was still clearly enjoying the remnants of his cigar.

"Want another drink?" he asked.

"No, it's okay," said Jamie, already angling to get away from the predatory gaze of his companion.

"Let's go and see if we can find something in duty free for you then," said George, winking and waving the waitress over for the bill.

"Keep the change," he said impatiently to the girl as he handed over a 10-pound note.

Jamie began to wonder whether he could bear a week of the man's company, even if it was under the Spanish sunshine. He already aimed to go off and do his own thing if things got too much but he was also aware George had been careful to hold onto the flight tickets, devious control freak that he was.

They were standing by the sunglasses in the plastic consumer paradise that was duty free. Jamie noticed the emporium was serviced by the same gormless, pale Sussex girls — no doubt dreaming of their discounted seven-day breaks in Tenerife, he thought — as the Sky Lounge had been.

"These would suit you," said George in a way that didn't brook any argument, pointing to a pair of pink tinted glasses with oversized lenses.

A sales assistant hovered over the counter but wasn't paying attention.

"Can he try those on?" said the director, rudely snapping his fingers in the girl's face.

She didn't answer but instead almost imperceptibly rolled her eyes, fiddled awkwardly with a key as she unlocked the vault and handed the item to an equally disinterested Jamie. Though as he turned the glasses over in his hand he saw they were Diesel Originals and he also noticed the 60-pound price tag. He certainly couldn't afford them but he wouldn't feel guilty about George shelling out, though he also knew he was racking up a tally of being indebted to him. Nevertheless, he removed the cheap sunglasses from the top of his head and replaced them with the new pair as he admired himself in the mirror. They looked good perched on top of his perfectly sculpted haircut.

"Yes, I'll take those."

George conspicuously handed over his credit card and the girl took an age rooting around for a case and then packing the item up.

"Poor cow," he said once the transaction had been completed and they'd moved on. "If she was a he I could have rescued her for one of my films."

"Thanks for the glasses," said Jamie sheepishly, but enthusiastically unwrapping the package and putting the glasses on top of his head.

They meandered around the sickly-sweet cologne scented mall for a few more minutes but Jamie finally excused himself for a cigarette break in the "Smoking Zone" and arranged to meet George at the departure gate.

"Don't be late."

"Okay," he replied, fiddling in his pocket for the cigarettes and sadly aware that even though it had crossed his mind to bail out while he could, Jamie knew he needed the money from the week's shoot as much as he needed the sunshine, the avalanche of expected cocaine and the lake of booze.

He lit up surrounded by the unwelcome fug of others' cigarette smoke. Jamie noticed from the departure screens that the flight to Barcelona was already boarding but he thought he'd make George wait as he puffed slowly on his Marlboro Light.

The director looked relieved to see him for last boarding as he anxiously ran a hand through his thinning hair. On entering the plane they were confronted by another battalion of the travel industry's inanely grinning and ultimately disinterested clowns, though Jamie was pleased to spot at least one cute trolley dolly.

The pair both accepted a selection of newspapers proffered by the film-star handsome, swarthy young thing in BA's tight blue polyester. As he handed over the dailies he gave a weak smile and continued working his way up the aisle.

"I'm going to give him my card, he's drop dead," said George.

"I wanna become a member of the mile-high club."

"You mean you're not already?" replied the director in mock horror and they both burst out laughing, drowning out the pre-flight spiel about life jackets and oxygen masks. Though when George's hand worked its way onto Jamie's leg it chilled his laughter. He sank back resignedly into his expensive seat and remembered bitterly who was paying.

A silence descended on them as the plane climbed through the gloom and into the brilliant blue. George had his head buried in page after page of sleaze, celebrities and sex in *The Sun*, while Jamie plugged himself into the seat-back "Entertainment System." It was a mix of sanitized Hollywood trash and BA sanctioned middle-of-the-road easy listening that was barely enough to sustain him for five minutes, let alone two hours; but he was grateful for the fact it shielded him from his companion.

*   *   *

When they touched down it was early evening but there was a ripple of excited chatter as the captain informed them it was a "balmy seventy-two degrees" outside.

"Want to get a drink in Barcelona before we head to Sitges?" asked George, smiling.

"Yeah, why not?"

It was a deluge of "thank you sirs" from the manically grinning cabin crew as they left the aircraft, though Jamie noticed none ever made eye contact.

"I'll take you to Las Ramblas, darling," said George as they made their way to the baggage reclaim.

There was no mistaking the aluminium ensemble next to the Louis Vuitton fake as they grabbed their belongings and headed for the exit.

"We'll take the train to the city and be just in time for a sundowner in the old town," said George.

They left the airport and Jamie felt the pleasant warmth immediately. George pointed to a footbridge a few yards away and the boy followed.

"You've never been to Barcelona before, have you?" said the director over his shoulder to Jamie, who was trailing behind like a pet dog.

"We used to come to Spain when I was a kid but I don't think we made it to Barcelona," he said, remembering those fraught package holidays on the Costa Del Sol. Bob would seem happy for the first couple of days, only to be followed by two weeks of heavy drinking, rows and violence. As soon as he was old enough to stay home alone he'd done so, though he'd also feared the consequences for Liz.

He remembered one particularly galling incident when they'd travelled abroad with family and friends to a Spanish resort — a big concrete-clad hotel on a beach. At the time Bob was under the strain of having to be constantly on his best behaviour. Jamie had pulled his dad into an ice cream parlour and ordered the works. The young guy behind the counter was a real clown, he recalled vividly, and flicked up the scoops of ice cream into a cone, topping it off with whipped cream and a cherry like a work of art. He gratefully took the ice cream but could sense Bob was impatient to get to the beachside bar. He fiddled in his pockets nervously and sent a handful of *pesetas* spilling out all over the floor. Having frantically picked up the coins as he rose he felt the agonising pain of his father's hand across his temple. Jamie held onto the change but the ice cream sadly plopped to the ground, looking faintly ridiculous as it landed whipped-cream side down, melting onto the tiles. Bob roughly jerked his son out of the shop to the uncomprehending stare of the Spanish man behind the counter.

"You'll love the city," said George, breaking Jamie's sad recollection as they walked across the footbridge.

He was struggling and sweating in the heat, as the director had given him one of the aluminium cases to carry as well as his own bag. Consequently George looked completely unruffled in comparison and was chomping away on a big cigar by the time they reached the railway station.

The waiting double-decker train was spotless inside and out and when it moved off it was only a few minutes before the green countryside transmogrified into the concrete urban clutter of Barcelona.

"It's a beautiful city, isn't it?" laughed George as he thumbed at the ugly tenement buildings they were rolling by. "Don't worry. It gets better than this, a lot better."

"Never go on first appearances, right?"

"Right."

When they disembarked at the other end George marched confidently through the busy station. It was much like any big city terminus but Jamie saw that despite the throng many of the Spanish held themselves with a certain degree of elegance. He could already feel the aura of style and character that marked all great cities.

As they got outside the director thrust his arm up and waved down a passing taxi. The English boy, now sweating profusely, struggled into the back with the two cases.

"Las Ramblas," directed George to the driver, who nodded his head as they moved into the heavy traffic.

Dusk was falling when they reached the large pedistrianised strip at the edge of old Barcelona. The pair sat down at the first outdoor café they came across. A femme waiter immediately spotted them and approached.

"Must be the aluminium cases," said George, smirking.

"*Buenos noches*," the boy exclaimed and then moved seamlessly into English: "What can I get you gentlemen?"

"A jug of sangria," said George, taking the liberty to order for both of them as the waiter bowed theatrically and made his way back to the bar.

Jamie sat back in his chair and was intent on enjoying the comings and goings of Las Ramblas but feared that time was very much money to his companion.

"We got a day at the beach tomorrow and then down to business okay?" the director said, as if the boy had any say in the matter.

"We're not going out in Barcelona tonight?" he replied, already excited by the possibilities of the city.

"No, I'm too old for all that, love," said George, chuckling.

Jamie couldn't believe the filmmaker had so selfishly discounted the fact he was only a youngster but he just shut up and took it like he used to from his own father.

An uneasy lull was broken when the waiter brought the sangria and fussed around filling their glasses. Jamie took a gulp and hoped he could successfully negotiate whatever was to come that night, but he could scarcely imagine being cooped up in a hotel room with George while all the young guys were out to play.

He sadly watched people walking to and fro, tourists mingled with locals, hawkers and street performers. Jamie felt they were free and an inner rage built inside at being tethered to George's side. The trip already felt like torture of the worst kind; he could see what a great place it was but it was like experiencing it all from behind bars.

"Come on, drink up," said George finally. "I told the guy at the Hotel Romantic we'd be there early evening."

"Hotel Romantic, that's a joke," said Jamie scathingly, but his companion ignored the jibe and waved over the waiter for the bill.

They walked in a deafening silence to the end of Las Ramblas that was buzzing with evening chatter. As they reached the main road Jamie contemplated whether to run for it but remembered he'd already exceeded his overdraft. Instead, he got into the back of a waiting cab with the filmmaker.

"All right?" he said, turning to Jamie as he placed a hand back on the boy's thigh.

He didn't answer but just nodded.

They were in a Mercedes and all the clichés about Spanish taxi drivers seemed to be true as he gave them a sickly psychotic grin and sped off towards Sitges, cigarette in one hand, steering wheel in the other.

"I'll take you to my mate's bar tonight and we can get more acquainted with the Spanish boys, if you know what I mean," said George above the trashy techno blaring from the car's expensive sound system.

"Great."

"Taff, he's a wonderful guy, Welsh. A former producer of BBC sports programmes. Must have been all those men in shorts because he turned to making porn before he retired and then bought the bar in Sitges. Lucky bastard."

They pulled up outside a whitewashed building in a narrow street. Jamie looked at the clock on the car's dash. The LED read 8.05pm.

"This is it," said George cheerfully.

The music was still on and the driver still had a cigarette in his hand as he rushed around to retrieve the luggage from the boot.

Jamie got out after George and their bags were already neatly lined up before the entrance. The director handed the driver a sheaf of notes as he got smilingly back into the Mercedes and roared off down a street that was barely wide enough for such a tank of a car.

The boy grabbed the Louis Vuitton and the remaining aluminium case and followed George inside. He was being fawned over by what Jamie guessed to be the hotel manager/owner — a camp, diminutive, elderly Spanish man with oily black hair, dressed in an old-fashioned blue blazer. The Spaniard spoke excitedly through mouthfuls of cigarette, oblivious as ash coated the front of his jacket.

"Ah, *Senor* George, I see you've brought another friend from England, no?" he said.

"I'm Jamie from London," he replied, speaking for himself, and shuddered as the old man gave him the once over.

"Such good taste," said the Spaniard in a stage whisper as he turned back to George, who was laughing hollowly.

"Room thirteen, I know you like the light in there, it's just perfect," he continued, addressing the director but staring at Jamie as he handed over the key. "*Buenos noches.*"

"*Buenos noches,*" said George jovially as he walked up the adjacent staircase.

The boy followed in silence but felt the old man staring at his behind as he climbed upwards.

Down a hallway George opened the door on a spartan whitewashed room, narrow but long with a high ceiling. Jamie was mortified to notice just one double bed.

"Cosy, isn't it?" George said with a chuckle. "Make yourself at home."

He looked at the four walls and felt imprisoned. The sinking feeling in his stomach was accentuated as the director whistled contentedly while he undid one of his cases and started hanging things in the wardrobe.

"Where's the bathroom?" Jamie asked.

"It's communal, love, as this is a gay hotel. Just down the hall on the right I think it is."

He grabbed a towel from the bed, kicked his shoes off and made for the door. But in the passageway between the wardrobe and the exit George confronted him and attempted to stick a fat tongue down his throat. Jamie smelled the foul, bitter taste of the director's breath and managed to push him lightly away as he left the room.

As he got into the emptiness of the corridor he felt such savagery that he wanted to kill George, though his murderous rage quickly dissolved into sobs. He'd vowed to be strong before the trip but as his tears merged with the shower water flowing down the drain Jamie knew he'd have to acquiesce or things would turn nasty. He'd managed to blunt Pete's advances but he was a pathetic drunk; George was a different prospect.

He spent a long time in the shower and returned to the room with some foreboding. Jamie felt it was odd the door was unlocked because he was shrouded in darkness as he entered. Looking uncertainly for the light switch he was grabbed tightly by the arm and felt the familiar hot breath in his face.

"You're with me, remember that. I'm not asking a lot, just the odd favour in return," said George flatly out of the gloom. "If you don't like it, you know where the door is."

He finally let go of the boy's arm and snapped the light back on. The director was already dressed for dinner and despite the outburst Jamie noticed his face was horribly dull and expressionless.

"I'll be down in the bar, see you in the next five minutes if you want to join me for dinner," he said as he walked out, not waiting for an answer.

Jamie was shaking and looked at his arm. It was bright red where George had gripped him and would probably bruise, he thought. Nevertheless he hurriedly got dressed, being careful to select a long-sleeved shirt, and headed cowardly downstairs to the bar like he'd been told. For the first time in his life he could understand in some small way why his mother was still with the abusive Bob; but it meant he hated himself as much as he despised George.

The director was chatting away to the man behind the bar and even though the boy knew he'd been spotted it barely registered.

"Like a drink love?" asked the aging but immaculate looking bar-man in a Manchester accent.

"Gin and tonic please," said Jamie, delighted to be finally noticed but looking into the guy's suntanned face and wondering how many pints of moisturizer he'd used to keep the wrinkles at bay.

"Right you are."

The barman smiled at the boy as he put a coaster down and his accompanying drink and then went back to washing glasses at the far end of the bar, leaving the two companions in silence.

"Got over your tantrum?" George said, finally turning to address Jamie.

"Yeah."

The boy was grateful for the drink as he looked around the desolate bar, which was chintz central. He thought the hotel was absolutely typical George too, expensive but simply no style.

"I've booked us a table here," the director said, nodding through an open door to what Jamie guessed to be the restaurant, which he noticed was totally empty.

"Oh. Hardly seems worth booking," he said, forcing a laugh.

"It's still low season love," said the barman, overhearing and bringing over some peanuts. "Don't worry; there's still a bit of action in town."

"Yeah, I've heard about El Horny," Jamie replied.

"Oh, El Horno you mean. Got to be careful in there, the whole second floor's a darkroom," the barman said, winking conspiratorially.

"Are you horno, I mean horny?" asked George to Jamie.

"Not really, it's been a long day," the boy replied, shuddering slightly and wishing he'd drop the subject of sex altogether.

"Want a refill love?" asked the barman, who'd noticed Jamie had already finished his drink.

"I think we're going through to dinner," said George, answering for him.

"Right you are, I'll show you guys through."

They walked through the doorway, led by the barman cum waiter — Jamie wondered whether he was the chef too — and into a smaller room with several tables and chairs. He sat down and looked uncomfortably around at the gaping, empty spaces.

"I know a nice place on the seafront, we'll eat there tomorrow," said George as the barman/waiter disappeared to get the menus.

When he came back the director ordered a bottle of the house red. Jamie perused the imitation leather-bound menu and was resentful all over again. The dishes just oozed tackiness, featuring the likes of prawn cocktail and chicken *cordon bleu*, with hardly an authentic Spanish dish in sight.

Wanting to get the ordeal over with he ordered as quickly as possible and went for the chicken Caesar salad, which looked the most sophisticated thing available. George chose the steak tartar, the most expensive dish.

"Both excellent choices, gentlemen," said the barman/waiter unnecessarily as he poured the wine and dashed off to the kitchen.

"You think he's the bloody cook too?" asked George.

"Probably."

The meal was passable but instantly forgettable and they made a point of skipping the "homemade" desserts. George paid the bill quickly and conspicuously refused to leave a tip, which Jamie happily noted finally shut the over-familiar barman up.

He enjoyed the anonymity of the dark street as they stepped outside following George's second exchange of pleasantries with the spooky hotel manager.

"He's going to let us use one of the big hotel rooms for a shoot but only if he can watch," the filmmaker said, laughing, but Jamie knew the laugh; it meant he wasn't joking.

It was cool outside but comfortable in shirtsleeves even though Jamie felt a dull throb in his arm that nagged worryingly at him like the night ahead. But George, seemingly ignorant of their earlier row, put an arm lightly across the boy's shoulders.

"Okay, I'll take you to my mate's bar — the Pink Parrot."

Romantic Hotel, El Horno and now Pink Parrot, thought Jamie, rolling his eyes. Could it get any worse?

George expertly negotiated the mostly deserted, winding Mediterranean streets. They eventually came to a fairly lively strip of bars but Jamie observed the age of the occupants was frighteningly high. His heart sank when he saw that the bars sported rainbow flags and other giveaway gay paraphernalia, which like the clientele he guessed was never discreet.

"Welcome to queer street," said George, leading him by the arm, his injured arm, under an awning that proclaimed "Pink Parrot."

Many men were sat at tables and chairs outside but they headed straight for a dimly-lit interior where a few people were scattered about. As his eyes grew more accustomed Jamie made out a lone, fat figure at the bar talking to a cute Spanish barman.

George sidled up, put a hand on the fat guy's shoulders and he wheeled expectantly around.

"Hi, Taff," George said as he kissed the guy on both of his ample cheeks.

"George, how the devil are you?" said the man, his singsong Welsh accent clearly audible to Jamie above the pop pap thudding across the near empty bar.

"Just dandy, if you know what I mean."

"And this must be Jamie," said the Welshman, turning to George's companion. "I've hard all about you boyo."

"All good I hope?" he replied, but his sentence was swallowed up by a techno version of "I Will Survive" as Taff turned his steely blue gaze back to George.

The pair huddled together in conversation as though thick as thieves but Jamie was more interested in the barman. He was a solid, masculine looking Spanish boy, possibly a couple of years older than himself, with a T-shirt on that proclaimed: "Spaniards Do It Better." It was certainly an improvement, he thought, on Taff's "I'm Not Gay But My Boyfriend Is" effort stretched across a sizable beer gut.

"Hi, my name's José and you must be Jamie," said the barman with a smile. "I'm Taff's boyfriend. Drink?"

"A beer please," he replied, looking at Taff, then back at the beauty staring at him from behind the bar, and felt deflated all over again.

"We can hang out tomorrow, go to the beach," said José, placing the bottle of San Miguel in front of Jamie.

"Yeah, cool."

"I see you two have already become acquainted," said George, laughing as he came between the pair of youngsters.

"Meet your new sex partner," exclaimed Taff, joining in.

The boys just looked at one another in the face of the gently mocking laughter. Jamie contemplated having his most intimate moments robbed again and could almost picture George and Taff salivating behind the camera as he and José made out.

"Is there anywhere to go after here?" he asked the barman once George and Taff had tired of toying with them.

"This is *Espania*, everywhere's open all night, not like your England," he laughed.

"Yeah, but a disco or something?"

"There's Limelight. It doesn't get going till about two o'clock, though, and Taff doesn't like me to stay out late," he said with a sigh.

"I don't think we'll be having a late one tonight," said George, rudely butting into the conversation. "Party time tomorrow night though."

Again Jamie focused back on the claustrophobic hotel room and a frighteningly powerful anger rose up in him. Not for the first time he wondered whether he and George would make it through the night, let alone the week. He looked across at the filmmaker, his normally expressionless face blotchy with cheap Spanish red wine above another immaculately-pressed cravat and he despised him, despised him as much as his own father. George noticed the boy staring disapprovingly at him and winked back nonchalantly.

Another few customers had come into the bar and José, under Taff's ever-watchful gaze, busied himself with the new clientele. The English boy sat and drank his beer alone because he wasn't in the mood to be sociable. If he'd been with his mates he would have been mad for it and already searching out his second pill but George wasn't conducive to waving inhibitions away, because he was always so ready to exploit vulnerability.

"Don't you think so?" said George, turning around on his stool and finally engaging Jamie, who'd been sitting next to him for almost an hour in virtual silence.

"What?"

"Nothing, just checking if you're still awake," the director said coldly. "But don't worry, we'll find something to keep you awake tomorrow night."

"Charlie's coming to town," said Jamie.

"But only if you're good," replied George, tapping his protruding nose with a long finger.

Jamie would have laughed along with the reference to cocaine before but he just sat stony faced as the filmmaker turned back to Taff.

"So you see me tomorrow?" said José, who'd come over between serving customers.

"Yes I see you," said Jamie, mimicking the Spanish boy's pidgin English. "Come to the hotel in the morning, Hotel Romantic, room thirteen, and we'll go to the beach."

"Si," said José, smiling as he moved closer and whispered in Jamie's ear, "You stay with him, the older guy?"

"Yeah," he said, rolling his eyes as the Spaniard shrugged sympathetically.

He winked cheekily as he went back to serving another customer and Jamie wished life could be as simple as him and José. It should be that easy, he thought, looking back across at the fool in the cravat who was virtually drooling over two Spanish tarts who'd entered the bar trailing a cloud of CK One. The English boy chuckled to himself at George's expression when the two boys sat themselves with a couple of shrivelled, septuagenarian tourists.

"I think it's time we were off," he said, turning back to Jamie.

"Okay," the boy replied meekly, even though he was only halfway down a new bottle of beer and even though he was aware he was adopting the "anything for a quiet life" mantra of his mother. He even waited patiently as George and Taff hugged.

"Smashing to meet you, Jamie," said the Welshman, with just a hint of sarcasm.

"Oh, you too," he replied acidly back.

José gave him a genuine wave from the bar where he was serving yet another beer and Jamie responded by blowing him a kiss.

They walked out of the Pink Parrot, ears ringing with pop trash, into the uncomfortable silence they'd made for themselves, the high shouts of laughter from the happy holiday bars seemed to mock their every step. Jamie nervously lit a cigarette even though it was only a mercifully short walk to the hotel. In reception the old manager was still behind his desk and, though slumped against a wall, managed to open half an eye and hand over their key.

George roughly unlocked the door and snapped on the light, illuminating Jamie's nightmare, the small double bed in the narrow whitewashed room. The director moved forward aggressively and kissed him on the lips. The English boy stood and took it, like he'd stood and taken it when Bob had hit him, just hoping it would all go away.

"This night has been on me," said George as he grabbed Jamie's injured arm and breathed his disgusting breath in the boy's face. "Now I want something from you."

Jamie grunted derisively but the director slapped him hard against the face and sent him reeling backwards into the hard wooden furniture.

"And I'm going to get it!" he shouted as he moved menacingly over the boy.

Jamie swiftly recovered his balance and as George reached to grab him again he instinctively took the hefty camera that had been placed so carefully on the dresser, raised it above his head like a dumbbell and brought it smashing back down onto the man's bald, pink temple.

George immediately fell back with a thud onto the floor while blood spurted from a big gash in his forehead and ran down, colouring his cravat as it crept scarlet across his white shirt. The film-maker was still conscious but prostrate and looked pleadingly up at the boy who was still holding the camera in his hand.

"Where is my fucking ticket?" shouted Jamie, hardly recognising the aggression in his own near-hysterical voice.

"In the smaller case," George croaked, now holding one of the Hotel Romantic's fluffy towels to his leaking wound as he lay back pathetically on the floor.

Jamie finally put the camera down and rifled through the case with half an eye on the director's prone body. As he flung articles of clothing out onto the floor he located the tickets, carefully stashed at the bottom.

"You won't fucking get away with this, I'll have you arrested. Arrested!"

Ignoring him, Jamie hurriedly threw clothes into his own case. He spotted George's wallet invitingly on the dressing table, from which he grabbed a wad of notes as its owner could only look on impotently from the floor. Without a word or a second glance he strode to the door, his heart beating almost out of his chest.

"Bastard!" called George from behind him, but he was already halfway down the staircase.

"Going somewhere?" upbraided the manager, who was now sitting up smoking, eyeing Jamie and his suitcase with suspicion.

"There's been an accident," he said breathlessly, nodding up the stairs. "You better check it out."

The manager moved to block Jamie's path but he simply barged the frail old man out of the way and fled into the street, frantically flagging down a cruising taxi.

"Barcelona Airport, please," he said through the driver's open window.

The cabbie shook his head and was about to move on when Jamie shouted: "Twenty thousand *pesetas*."

"Okay, okay," said the driver and nodded for the boy to climb in the back.

He jumped in gratefully and as they moved off watched the figure of the hotel manager, who'd run out into the street, recede in the rearview mirror.

"*Problema*?" queried the driver.

"No, no everything is just fine," he replied, smiling, as he shakily lit a cigarette.

CHAPTER FOURTEEN

Craig's time in Thailand was ebbing away and after his trip to Samui he felt like being more selfish, the prerogative of all lone travellers. He didn't want to encounter another Leo or another John because he'd been emotionally drained by the journey to the south.

He'd only spent a couple of days in Bangkok since Samui and resolved to see Eddie one last time, but only after he'd visited Pattaya. Craig had heard the beach resort was less than salubrious but still he was curious, wanted to see for himself and more crucially wanted to be anonymous again. He'd checked out of the Malaysia Hotel to a chorus of "Where you go?" and he hadn't replied.

Craig caught a cab to Ekkamai, the Eastern Bus Terminal. Stained with diesel oil and reeking of fumes it was down-at-heel and no different from any other busy terminus. In the Thai tradition it was a playground for stray dogs, most sporting terrible afflictions. The clientele were a motley crew too. He noticed the backpackers heaving under huge rucksacks off to Koh Samet and Rayong, clutching their *Lonely Planets* and *Rough Guides* as if their life depended on it. Then there were what Craig deemed — naturally excluding himself — sex tourists, far more prevalent in the queue for tickets to Pattaya, he noted. Most were older Caucasian men, sprinkled with Middle Eastern and Indian too, more often than not with a young Thai girl or, occasionally, boy. As for the Thais, he observed, like bus travel everywhere, a pretty rough cross-section of society represented — anything from a farmer carrying a clutch of chickens to a young executive with a mobile phone clamped to his ear.

Craig picked up his ticket, then made his way to the bus, having already been eyed up by a lone boy in the give away stack-heeled boots and sporting a too ready smile. But of course he smiled back.

He didn't normally speak to people on buses, though was relieved to see some plump, jolly looking, thirtysomething foreigner sitting in the adjacent seat he was assigned to. The guy didn't seem to fit the sex tourist or backpacker model and he was intrigued.

"Hello, my name's Louis," said his neighbour, proffering a hand.
"Craig."

Louis had a mischievous twinkle in his eye and it was only nine o'clock in the morning. Craig knew it could be fun.

"Are you on holiday here?" he ventured.

"No, I'm working in Bangkok," Louis replied.

There was something in his nature that made Craig feel uninhibited and at ease.

"What do you do here?"

"I'm a broker for Lehman Brothers, been doing it about two years," Louis said in his obviously educated but London-tinged accent.

"But why Bangkok?"

"Hey, personal question," said Louis, laughing as the bus pulled out of the terminus. "I came here on holiday and fell in love, not with the place but with the people."

"You have a girlfriend then?"

"Nope."

As silence fell between the pair, Craig looked out of the window and watched the bus slip out of Bangkok and onto an ugly elevated concrete highway. He got out a month-old copy of *Attitude* magazine, more as a test for his companion, who he had a sneaking suspicion was gay, rather than any real desire to read.

"I see you've got good taste," said Louis on spying the magazine, prompting them both to laugh aloud.

"You have a boyfriend then?"

"No, love, but I'm extremely good at picking up trash."

"Yeah?" said Craig uncertainly at his companion's sudden arrogance.

"Well, everything's a transaction here, everything and everyone has a price," explained Louis, exuding the scary kind of confidence that money bought in the Third World. "And you?"

"Well I've only been here a few weeks but I'm kind of seeing someone."

"I see," said Louis with a smile.

Despite the expatriate been there, done that demeanour, his neighbour at least seemed interested and interesting and had a sense of humour, though Craig sensed a streak of ruthlessness behind the personable façade.

"Why are you off to Pattaya? If it's not a silly question."

"Definitely pleasure, not business, darlin', that's for sure," said

Louis with his infectious laugh. "Take in a couple of shows, bring a couple of boys back and knock 'em around a bit. You know, that kind of thing."

"Where do you normally go, then?" said Craig hesitantly, still unsure whether Louis was winding him up or not.

"The action takes place in Boyz Town, which is just a whole lot of boy bars. I usually watch the show at Muscles, 'off' a boy then take him to Marine Disco and pick up another one, then head either to the next club or back to my hotel room," he said with an assurance that led Craig to believe he was a regular and far from joking. "Wanna join me?"

"Yeah, why not?"

As they pulled into Pattaya the pair arranged an evening rendez-vous in Boyz Town. Louis headed off to his swanky five-star hotel while Craig was booked into a cheap guesthouse on Jomtien beach, as recommended by Eddie.

The *songthaew* drove through the dusty town slow enough to give Craig a glimpse of what the place was exclusively about. The streets were quiet but his experience was illuminated by one scantily-clad Thai girl tottering along on platforms, ashen faced and probably hung over he surmised, no doubt returning from some *farang's* spacious, well-appointed hotel suite to her stifling little room that she shared with two others. She had a mobile to her ear and was probably arranging another appointment, he thought sadly. An overweight, shirtless white man passed her and Craig watched as he stared at the girl while swigging from a bottle of beer. It wasn't even midday.

He also noticed the shuttered street-side bars with names like "Pussy Galore" and "Big Jugs" that would open in the evening in all their ugly neon glory. The English boy imagined the desperate painted girls reeking of cheap scent, manhandling their willing victims into the bar and parting them from their *baht* for a not-so cheap thrill, a beer and often a lot more.

The town was a horrible concrete mess, though it became less imposing as Craig reached Jomtien. He alighted at the KFC as instructed by Eddie and was already aware of catcalls from across the street. Boys in colourfully cheap hot pants and bright-red shirts beckoned him into their bar as though their lives depended on it. Laughing to himself he made a mental note of it and followed Eddie's scrawled map to his guesthouse.

As he looked at the sagging mattress framed by the blue nylon sheets he wondered how many "transactions" had taken place on it. The room smelled of post-coital cigarette smoke and the only thing lacking was a porn channel on the TV, though Craig was surprised to find something as sophisticated as a television in the almost bare room. It saved the awkwardness of the morning after for all those newly acquainted couples, he supposed.

He came out of the guesthouse and turned right as indicated by the map, though it was quite apparent where the gay beach was anyway. Early afternoon and there was a procession of skinny, very dark and exceedingly young looking boys heading in one direction, accompanied by a legion of old foreigners. To Craig it was all still quite surreal but everyone else, including the Thais, seemed to turn a blind eye, even on occasions when obviously under-aged boys in little more than cheap white briefs clung to their sugar daddies.

His time on the Internet seemed to have paid off because the copious postings from fellow "enthusiasts" on cruisingforsex.com's Web board had laid out Jomtien in fanatical detail. Yes, there was the pillbox hut housing the toilets he noticed, which was also allegedly a popular "cottage". Next to it were the "straight-acting" masseurs that also provided an "out" service in hotel rooms. And just further up the beach, as promised, Craig was pleased to find the volleyball, which was apparently the centre of daytime "action" where the city's money boys kept themselves lean, toned and tanned. Though things didn't get going till late afternoon when the heat of the day had subsided and tourists "felt in the mood for company," the website concluded.

Craig found a deckchair as close to the volleyball as possible without appearing too conspicuous, but even then watched several pairs of eyes watching him. There were even one or two smiles but he recognised it as the hollow gesture of the prostitute. He wondered whether Louis had already ordered a couple up to his room and was enjoying the delights of room service Pattaya style. Sex was like fast food in Thailand and the Englishman was realising this would be his very last foray before moving on. The heat, the poverty and the ever-smiling boys were a concoction that brought out the worst in people, the worst in him.

"Where you come from?" said a voice from behind Craig.

It sounded almost feminine in quality but had just enough depth to convince him it emanated from a young boy. He whipped around and sure enough was confronted by a svelte Thai with almond shaped eyes, flashing smile and a pair of white bikini briefs around his tiny waist.

"My name's Craig and I'm from England," he replied, burying his nose back into his book because he'd heard the same banter so many times before.

"Pleased to meet you," said the boy as he turned on his heels and went back to join his giggling young friends.

Nevertheless, Craig found it difficult to concentrate on his reading matter. He witnessed boys constantly parading up and down as tourists watched from their deckchairs, taking surreptitious photos with their expensive camera equipment for closer scrutiny later. The foreigners were typically three times older than their concubines and it made for a rather desperate spectacle.

At about four o'clock the piercing screams of the volleyball ensemble proved the ultimate distraction for Craig. Each player was impossibly lithe and they seemed to play not only for the benefit of themselves but also to the avidly watching gallery. Each had on a pair of identical figure hugging shorts and were unashamedly — on the surface at least — selling themselves.

The shrieks and laughter of the players filled the afternoon and in some way was uplifting but the English boy couldn't help thinking there was something a little unhinged in their manic, neurotic energy and in his keen interest.

As he headed out of Jomtien in a *songthaew* towards Pattaya a couple of boys theatrically waved down the vehicle. The Englishman sighed inwardly when the pair sat opposite him and the whiff of perfume hit his nostrils. The guilty allure he felt about such youngsters was beginning to repulse him and he resisted looking their way, knowing that he could use and then discard them like a piece of rubbish. Craig didn't feel sexually aroused but suffered a pity bordering on hatred for their tacky, seductive clothes, overpowering cologne and desperate stares.

In Pattaya itself he noticed not so much a transformation from the daytime but a horrible kind of evolution. The sprinkling of prostitutes and their prey had multiplied by the dozen. The shuttered bars had a horrible neon halo around them, and inside, for they were all open to the street, Craig noticed the young Thai women dripping all over their fat *farang* daddies like some obscene cliché. The red lighting gave the cheap scene an even more hellish glare.

He got off the *songtaew*, along with the two boys, when he saw the huge sign advertising "Boyz Town." Craig strode purposefully away from the pair, who were still waiting for a reaction and as he walked down the street saw youngsters of various ages in varying degrees of undress. Each boy was offering something different but essentially the same — bodies competing in a human meat market and packaged for quick consumption.

He looked at the various bars and, like their employees, they were all similar. He noticed Rice Bar where he'd made his appointment and headed there, passing the perennially smiling waiters on the way in. Almost inevitably he spotted Louis with his earlier encounter from the beach.

"Hi darlin', you all right? This is Pom by the way," said Louis with a playful smile at his lips as he introduced the volleyball player.

"Yeah, we spoke at the beach."

"Oh," said Louis, grinning again as Pom flashed his infuriatingly insincere smile.

"I didn't meet anyone else."

"Well you don't mind if he joins us, do you? I'm hungry," said Louis, crudely motioning to Pom's disappearing backside as the boy left to the bathroom. "Don't worry love, we'll find a couple of others for you."

"A couple?" questioned Craig, laughing, but aware his new acquaintance probably wasn't joking.

Looking around the bar he noticed any number of sunburned old queens dripping with gold, looking into their drinks as though desperately trying to think of something interesting and vital to say to their childlike companions.

They were sitting on a terrace opposite Muscles and Louis pointed out a *farang* in the entrance of the club. Craig looked over at the slip of a man illuminated by a shock of peroxide blond hair, rat-like features made sickeningly prominent by thick make-up. Dressed in a billowing silk blouse he impatiently thrashed his arms around as he appeared to give instructions to the several half-naked boys that surrounded him.

"That's 'Keith the Scouser'," said Louis. "He owns half this bloody *soi*, I can introduce you later."

"He looks a bit scary."

"No, heart of gold really but there's a rumour going around that he had an errant business partner put out of the picture, shall we say," said Louis, still grinning.

"How?"

"Well the guy apparently had a stake in Muscles but then pulled out and planned to open a bar opposite. He also owed Keith money."

"What happened?"

"The guy burned to death in his own apartment. You can get rid of someone for a few thousand *baht* here you know," said Louis, clicking his fingers. "Just like that."

Craig looked across as Keith continued to manhandle his young employees and wondered. "Do you know him, Pom?" he asked.

"Keith? Yes, I go to a couple of his house parties. Very crazy, I not like him."

"Why not?"

"He's not so good to my friends," said Pom, turning back to a Thai newspaper he'd been reading, signalling he wasn't willing to elaborate.

"Yeah, his parties are a bit wild," said Louis with a chuckle.

They walked over to Muscles where Louis was greeted by staff who seemed in awe of him. He led the way hurriedly passed a stage area full of boys in underwear and headed up a narrow staircase into a well-lit corridor that contrasted with the semi-darkness below. They reached a door at the end marked "Office." Louis knocked confidently.

"Come in," said someone a little harshly from the other side.

Louis entered first — they'd left Pom downstairs because Keith apparently didn't like Thai boys in his office.

"Oh, hiya love," said the man Craig recognised as the one from outside the club, the harshness in his voice replaced by an annoyingly shrill Liverpudlian accent.

He got up from behind his vast desk strewn with photographs of what Craig noted were young boys. The whole place reeked of tobacco despite the obvious efficiency of a large air-conditioning unit and was framed by a two-way mirror allowing Keith a view of his boy empire, perched as he was directly above the dance floor.

A cigarette burned absently in an overflowing ashtray as the club owner embraced Louis while Craig shifted uncomfortably in the ice-cold room.

"How's business?" ventured Louis.

"Sound, sound but shame about the fucking new kids in town. So many guys set up here thinking it's a license to print money. Well I've got fucking news for them," Keith said as his voice rose to an aggressive howl.

"Oh, by the way this is my friend Craig."

"Don't worry about me dear, I'm just a silly old fart," said Keith, finally turning to acknowledge the English boy with an unflinching stare. "But I do own half of Pattaya."

Craig didn't answer but looked back at the painted face just a few inches from him. The cold grey eyes below the peroxide fringe said more than enough.

"Come now, please sit down on my casting couch and have a snifter both of you," said the club owner, switching awkwardly between intimidation and terribly cloying niceties.

Craig watched as the show unfolded below on the stage from behind the mirror while Keith busied himself making the three of them drinks. Quickly losing interest he turned away from the tired song and dance routine and sat next to Louis on the sofa as the diminutive Scouser handed each of them a drink and returned to glower at them from behind his desk, somehow seeming to dominate the entire space.

"Louis, we've got some lovely new boys in from the northeast. Handpicked by yours truly," Keith said as a smile returned to his glossed lips.

"We'd like three," Louis replied poker-faced as he glanced at Craig.

"No probs, I know just the boys. Numbers one, two and three are all yours and they're almost virgins," said the Liverpudlian, unleashing a filthy laugh.

"Ain't no virgins in this city, is there love?" said Louis as he nudged Craig.

But he didn't reply because he didn't find it funny. He just wanted to get out of the office, away from Keith's piercing gaze and the sordid business he presided over. Though it was obvious his associate was anxious to get away too given the rapidity with which he finished his drink.

The club owner swivelled around in his chair to face the glass and the window onto his world. He theatrically threw his arms up. "The show must go on," he bellowed. "Go enjoy yourselves boys, I'll be down soon."

Louis patted his friend on the shoulder as he continued to peer out through the gloom and into his club, no doubt gleefully watching the punters sip their expensive drinks and leer at the expensive boys, boys, boys that he'd undoubtedly "handpicked".

"Creepy," Craig said once he'd followed Louis out of the office and shut the door resoundingly behind him.

"Oh, he's all right really," said Louis, shrugging it off with a laugh.

Not surprisingly Pom was "entertaining" someone back in the murkiness of downstairs. His youthful, spiky blond 'do contrasted sharply with his new companion's balding pate. The Thai was holding court by courtesy of his man-child looks and twenty-eight-inch waist, thought Craig, not his scintillating conversation. But he obviously knew what his options were because on seeing the pair approach Pom ruthlessly dropped the guy, a smile still fixed to his lips.

"Keeping busy I see," chided Louis, cuffing the boy not so gently round the ear. The look on his face said he wasn't kidding.

"Just talking," the Thai replied sheepishly, looking both hurt and resigned.

"That's all right, we've got a couple of your Issan friends joining us later. Number One, Number Two and Number Three," shot back Louis cruelly, referring to the identifying numbers the boys wore so excruciatingly close to their crotches on their skimpy briefs.

They didn't have names because they could be who the punters wanted them to be, Craig supposed. Numerical figures were fantasy ones too because the customers were paying and he imagined there was little a couple of thousand *baht* couldn't buy in a place like Muscles.

Keith had come out of his lair and was prowling around. He collared Louis and briefly joined the three of them, his voice clearly audible to Craig above the pumping music.

"You all right then, yeah?" he said, puffing nervously on a cigarette. "I see you've got your drinks."

"Looking forward to another crazy night," replied Louis, raising his glass.

"The boys will be over soon. Don't do anything I wouldn't do," said the Scouser as he pecked his friend on the cheek and departed with a cackle.

As promised, lined up in front of them on the stage were the three boys.

"Are we really going to take them home?" said Craig, taken with their dark good looks.

"Yeah, to my place — two for you, one for me as I have Pom too. Don't worry, love, they won't bite, only if you want them to," said Louis, laughing uproariously and motioning for the three boys to join them. "Fresh from the farm and finger lickin' good."

Close up the boys looked shy and totally unsure of themselves. Nevertheless, they went through the motions and introduced themselves, though the conversation pretty much dried up after they'd trotted out their rote learned phrases. But the trio were affectionate and obedient as trained dogs as Number One sat his slender frame down on Craig's lap and Two tugged at his arm. Pom looked an unwilling party to Louis' plan but held onto him as things got animated with Three.

The six of them piled out onto the street, shocked by the glare. All of them were high after a snort of K in the toilet cubicles and glass after glass of whisky. Louis had generously supplied the amphetamines and the alcohol for the sole purpose of "softening them up" as he put it to Craig in a not-so diplomatic aside.

When they reached the hotel Louis cautioned the five of them to wait in the lobby as he negotiated with the concierge. It was clear money had smoothed their path because he returned with a smile and casually ushered the group upstairs.

Pom had obviously seen it all before but Craig watched the three Issan boys who looked cowed by the opulence of five-star luxury. They seemed grateful, intimidated and obliged all at once and that was a combination Louis thrived on, he thought, as the banker dramatically threw open the door of his cavernous penthouse.

"Welcome to the honeymoon suite, boys," Louis said, laughing. "Pom, dial room service and order two bottles of champagne."

The other boys were careful to take their shoes off at the door and sat tidily on the floor, presumably leaving the chairs free in deference to their foreign hosts.

They didn't have to wait long for the drink to arrive. Craig observed as the prostitutes swigged theirs back nervously, the only way they knew how, seemingly oblivious to how expensive it was. Louis laughed unkindly at them while Pom sat in a corner and disdainfully fingered his flute of champagne. It wasn't long before they paired off to the two separate bedrooms.

Craig fooled around with his two boys as all three of them writhed naked on the king-size bed. However, the whole night had left a bad taste and was way too similar to the party with Stefan and Devon at the Sheraton for him to lose his inhibitions once again. He really didn't feel like demanding anything of the pair as they fell asleep, even though he was sure Louis felt differently about his own "guests".

He listened with horror to the pitiful yelps and cries from the bedroom opposite that had woken him. Craig was sure the other boys had heard it but were too paralysed with fear to react.

Still groggy from the alcohol he nevertheless rose to his feet and listened again intently in the darkness. There followed the loud bang of the front door slamming, then a hammering on his own, which opened even before he had a chance to answer. The light was snapped on and Louis stood facing him, shaking with rage, a bloody gash leaked copiously above his eye.

"Okay, I want them out of here," he snarled, indicating the boys cowering on the bed behind Craig. "You two leave, okay?"

"But it's five in the morning," said Craig pleadingly in their defence. "What the hell happened?"

"The other fucker wouldn't do what I wanted despite the amount I paid. I want them out now. And if you think this cut is bad you should see what I did to him."

The boys looked confused but sensed they were being thrown out. Obviously concerned for their friend they hurriedly got dressed as Louis remained in the bedroom doorway, uneasy and aggressive and dabbing at the bloody wound with a towel already soaked crimson.

"Take this money and look after your friend," he said to the pair as he flung a wad of cash onto the bed. "He'll need hospital treatment."

One of them bowed down pathetically and guiltily grabbed the money. The other clung to his friend's arm as they both made to *wai* Craig and Louis and then quickly fled.

"He didn't mind being tied up but he objected to where I wanted to position the champagne bottle and got really aggressive. But they shouldn't fuck with me, I fuck back," said Louis, all trace of humility frighteningly drained from him. "I just hope for his sake that I never see him again or I'll finish him off next time."

"I've got to get some sleep," Craig replied meekly.

"Sure, at least I've got Pom to indulge me and I can get away with anything with him."

He watched in silence as Louis stalked back to his bedroom and listened as the key turned in the lock, wondering what hell was about to be unleashed on the blond volleyball player.

*   *   *

He woke in the morning to an empty bed, hating himself and despising Louis for what had occurred the night before. He decided then that he would head back to Bangkok and leave for Sydney as soon as he could. His companion had been charming, funny and generous too but he'd used such virtues to hide a multitude of sins and for Craig it was a final warning.

CHAPTER FIFTEEN

Jamie sank back in his business-class seat courtesy of George but didn't feel a shred of guilt — he believed he'd earned it over the course of their turbulent association, though he'd experienced a nervous night in a soulless airport hotel waiting for a flight back to London.

As the aircraft roared down the runway and into the beautiful blue of the early morning Barcelona sky, however, he did feel a tinge of regret that his dreams had led him to such a point with no job and no prospects once again. There was the couple of hundred pounds in his pocket he'd taken from George but it was hardly enough to maintain his now burgeoning coke and perennial club-bing habits.

Philippe had recently ventured the idea of joining an escort agency as a way of making "pocket money" but Jamie felt he'd gone as low as he could go with Adam Films. He still felt having sex with guys like Aiden, albeit on film, was a step up from servicing some sweaty old freak.

He hadn't switched his mobile on from the day he'd left for Spain in the hope of deterring Gary and was still loath to, fearing George would try to contact him, though Jamie felt he was always running away from things yet finding more trouble. The problem was, he didn't know how to stop running as it was ingrained from his abu-sive childhood and he feared the day something would stop him dead, forcing him to confront his problems directly.

"What do you do, then?" asked the businessman next to him, rudely breaking his train of thought.

He was wearing a wedding ring and probably had a picture of his kids in his wallet but Jamie sensed he was making a move.

"I don't," he replied obnoxiously, to which the guy blushed and hid behind his *Financial Times* for the remainder of the journey.

*　　　　*　　　　*

Jamie almost expected flashing blue lights on the Heathrow tarmac and fantasised about being led from the plane in handcuffs by burly police officers. Instead he witnessed the usual muted reception and anti-climax of arriving back in London. He felt totally empty with no one to surprise with his unexpected early return as he followed directions to the Tube.

When he arrived home the flat felt damp and the answer phone blinked menacingly at him. He knew he'd been dreaming when he thought some time away would put off someone as determined as Gary — the more he ignored him, the closer he seemed to get.

The answer phone had stored twenty-six messages and he'd bet the only reason there weren't more was that the tape had run out. He also guessed virtually all would be from Gary since everyone he knew, which didn't amount to many, had been informed of his "holiday" to Spain.

He tentatively pressed "play" and listened to the first message: "Hi, it's Gary, I'm sorry about the other night but I really think we can mean something to each other. Could we meet up again?"

So far, so mellow, he thought, but he reeled through to the end of the tape: "Why the fuck don't you call me? It's fucking over between us, over! Why are you such a fucking bastard?"

The final message brought back to Jamie the occasion he'd been followed home and his stalker had veered frighteningly between Mr Nice Guy and psycho. He knew he couldn't face another night like that and vowed to go out the following evening with George's money and get trashed with Philippe to forget about life for a while.

He also planned to see Liz, because he needed money. Jamie knew he could still go to her for cash; she always fell for the one about him being threatened with eviction — when twenty years of maternal guilt came readily to the surface. He resolved to call her and make some noises about being laid off as a "runner" at the film company he'd worked for.

He switched on his mobile and within a couple of minutes it was ringing. Jamie looked at the digital readout and didn't recognise the number but guessed it was Gary. Hesitantly he pressed the "answer" button just to make sure.

"Hi," said a shaky but sickeningly familiar voice at the other end. "Where the fuck have you been?"

"Sorry. I was called away on an urgent trip to Spain."

"Well, didn't you get my messages?" said Gary, seemingly oblivious to the fact that his bombardment bordered on the insane.

"I said I've just got back."

"What about the mobile!" bellowed Gary.

"It was switched off and I haven't checked the messages, for fuck's sake."

"Well, can we meet today? I've missed you so much."

"Gary, look, I've just got back from a busy trip to Spain. I'm not seeing you today but I'll call, okay?"

"How about tomorrow?" pleaded his pursuer like a child.

"Look, once I'm feeling more chilled I'll call you."

"Can you promise we'll meet tomorrow?"

"I'll call you," Jamie replied, exasperated.

"Fucking promise to meet me tomorrow!"

"Okay," Jamie sighed, just to get him off his back, and hung up but felt sick to his stomach. It seemed like the nightmare wouldn't end until something drastic happened.

He went into the kitchen and was hit by the stench of rotting food. There were pizza boxes and fast food cartons strewn around, cigarette ends in an overflowing ashtray and a sink full of unwashed plates. Jamie opened the fridge more out of curiosity than anything else and nearly retched at the smell of fermented milk. Knowingly, he reached in the cupboard under the sink and resignedly pulled out a bottle of whisky. He glanced around but there were no clean glasses so he tilted the bottle to his lips and felt the liquid burn down his throat and warm his stomach. Feeling a little better, he dialled Philippe's number.

"Hi, it's me," said Jamie to his nominal best friend.

"And who's you?" said a sceptical voice at the other end.

"Jamie."

"Oh."

Jamie ploughed on regardless but felt tears sting his eyes, he was so lonely. "Just wondering whether you wanted to come out tomorrow night?"

"Who are you again by the way?" said Philippe, thinking he was funny. "Let me see, I think I can find a space in my social diary even though it's Friday tomorrow and it's all going off at Heaven."

"When and where?"

"I fucking hate all the gay bars, they're just so gay," said Philippe coolly. "I'm really over them."

"Got any other bright ideas?"

"No, let's just do Freedom Bar."

"Oh great, a gay bar pretending not to be, how radical," said Jamie disparagingly. "See you there at nine-thirty."

"Okey dokey," said Philippe and hung up, leaving his friend with nothing but dead air.

A heavy rapping on the door raised him from his slumber. It was light outside and Jamie guessed early afternoon. Still tired after that morning's trip he rolled over in bed as if to sleep again thinking it was the gas man, the postman or any one of those annoying, officious people that wore starched blue uniforms.

"Just go away," he shouted in the safe knowledge no one would hear him, as his bedroom door was firmly shut and locked.

"Jamie, I know you're there, open the door. I've got to see you," bellowed Gary through the letterbox, sending a chill down his spine and no doubt alerting the whole corridor.

Most in the flats were either unemployed, retired or on sickness benefit so Jamie could just imagine curtains twitching all down the passageway, though after the event no one would have seen or heard a thing of course.

As he left the sanctuary of his room he could see Gary's burly frame horribly silhouetted against the flimsy glass of the front door. His heart was thumping hard as he made his way toward it but he had to do something to shut him up.

"Okay, okay I'm coming," Jamie shouted frantically as he saw the door bow from the pressure applied from outside. "Hey, can you hear me?"

"Just let me in!"

"Can't you come back later? I want to sleep," pleaded Jamie, shivering in the dank hallway.

"I want to see you now! I'm not waiting any longer."

He was careful to put the chain on and edged the door open. As soon as he did the stalker stuck a large booted foot between door and frame making a mockery of the slight link of metal keeping the two apart. He could see Gary's face through the crack in the door, flushed with anger, and as Jamie looked into his eyes it was as though he didn't even register, so focused was he on getting into the flat.

"Gary, look just leave me alone. I'm going to call the police if you don't go."

"Call the fucking police then. Look, don't be silly; just let me in."

"I'm not ready to see you now. I was sleeping."

"I came all this way to see you, took the day off work sick. And you won't even open the fucking door," he said, his voice hysterically loud as the tears streamed down his face.

Jamie, sensing weakness, moved the door as far back as the chain would allow and then slammed it as hard as he could on the intrusive boot. Gary let out an animal-like howl and went staggering backwards into the corridor, allowing the boy to shut the door with an explosive crash.

"I'm calling the police, now fuck off," he screamed through the pane of glass.

"Eh! Clear off, you're not wanted round 'ere," shouted someone from further down the passageway who'd obviously been riled by all the commotion.

Another party getting involved seemed to have the desired effect. Jamie watched in relief as Gary finally sloped off with a pronounced limp. He knew it was far from over as he walked dejectedly back to his bedroom and curled up under the covers in a ball.

He hadn't even dared switch his mobile back on because he knew there'd be more harassment. Jamie was also against getting the police involved as he'd come up against them when he'd previously had some trouble on the estate, like dog excrement through his letterbox, that kind of thing. The two officers assigned had been pure machismo stuffed into blue uniforms and were totally unsympathetic, almost to the point of suggesting he deserved it. They'd told him to "tone it down" and be "more discreet", whatever that meant. So he waited for the queer baiting to fizzle out, which it did, but Gary was showing no sign of losing interest.

After a fitful sleep, where he kept one ear open listening for any slight noise, he woke up around teatime. He left his bedroom and peered out of the front room curtains, half expecting to see Gary loitering outside. He breathed out as he took in the silent passageway.

Jamie slipped into some tracksuit bottoms and an oversized sweatshirt and left the flat cautiously, bound for the local supermarket. He was careful to deadbolt the front door and looked over his shoulder as he made his way warily to the grimy concrete stairwell, all senses on alert. At the bottom he noticed a shadow cast by the fluorescent light but his attention was suddenly diverted as a figure entered the bottom of the stairs. He was relieved to register the hunched figure of the dotty old cow from his floor that sometimes talked to him about the weather.

"Hello dear, miserable one today," she said, weighed down by the requisite couple of shopping bags.

"Hi," he replied as evenly as he could since he'd noticed what was responsible for the shadow. Gary was lurking at the foot of the stairwell and their eyes inevitably locked but the stalker's path to Jamie was blocked by the old woman's bulk.

"I'm gonna kill you," he said so matter-of-factly that Jamie believed him.

He sent the pensioner tumbling out of the way as he ran into the street and she collided with Gary. The boy quickly glanced back to see his stalker brushing the woman off and giving chase, something metallic flashing in his outstretched hand. His pursuer was big but he was moving quickly and to Jamie he looked huge as he bore down closer and closer.

He was aware of other people on the pavement but they just became obstacles to be brushed aside as he ran. Jamie knew no one was going to be a hero or rush to his aid; it was his personal nightmare. He could hear Gary shouting things behind him against the roar of traffic on the busy main road. It was mostly mangled, incomprehensible stuff but he listened intently for the sound getting closer. It was.

He wheeled around again and his stalker was just two or three metres away, a jagged knife clearly visible in one clenched fist. Jamie darted into the road and closed his eyes. He ran as fast as he ever had, the air feeling it was going to explode in his lungs. He sensed the rush of traffic and felt the vibrating tarmac under his feet. Hearing a huge bang followed by a terribly human cry he turned around to see Gary somersaulting over a car bonnet.

From his new vantage point at the other side of the four-lane carriageway he was captivated by how graceful his stalker looked plummeting to the ground. Traffic squealed to a halt in both directions as Gary lay motionless. Jamie, still rooted to the spot, watched as the driver of the car that hit, a woman, got out slowly, zombie-like, face creased in anguish as she moved helplessly to the body. It was like she could barely look at the victim when she stood above him, shaking, arms flailing.

Amazingly traffic in the other three lanes began moving again but Jamie still stood as another motorist who'd been behind the woman got out, walked over and put an arm lightly around her shoulders. A small crowd had already gathered on the pavement to gossip and leer, while several vehicles further back in the stationary line honked their horns, but the body stayed eerily still.

Jamie slowly turned his back on the scene as he heard the wailing of sirens from the emergency services on their way to clear up the whole sad mess.

He'd called Liz solely for some financial aid and she'd agreed to meet on the pretext of one of their regular chitchats. So much had happened in the time since they'd last met.

Even after Gary had been killed in the road accident his ghost still haunted Jamie. He'd switched his mobile on the previous evening, the one of the accident, and there'd been several abusive messages on his voice mail. As he listened to them he was morbidly fascinated by Gary's anger but imagined the stalker lying silently on a cold slab in a hospital morgue.

Then there'd been the call from George that he'd been dreading. He sounded as unflappable as ever, his voice low and moderated, though Jamie knew he'd beaten him. Neither of them could forget how helpless and pathetic he'd looked on that hotel room floor in Spain. Nevertheless, the phone call was intended as a warning and the director reminded Jamie that he was well connected and that he'd make sure his former employee "never walked again" if their paths crossed in the future. This time he wanted the last word.

Jamie was suffering an inner turmoil that he felt wouldn't recede but at least George and Gary were both out of his life. He didn't want to confess the incidents to Liz, however, for fear that everything would spill out and she'd shrink before his eyes as though he was the devil. He knew she never wanted to hear the truth about his life, like she always shielded him from the truth of hers.

On the way out to meet her he was about to step over the accumulated mail on the mat but a postcard at the very top caught his eye. He flipped over the garish picture of a tropical beach and read the first few lines, niceties from Craig, who was still in Thailand. He threw it back on the pile with abandon, resolving to bin everything when he got back home.

"What was that all about the other day dear? You knocked me flying," said the pensioner, weighed down with shopping in the corridor. "Frightened the life out of me."

"Sorry, we were just messing around," Jamie said, anxious to get away from the nosy old dear.

She was about to say something else when he rudely nudged her out of the way and trotted down the stairs towards the Underground, wishing the stalker had stuck the knife in and put her out of her misery.

He passed the point where Gary had performed what he thought of as a rather good triple-axle jump. Jamie scoured the ground for signs of blood but all that was left was what looked like some broken pieces of a car's indicator light. A couple of lines in the week's local rag speculating about "a knife found at the scene" and a few bunches of flowers left on a fence opposite were all his pursuer had warranted in death, as far as he knew. The newspaper report concluded that no witnesses had come forward. Jamie whistled to himself almost contentedly as he walked on to the Tube station as the sun shone on an early spring day.

Liz was already seated at Harvey Nichols' fifth-floor restaurant when he arrived. He was beginning to regret their meeting as he moved closer and saw she was wearing sunglasses. He mused whether the eye wear was to cover up yet another bruise or an elaborate attempt to hide her tears.

"Hi Liz, how are you?" he said, leaning across the table to kiss her cheek, and awkwardly knocked the expensive tortoise-shell frames, though they both stubbornly pretended to ignore the presence of the glasses.

"I'm fine," she said.

But looked far from it, he thought, nervously fiddling with her wedding ring as a half-finished gin and tonic sat in front of her.

"Sorry I'm late," he said. I was held up looking at where my stalker came to a sticky end, he contemplated saying, but instead smiled up at the bitch of a waiter they'd had last visit and said, "A gin and tonic please."

"You weren't late, I was early," she said, swilling around the ice cubes in her now empty glass.

It was unbelievable, thought Jamie; he was the one who was late yet she was apologising. The spectre of his father hung over her always.

"Bob and I are off to Thailand next month, a week in Bangkok and a week in Pattaya. He insisted on spending a week at the beach."

"Pattaya, isn't that where all the sex tourists go?"

"Oh, I don't think so..."

"And are you ready to order?" queried the waiter as he unprofessionally butted in and slapped Jamie's drink down.

"Just give us a minute," he replied, taking a welcome gulp of the drink and leisurely perusing the menu. "Liz, you should try the Thai green curry. It'll get you in the mood for next month."

"Yes," she said, always one to be bullied. "The green curry please, with chicken."

"I'm watching my weight as summer's coming, the chicken Caesar please."

"Excellent choices," said the waiter, with the most insincere of smiles.

"That guy is an asshole," said Jamie as the waiter minced almost out of earshot.

"Jamie!" Liz admonished, though he knew his father had called her far worse. "But you're absolutely right."

And they both started to giggle, which was a very unusual sound at their monthly lunches.

"So how's your job?" Liz finally asked.

"That's what I meant to tell you. The company is downsizing, which means I get the boot. You know it's all down to mergers and acquisitions these days. Adam Films was acquired by a larger company and had to lay people off."

"Oh, I see. So what are you going to do?"

"Well, I was hoping you could lend me some money while I get myself sorted," Jamie said pleadingly as the waiter made his presence felt again and banged down their dishes.

"Two more G and Ts," Liz said before he disappeared.

"Well?" asked Jamie insistently, looking at the plate of food that he really didn't think he could manage.

"Well," replied his mother cautiously, ladling some curry into her mouth and chewing it over, sunglasses seemingly glued on. "I talked to your father about this and he's decided that you're not to have any more money."

She'd said it so meekly that Jamie almost felt like giving up himself as he sat in silent contemplation. He knew it would happen eventually; the bastard Bob would cut off his lifeline simply because he could. And he'd bet that she'd just sat there and nodded in agreement, his *so-called* mother.

"You really are fucking pathetic, you know that?" he said, leaning over and ripping the sunglasses off. Not only did it reveal an ugly yellowing bruise but eyes filled with tears.

"How am I meant to live?" wailed Jamie, on his feet now and feeling other diners' eyes boring into him. He turned and strode to the exit, leaving his mother inconsolable and sobbing uncontrollably in his wake.

Jamie arrived home from the draining afternoon with Liz and planned to take it easy before meeting Philippe later that evening. He moved into the front room and went over to the pile of videos scattered on the floor and chose one of the no-holds barred Eastern European films he'd picked up in Amsterdam a while ago.

He lay on the sofa, falling in and out of consciousness as three Czech teenagers took turns fucking another boy in a barn — a slight variation on a very common theme.

Jamie had finally moved to full-on dozing when his mobile rang. He looked at the TV screen that belied the earlier action and was a snowy blank, then glanced with concern at the clock on the wall.

"And where the fuck are you?" was Philippe's knockout opening line.

"Er ... at home."

"It's nine fucking thirty," spat the French boy.

"Sorry, I fell asleep. I'm still recovering from Spain."

"How can you be jetlagged? It's only a couple of hours away," said Philippe, finally lightening up and laughing. "Why are you back anyway? I thought you were going for a week."

"Er, I was but I'll reveal all later."

"That's if I hang around. I'm standing alone and being hit on by 'Mr Fucking Gorgeous'."

"Lucky you, look I'll be there quick as I can."

"Time?" snapped Philippe.

"Ten," said Jamie, waiting for some confirmation from the other end, but the precocious French boy had hung up.

He went through to his bedroom and opened the wardrobe, which was the only thing in his flat that was ordered. There were row upon row of immaculate clothes and probably enough shoes to have made Imelda Marcos smile.

Keep it simple, he thought, as he pulled out a pair of jeans and another singlet, which would show off his muscle tone. He quickly showered and lathered a wad of gel into his hair.

Jamie slung on the clothes, checked his hair yet again in the hallway mirror, grabbed his leather jacket and was gone. Out in the graffiti-covered corridor he held his breath as he walked down the rank smelling stairwell. A lad bouncing up the stairs gave him the once over as if to say "fucking queer", or maybe out of lust, fantasised Jamie, even though he hurried his step. He fought the urge to look back but would have seen the snarling guy marvelling at his beautifully rendered arse if he had done.

The estate was what Liz would call "rough" and he did have to watch his step. He'd had all the usual like verbal abuse, funny looks and broken windows. It was juvenile stuff, scary at first but not amounting to much. His real fear was being cornered by a group of skinheads and he tried not to think about it, though sometimes he caught the eyes of the estate's teenagers and saw only hatred staring back.

The council had made improvements; it was brighter and CCTV cameras watched around the clock. But Jamie knew these were merely cosmetic measures and didn't tackle things like alienation, unemployment, racism and homophobia or simply the fact people could be evil. Every time he saw a gang of local lads in the glow of the amber street lamps he felt a frisson of fear and instinctively crossed the road while feeling in his pocket for his mobile in the vain hope that it could save him.

Jamie felt safer when he was on the Underground heading towards Soho's gay ghetto, where two men could actually hold hands and a rainbow flag could flutter freely outside a venue without fear of the windows being smashed in.

He surfaced at Leicester Square Tube and headed down Charing Cross Road, turning left at Old Compton Street, which was buzzing with people. Jamie had timed it wrong, though, as the threatre goers were all pouring out of *Abba the Musical* under the watchful eye of the local dealers, pimps and cabbies.

So naff, Jamie thought, as he saw couples like his mum and dad bright-eyed and bushy tailed after an evening of wholesome entertainment, intent on getting back to their suburban, pebble-dashed palaces. He knew Bob was a big Abba fan but only because he liked "that blonde piece". He'd absolutely insisted on taking Liz to the musical. She hated the Swedish band and Jamie could imagine her fake smile, as his dad clapped along to the simple tunes, desperately trying to have a good time but fearing another beating.

He turned right onto Wardour Street and strode past the doorman at Freedom, who was accessorised with a stupid Madonna-style microphone set on his head. As Jamie entered the bar he was pleased to see Philippe alone and turned on by his choice of translucent top, advertising that buff body. He felt fat just looking at the French boy and worriedly brushed a hand across his own washboard stomach.

"The top's just darling," he said, pinching his friend's nipple through the delicate cloth and pretentiously kissing him on both cheeks as was the custom in Freedom.

Unimpressed, Philippe looked at his Gucci watch, which read 10.10pm. "You're lucky. I was going to leave in five minutes."

"Sorry but you said you were being hit on, I thought you could keep yourself amused."

"Yeah I was being leered at by a thirtysomething, a *thirtysome-thing* for fuck's sake," Philippe shrieked as he rolled his eyes at the indignity of it all.

"Well I've just been on a so-called holiday with a fortysome-thing," said Jamie, sighing.

"But at least *he* was paying."

"Yeah, he paid for it all right," replied Jamie. "He fucking hit me and demanded sex, so I slapped him one".

"Jamie you went there knowing he was paying for the trip in or-der to make a porn film, surely you knew he was part of the deal?"

"I didn't sign a contract to that effect, no, and I'm not letting someone treat me like my mum's been treated all these years," said Jamie with the unwelcome sting of tears in his eyes as he looked at the impassive Philippe sipping away on a cocktail. "Anyway I need a drink."

"You go girl," sang Philippe as Jamie walked sullenly to the bar.

He didn't want to discuss anything deeper with the French boy than the latest soap opera and was glad not to have elaborated on Sitges as he ordered a gin and tonic from the unspeakably beautiful barman. Though the server was clearly disinterested in everything apart from his own reflection in the mirror behind the bar. As Ja-mie gave him the eye the barman might as well have just replied, "You are not fucking pretty enough."

"Your change," he muttered almost unintelligibly instead while staring off into the far distance.

Oh well, fuck him, thought Jamie, looking around to see if he could see anything more interesting and instantly met Philippe's gaze. The French boy looked away. If only, he sighed.

"So why *are* you back early?" said Philippe, all studied indiffer-ence but obviously eager for the full story.

"I told you, we had this fight and I just left," he replied, attempt-ing to brush it off and wary of admitting any flaw, particularly something that reminded him of his dad's failings. Because Jamie did have a violent streak; he'd even hit Craig once.

"I thought George was meant to be a control freak. He just let you go?"

"He was on the floor after I decked him."

"Jesus, it must have been a hard punch," said Philippe, looking sparkly eyed and impressed for once. "Was there any blood?"

"Look, I hit him over the head with a camera," said Jamie, finally confessing and taking a couple of welcome swigs of his drink.

"Wow, that's serious."

"He was groaning on the floor as I left. He was fine," Jamie insisted. "He's phoned me since."

"You could have killed him."

"No, he's gonna be all right. He deserved it anyway."

"Well, that's the end of your film career, honey," said Philippe, laughing mercilessly.

"Short and legendary like Jimmy Dean."

"Yeah the difference was Dean died himself. He didn't try and murder his director."

"I could always plead artistic differences."

"You call that art?" said Philippe, and they both started giggling. "Anyway, it's my round."

"Same again," said Jamie as he watched his friend move gracefully to the bar.

As he scanned London's so-called beautiful people — everyone was so fashionably dressed and such a picture of studied cool a nail bomb could go off and facial expressions wouldn't change, he thought — it dawned on Jamie that Philippe had been longer than usual at the bar. When he turned he felt a pang; the French boy was chatting to the surly barman who now had a big "come get me" grin on his model-type face.

"Barman's hot, huh?" said Philippe, all smiles as he handed over Jamie's drink. "And he gave me his email address."

"His email address?" replied Jamie, unable to contain his derision. "Doesn't he have a mobile?"

"Maybe he lives with a rich uncle and he's got to be discreet," said Philippe, winking. "Besides he's modelled for D & G, which raises his standing just a tad."

"Oh please, who in here isn't an out of work actor or aspiring model?"

"Sorry, being pounded in some nasty skin flick by a well-hung gringo doesn't count."

"Oh fuck you."

"One night in heaven, one night in heaven," sang Philippe in a not too accurate rendition of the M People hit, while nudging his friend in the ribs and thumbing over at the barman. "I think he knows how to show a girl a good time."

"Whatever," said Jamie disinterestedly. "Bet he doesn't have a stalker."

"He does, me."

"No seriously, I had a stalker," said Jamie.

"You?" replied Philippe, creasing up with laughter. "Where is he now then?"

"I'm not sure," said Jamie hesitantly and reddening, not wanting to go into the desperate details.

"Did you order him from the Shopping Channel?"

"No, he's for real. I met him at CXR."

"In that hell hole, well it figures," the French boy said with disdain.

"He wouldn't leave me alone."

"Enjoy it while it lasts," said Philippe, laughing off his friend's problems as he headed back to flirt with the barman.

Jamie was left staring at the empty space so rudely vacated by the French boy and pulled out the packet of cigarettes in his pocket reserved for such emergencies. He lit up and began leafing through a copy of *Boyz* from a nearby table. He turned straight to the contact ads that actually formed the bulk of the magazine. He liked looking at the cropped pictures of people's appendages — it was like shopping in a supermarket with such a variety on offer, he thought. Running a finger over the numerous ads he spotted Latino, Scottish, Brazilian and Oriental boys among others, all willing to do virtually anything *for a fee*.

"He's going to heaven tonight," said Philippe, returning with a big grin on his face. "And so am I."

"I've been with guys like that before; they have to look at themselves in the mirror before they get a hard-on."

"Just jealous," Philippe replied. "Anyway the next round of drinks are free so stop dissing him."

"I just hope we can score."

"Well that's where I can help you, Mr Jamie. I've still got a couple of pills left over from the weekend," his friend said, winking.

Jamie was disbelieving when Philippe hailed a black cab instead of taking the less-than fifteen-minute walk to Villiers Street and

Heaven nightclub. But that was Philippe, who Jamie knew always liked to be extravagant simply because he could.

"Where to, lads?" said the cabbie, rolling down his window, the archetypal Cockney geezer.

"Heaven," they chorused.

"All right, boys," said the driver, with the hint of a mocking lisp.

Drawing up on The Strand Philippe paid the ridiculously expensive fare for the short ride and left a tip.

As they turned on to Villiers Street the queue from Heaven snaked around the block but the pair strode nonchalantly to the front. Philippe had once turned tricks for the head bouncer just so he'd never have to line up like all the rest. Indeed the portly, aged doorman gave the French boy a wry smile and waved them both past the velvet rope, though Jamie couldn't resist one last look back and had a chuckle to himself at the column of preening queens shivering in the cold.

They'd once had access to the club's hallowed inner sanctum, the VIP Lounge. That was until one of Philippe's fag hag friends took umbrage at a boringly rehearsed put-down from a camp, misogynist comedian with his own unfunny TV show. Secondary to the cult of celebrity, they were unceremoniously ejected. It was B-list territory anyway; for instance Jamie had once seen the light entertainer Michael Barrymore sidelong on one of the sofas knocking back sparkling wine from the bottle with one hand and groping a teenage boy with the other. Though he immediately felt comfortable in Heaven as he looked around at the carbon copies of himself sinking Bacardi Breezers, arms angled to accentuate gym-toned muscles.

"My round," he said. "What do you want?"

"Get me a Breezer," replied the French boy.

He elbowed his way through a sea of tight tees and high maintenance 'dos without an "excuse me", as tradition demanded. Edging towards the bar the requisite cutie barked at him for his order and Jamie suddenly recognised him. It was Aiden. Recognition rendered him momentarily speechless but there was not a glimmer in the barman's cold eyes as the delay simply saw him impatiently move on to serve the next customer. He knew the Scotsman was only a couple of years older than he was but close-up looked haggard and resigned, like the commodity of his youth had simply been squeezed out of him.

The boy's mind briefly wandered back to that cocaine-addled shoot as another barman came across and took his order. Jamie remembered how he and Aiden had barely grunted at each other but been totally intimate. He felt crushed as he walked away from the bar with the drinks, popping a pill into his mouth.

"You never guess who I just saw." said Philippe.

"Not that alcoholic Barrymore?"

"Nope, Boy George looking fatter than ever."

"Don't you mean Boy Gorge?" said Jamie, feeling relieved to laugh. "He always wears those hats to hide his chubby cheeks."

"Can't disguise the chubby butt cheeks though."

"I've taken my pill," said Jamie, heading for the dance floor and beckoning his friend to follow.

"Darling you're just insatiable."

For Jamie it wasn't a good trip as he came up but he remembered to keep smiling. His legs felt strangely leaden as he swayed from side to side rather than danced as the rhythm pumped monotonously on.

"C'mon," said Philippe encouragingly, putting an arm around his friend and gently kissing his earlobe. At that moment the barman from Freedom appeared in a singlet displaying the to-die-for pecs and the French boy dropped Jamie like he was the Elephant Man.

The English boy excused himself from the dance floor, disturbed to note not a flicker of disappointment in Philippe's eyes at his sudden departure.

Again he had to fight his way through a crush of people and was thankful to steady his hands on the bar top. Jamie felt uncomfortably high and worried if he blacked out then and there there'd be no one to save him. The warm and fuzzy thoughts that normally flooded his brain when he was on a pill had been replaced by screaming demons with the incident in the Sitges hotel room on an almost constant loop. He looked around as he propped himself against the bar and found it hard to believe that in a club bursting with so many people he could feel so alone.

"Yes mate?" said Aiden, bringing Jamie out of his trance as he came across to serve him, though the Scotsman obviously hadn't meant to, given the embarrassed look on his face.

"Hi."

"All right, how are you?" Aiden mumbled while averting his eyes.

"Fine, get me a pint of Fosters," he replied as though it was all one word, so anxious was he to get Aiden out of his face.

"Fosters you say?"

"Yeah."

Jamie caught a glimpse of his own reflection in the smoked-glass mirror behind the bar and smiled because despite the chaos of his life he still liked what he saw. He looked admiringly at his side profile and ran a hand over his pumped pectoral muscles, feeling slightly better.

Aiden came back with his pint, his change and a weak smile. Jamie left a few coins in the tray just for the sake of appearances and gulped down some beer that tasted bitter against his parched throat as he turned his back on another mistake.

He moved back to the dance floor but stopped in his tracks when he saw Philippe and "Mr Freedom", Ronaldo he thought the French boy had said, in a deep, druggy embrace — a bundle of muscles awkwardly entwined.

"This sucks," he said aloud and was eyed hatefully by an inanely smiling disco bunny as he headed for the coat check on his way to the exit.

Jamie and Philippe normally left clubs together because both liked having someone by their side on the cold, dark streets of early morning. Though on the scene it was another unwritten rule that sex came before friendship, so he was alone as he headed out into the faded Victorian grandeur of Villiers Street, the pavement stained and stinking of urine from the homeless congregated and huddled against the chill.

"Spare some change man," said a figure crumpled in a shadowy doorway, making him jump.

Jamie nervously waved away the beggar's cries and walked on faster, knowing he'd be safer once he reached the buzz of Trafalgar Square. The warmth and sound of the club quickly faded on the near deserted streets and he concentrated on the sanctuary of his bed, willing himself home.

He rounded a corner and the emptiness was punctuated by the high shouts of a group of four or five lads on their Friday night out. Jamie knew they'd seen him and guessed it would look feeble if he turned around so he carried on walking towards them and their loud and boisterous banter. He looked straight ahead hoping to remain anonymous, invisible, just like he had in the school playground. But just like at school they couldn't let him walk by without abusing him.

"Fuckin' queer," said one.

"Shirtlifter," wailed another.

Jamie tried to ignore their cries, the pathetic playground taunts that still cut deeply, and kept on walking. But one of them had doubled back and blocked his path. He registered for the first time the shirt outside the jeans, the sovereign rings, the razor-cut hair and the silly, mocking grin of just a teenager with only hatred in his eyes.

Panicking, he tried to push past and run, but was sent reeling by a hard fist. As he staggered back and felt the warm blood leak from a wound just above his brow the rest of the group circled like sharks and senselessly joined in. They took turns mauling him all over his body with fists and boots as he fell uselessly to the pavement.

Jamie didn't have time to think, just to fear, as the boys' hysterical hail of abuse registered as hard as their blows — sheer cold-bloodied hate.

"Cocksucker, bum bandit, shit stabber, faggot," they spat out almost in unison, practised like some religious chant.

Then through the terrifying melee Jamie saw the flash of a blade and felt a hot, sharp surging pain across his face again and again and again. The echo of insecure, excited young voices trailed off as he slipped consciousness.

He came to with a flurry of activity going on around him. The starched white nurses' uniforms and the bright, clinical hospital light was all it took to bring the horror back to him. Jamie moved a hand hesitantly to his face but touched a swathe of bandages, as though he was being held together.

"Just lay back, there's a good boy," said an orderly as though Jamie was a young child.

He saw Bob and Liz standing ominously in the corner of the room, silent with heads bowed like someone had just died. Jamie was anaesthetised and could no longer feel any pain, but could still hear, and discerned the gravity in the voices of the medical staff. He feared seeing himself in the mirror again and he was right to.

CHAPTER SIXTEEN

"It'll be good to be going home. I miss my friends and that," said Craig's young English companion on the bus back from Pattaya to Bangkok.

"Yeah," replied Craig as he felt his stomach cramp at the thought of England, and looked out of the window as the grim allure of Bangkok came into view, shimmering in the morning sunshine.

"I'm booking my flight today," said the backpacker, gleefully rubbing his hands.

Craig didn't reply but continued to stare out of the window at a sea of possibilities. It would be a while yet before he climbed back on that plane to Heathrow, he thought.

When the bus pulled into the Ekkamai terminal he curtly said goodbye to his neighbour, grabbed his travel bag and quickly hailed a cab to the Malaysia Hotel, ready to experience Bangkok one last time.

Waking from a fitful nap Craig looked at his watch and was pleased to note it was only lunchtime. He was aware he had plenty of time to himself, guiltily aware. He'd come back to Bangkok for a reason and he nervously fiddled with Eddie's business card, hoping the boy would agree to spend a couple more days with him before he flew to Sydney. He dialled the Thai's number and held his breath. It rang several times.

"Hello," a voice said finally at the other end.

"Hi, Eddie?"

"Ah it's Craig, where are you?"

"Malaysia Hotel."

"Really. You come back to see me?"

"Yeah, just for you," Craig said sarcastically. "Can I see you this afternoon?"

"I come to your hotel room now," Eddie replied, laughing.

"No, look, I want to see the Grand Palace this afternoon."

"Okay, I'm free after lunch. Meet me outside the Oriental Hotel at two o'clock and we can travel along the river. Just ask the taxi driver for Oriental Hotel."

"See you then," said Craig, and smiled to himself, recalling the earnest boy with the boxing scars, the devilish tattoo on his chest and the crew cut.

He walked purposefully through reception, avoiding eye contact with several boys sitting languidly around waiting, though he guessed most had vacated to the poolside or tourists' hotel rooms.

Outside and into the syrupy heat he hailed a cab. Craig climbed in, told the driver his destination, sank bank in his seat and closed his eyes to the maelstrom of the city.

"Oriental Hotel," said the driver as they pulled up outside a smart colonial-style building.

Craig paid the fare and saw Eddie waiting for him with a welcoming smile on his face. He got out and embraced the boy.

"You look very good," the Thai said, holding him at arm's length.

"So do you."

"I look the same as yesterday," he replied, giggling.

Craig laughed too as he remembered his friend's quirky sense of humour, his frown and his unwillingness to take a compliment.

"Do you want lunch at the hotel?"

"No, very expensive there," Eddie said, grimacing. "We can just have a drink in the bar and eat later."

They were shown onto the terrace by a young boy in a starched white uniform. Craig was already smitten by the waiter, no more than a teenager, and even though he felt guilty he didn't feel nearly guilty enough. The youngster handed them menus and the English-man wondered how the server kept so cool as he sat and sweated unfashionably under the boy's gaze.

"You like him?" hissed Eddie as the waiter returned, balancing their drinks expertly on a silver tray.

"He's okay."

"Up to you," he said, lighting up a cigarette. "*Farang* are all the same; they move from one boy to the next like a butterfly."

"Sorry," said Craig, realising he'd hurt his friend, but he knew *sorry* could never be enough.

"Forget it," replied Eddie, raising his glass. "Good luck."

"Cheers."

The breeze from the Chao Pharaya River made the unbearable afternoon sun almost bearable but Craig saw the sweat forming on Eddie's brow and wished he hadn't upset him. He reached his hand across the table and touched the Thai's.

"Do you want to go out tonight?"

"Okay," said Eddie, grinning through the tears in his eyes. "But you're leaving me soon."

They both walked in a contemplative silence to the riverside. Eddie led Craig to the welcome shade of a primitive shelter next to the jetty, from which they could catch the ferry.

Craig enjoyed the river since it broke the monotony of concrete that marred the city. The waterway was a mixture of traditional and the ultra-modern, brightly painted long-tail boats chugged along in the shadow of huge cigarette-shaped condominiums, and he imagined the wealthy sitting high above toasting Bangkok with their perfectly chilled aperitifs prepared by underaged waifs. He remembered Louis saying he had a place "on the river".

Eddie looped an arm through his, happily oblivious to the tourists that surrounded them. They jumped on the boat that sidled up to the jetty. Craig trailed his hand in the dark green water and felt the cool spray on his face. He turned to his companion and kissed him lightly on the cheek. The Thai grinned back.

It was quite a meandering journey and he was happy to relax to Eddie's rather dozy commentary, identifying various landmarks along the way. Craig looked at the little boys from the shantytowns splashing around at the fringes of the river, dwarfed by the towering penthouses, and noticed they never looked up.

Finally, Eddie pointed to the outline of the Grand Palace in the distance, signifying something exotic and unspeakably foreign for Craig, but the holidaymakers fumbling awkwardly for their cameras and clicking away somehow managed to destroy the moment.

He was disappointed as they alighted and joined a stampede of other Westerners on a whistle-stop tour that seemed to belittle something so apparently sacred. The temple was just another tourist attraction, Craig found.

"It's very beautiful, no?" asked Eddie proudly as they completed the visit and stepped outside the gates.

"Yes," said Craig, not wanting to hurt his friend's feelings again. "It's amazing."

Once they'd caught the boat back upriver he left Eddie at the bus stop to go back to what he imagined to be his squalid little room somewhere in the warren of streets that made up Bangkok. He'd asked to go with his friend but the Thai said he was embarrassed of his home and wanted to go back and get changed before they met later that night. As he waved him off Craig imagined the dark, stuffy little cell inhabited by the four laughing boys and embarked on the relatively short walk back to the air-conditioned Malaysia Hotel as darkness fell.

He enthusiastically answered the knock at the hotel room door, knowing it would be Eddie.

"Hi," said the boy, smiling, his skimpy singlet only accentuating the muscle-bound body.

Craig didn't say a word but instead grabbed Eddie around his ample shoulders and dragged him onto the bed. He lifted off the boy's vest and pinched the rock-hard brown nipples. He then wet them with his tongue and squeezed them between his teeth as the Thai gave little gasps. Craig followed with his tongue over the rigid body to the cute navel and nosed the tuft of hair that spilled out over the top of red silk briefs.

After they'd both come Eddie grabbed his crumpled trousers from the floor and took out the obligatory phial of Special K. Craig wasn't too keen but he was still in the boy's thrall and snorted up the white powder anyway. He winced as it burned the back of his throat but the Thai turned to him and offered just that little bit more. Pathetically he accepted even though he couldn't get the image of Devon, the young American lolling helplessly on the sofa in his death throes, out of his head.

"I love you."

"Yeah, I know," Craig replied harshly, because he saw not love but desperation in the boy's eyes, and it was at that moment he thought of Sydney and how glad he was to be leaving soon for Australia as he guiltily turned away from Eddie.

He felt lightheaded as he stepped out of the lobby and sweat pulsed from his body after the artificial coolness of the hotel room. Eddie waved at a passing cab and they both lurched towards the illuminated yellow taxi sign in the dark street.

"You hot?" the Thai asked as he wiped the drug-induced sweat from Craig's brow.

They got out at Silom Road where the tourist throng had descended and were picking their way along the street market. Eddie held Craig's arm and led him unsteadily towards DJ Station.

Craig noticed a salesman on the opposite side of the road showing off a laser pen to a prospective buyer. He followed the arcing red circles; faster and faster they spun. His senses were sharpened though he found it difficult putting one foot in front of the other. The vendor with the laser played a pattern on the front of his shirt. He waved over. The salesman smiled back.

In the bars surrounding DJ Craig noticed the same desperate boys but with different foreigners, though many of the tourists had the same hungry looks on their faces.

"Drinks are on you tonight."

"Fine by me," Craig replied, smiling thinly at the bitter reminder that almost everything in Thailand amounted to a transaction.

It was frantically busy in DJ and he left Eddie on the dance floor while he went to buy the drinks. Wanting a break from the tumult he climbed the three floors to the top of the club where it was emptier and looked down. He picked out his friend and saw him smiling and flirting as he bobbed around in a sea of people. As he was about to turn away the Thai looked up and waved.

He pushed his way back down towards the dance floor. His heart sank as he saw Leo from Koh Samui climbing the stairs in the opposite direction and draped over a fat European looking man who was covered in chunky gold jewellery and flushed from the sun. A man that obviously denied himself none of the excesses he could afford, Craig thought.

He looked straight at Leo but, far from colluding, the pretty Thai boy blanked him, acted like he'd never seen him before in his life. Craig felt not only sorry for the boy, who was probably on a good thing with the rich foreigner, he mused, but also hurt himself. He turned around and watched forlornly as the Thai blindly followed his sugar daddy.

He rejoined Eddie, who was too busy enjoying himself or too high to notice. He pulled the Thai close, kissed him, but couldn't get the cameo just played by Leo out of his mind.

He frantically looked around the fashionable boutiques of the swanky Emporium shopping mall. Craig was desperate to find a gift for Eddie on his last day in Thailand but realised he couldn't give him want he really wanted, a one-way ticket out of the heat and chaos.

Craig settled on the red Casio G-Shock watch because he was aware of how label-conscious the Thai was. Though he guessed most of the labels the boy paraded were fake. As he handed over the sheaf of notes in the gleaming showroom he imagined Eddie and his friends haggling in the cluttered, dusty bazaars of downtown where there were no guarantees or warranties.

He sat in a coffee shop after the purchase and watched city society walk by, strutting like peacocks in the polished, cavernous mall. A group of *kathoeys* sat adjacent to Craig despite the wealth of empty tables. They were loud and flirtatious and whereas once he would have been intimidated — remembering his first day in Bangkok and meeting Natasha — he enjoyed their sense of fun and amused stares.

"You join us?" asked the most voluptuous of the group.

"No thank you," replied Craig, to which she comically turned her head up and away in disdain, dramatic bouffant silhouetted against the artificial light.

The driver put his foot down on the expressway, weaving in and out of the heavy traffic, seemingly anxious to dispatch Craig and get on with earning a living.

He thought of his first day in Bangkok as he was driven in the opposite direction into an unknown world and the trepidation that had accompanied him. Now everything made more sense than it had done then, he thought, *just*. And while Craig could never forget his chronic illness, he had found it within himself to smile at the future.

As they pulled up to the airport building Eddie was already waiting. Craig was thankful as the Thai rushed over when he saw him struggling out with his backpack and chivalrously slung the bag over a broad shoulder.

"Good day at work?"

"No," replied Eddie glumly. "You must come back soon, I am so sad you are leaving."

"I will," said Craig, sick at having to make a promise he instantly knew he wasn't going to keep.

He handed over the gift and enjoyed watching Eddie ripping off the wrapper in expectation. His eyes widened in pleasure as he revealed the watch and put it straight onto his right wrist because he was already wearing one on the left.

"*Kupkawnkrap*," Eddie said as he hugged Craig unselfconsciously outside the busy terminal building.

"Goodbye," said Craig, giving Eddie one last hug as he strode towards the airport.

He turned expectantly around as the electric doors swished open but the Thai had already headed off back into the crowd, back to get on with his own life.

He looked out of the aircraft window, several thousand feet up, and the huge mass of Bangkok blinked back at him. The sprawling city would always have a very human face to him now, for better or worse.

CHAPTER SEVENTEEN

Jamie brushed his fingers lightly over his swollen face. He could feel the protrusion of stitches that formed a crisscross pattern, holding the lacerated flesh tightly together. His breathing was uneven and shallow and sweat glistened off the palms of his hands. Drugs had successfully numbed the physical pain but the mental scars yawned open. His mind retrieved the horror of the attack at frequent intervals — it all came back like a grainy half-speed cine film.

Doctors and nurses bustled about in their white uniforms. They tried to look busy and unconcerned at the sight of Jamie but he wasn't fooled. He'd watched the looks on their faces and witnessed the whispered asides. Bob and Liz visited every day but others had tended to come only once. Most visitors didn't address him directly but fixed their attention at the blank wall behind his bed and fussed around fixing his blanket, plumping up his pillows or reading his "Get Well" cards.

The medical staff put on a positive gloss and promised he could go home soon. But going home was what Jamie dreaded the most because it meant going back to the real world. He knew his face was horribly disfigured and it would be a world where he'd be even further alienated than he felt before.

All Jamie saw when he thought of the future was a chilling emptiness. Doctors had mentioned plastic surgery — several months for this to heal, several months for that to heal — but he hadn't really listened. He wasn't interested because he knew he'd never look or feel the same again.

His parents had said he could move back to Carshalton to recuperate, as though it was some compensation for what he'd been through. He feared moving back to their soulless, suburban pebble-dashed grave where Bob could control and manipulate his life once again. Although he couldn't imagine living alone and looking in the mirror every day with no one there to console him.

The morning he'd spied his reflection and saw a deformed monster staring back destroyed him. Jamie had cried and cried into his cupped hands and he was crying again as he stood at the top of a multi-storey car park at Heathrow, several hundred feet above the hard asphalt of the road below.

Teetering on the edge he remembered Liz bringing him to the airport as a kid, where he'd watched the planes take off and land. He had a childlike wonder of where people were going or where they'd come from but he was too selfish to let his mind recall those that actually cared a little like Philippe, which is probably what had helped propel him to this point.

He stood transfixed now as an aircraft seared through the grey sky overhead, engines screaming like his thoughts. Jamie imagined its passengers were off to somewhere bright and sunny and hoped he was too as his body hurtled towards the cold, black concrete several storeys below.

CHAPTER EIGHTEEN

He arrived at Sydney International and was shocked at how clean — almost clinical — everything seemed. Craig felt the grime of Thailand still oozed from every pore like a comforting second skin.

The immigration officer peered at him suspiciously under the bleak lights and, as he tried to move through customs, the burly man blocked his way and grunted at him to open his backpack. The official turned his nose up as the smell of the Third World flooded from the bag.

Craig was relieved that he didn't have to declare what he'd experienced over the last few months as his belongings were rummaged about and smiled to himself wryly after being finally waved through.

He'd called his mum when he reached the hotel and she told him that Liz had telephoned her about Jamie's tragic death. Craig had felt numb when he put the receiver down but as he watched the sunrise over the famous harbour, turquoise sea bisected by the brilliant white sails of the Opera House, tears rolled slowly down his cheeks — he was overwhelmed just to be alive.

About the author

Robin Newbold is a Londoner born and bred, though for his sins he now spends far too much time in Bangkok. A freelance journalist, he's written on gay and lifestyle issues for a number of publications such as *Time Out, The Times, Traveller, The Nation* and *Bangkok Metro* magazine. *Vacuum-Packed* is the first of, what he hopes, many works of fiction. He is a Crystal Palace fan.

www.geocities.com/robinnewbold

Printed in the United States
18027LVS00003B/202